University Reader

英汉对照·中国文学宝库·现代文学系列
English-Chinese·Gems of Chinese Literature·*Modern*

老舍小说选
Selected Stories by Lao She

老 舍 著
Lao She

中国文学出版社
Chinese Literature Press
外语教学与研究出版社
Foreign Language Teaching and Research Press

图书在版编目(CIP)数据

老舍小说选:英、汉对照/老舍著.—北京:中国文学出版社;外语教学与研究出版社,1999.8
(中国文学宝库·现代文学系列)
ISBN 7-5071-0562-8

Ⅰ.老… Ⅱ.老… Ⅲ.小说-中国-现代-对照读物-英、汉 Ⅳ.H319.4:I

中国版本图书馆CIP数据核字(1999)第29857号

中文责编:季晟康
英文责编:殷 雯

英汉对照 中国文学宝库·现代文学系列
老舍小说选
老 舍 著

中 国 文 学 出 版 社
(北京百万庄路24号)
外语教学与研究出版社   出版发行
(北京西三环北路19号)

北京市鑫鑫印刷厂印刷
新华书店总店北京发行所经销

开本850×1168 1/32 10.625印张
1999年8月第1版 1999年8月第1次印刷
字数:160千 印数:1—5000册
ISBN 7-5071-0562-8/I·502
定价:12.90元

总编辑　杨宪益　戴乃迭

总策划　野　莽　蔡剑峰

编委会（以姓氏笔划为序）

　　　　　吕　华

　　　　　李朋义

　　　　　赵文炎

　　　　　凌　原

　　　　　野　莽

　　　　　蔡剑峰

目　　录
CONTENTS

大学生读书计划 ……………………………… 编　者（Ⅰ）
　　——中国文学宝库出版呼吁
A Vision ……………………………………………（ 2 ）
微　神 ………………………………………………（ 3 ）
Black Li and White Li ……………………………（ 36 ）
黑白李 ………………………………………………（ 37 ）
The Eyeglasses ……………………………………（ 84 ）
眼　镜 ………………………………………………（ 85 ）
Brother You Takes Office ………………………（110）
上　任 ………………………………………………（111）
The Soul-Slaying Spear …………………………（162）
断魂枪 ………………………………………………（163）
The Fire Chariot …………………………………（194）
火　车 ………………………………………………（195）
Crescent Moon ……………………………………（246）
月牙儿 ………………………………………………（247）

大学生读书计划
——中国文学宝库出版呼吁

在即将开机印刷这第一批50本名为中国文学宝库的英汉对照读本时,我们的心情竟然忧多于喜。因为我们只能以保守的5000册印数,去面对全国400万在校大学生。

虽然我们并非市场经济的局外者,若仅为印数(销售量)计,大可奋起而去生产诸如TOFEL应试指南,或者英语四六级模拟试题集一类的教辅图书,但我们还是决定宁可冒着债台高筑的风险,也有责任对大学生同胞发出一声亲切的呼唤:请亲近我们的中国文学。

身为向世界译介中国文学和向国内出版外语读物的,具有双重责任的出版社,我们得知目前大学生往往仅注重外语的学习而偏废了母语的提高,以及忽视了中国文学的阅读,放弃了人文知识的训练。有统计表明,某理工院校57%的同学不曾读过《红楼梦》等四大名著,以致校园内外流行着"样子像研究生,说话像大学生,作文像中学生,写字像小学生"的幽默。还有一副这样的对联,说大学生的文章是"无错不成文,病句错句破残句,句句不堪入目;有误方为篇,别字错字自造字,字字触目惊心",横批"斯文扫地"。作为未来社会中坚和整个社会发展关键力量的大学生,这种"文弃"现象的流行,势必导致一场人文精神危机的爆发。对照以科学与人文精神追求为主题的五四新文化运动,八十年的历程告诉我们,以上提醒绝非危言耸听。

我们已经迈入知识经济时代,在追求科学知识的同时,创新精神已成为关键;而创新的源泉其实有赖于多学科多领域知识的交融,依靠的是新型的复合型人才,所以,文学对于新一代的大学生来说绝非装点,而是沟通自然科学与人文科学的桥梁,使我们在汲取知识的同时更能获得智慧,于创造物质的同时还进一步丰富和完善着精神;无怪乎爱因斯坦认为自己受影响最大的竟是陀思妥耶夫斯基。由此证明,一个真正的科学家应该拥有丰富的文学和文化知识以及完整的人格。十年前,七十五位诺贝尔奖得主聚会巴黎,当时他们所发表的宣言开篇就是,"如果人类要在 21 世纪生存下去,必须回首 2500 年去吸收孔子的智慧。"确实,十年的时间让我们有目共睹,现代经济科技的飞速发展何尝不是一柄双刃的剑?只有文化的力量才能抵消随之而来的负面后果。可见,知识的获取与技能的训练对于大学生来说固然重要,但文化与修养却尤需关切。正因为大学生代表着社会先知先觉的知识力量,置身当前的文化现实,就应有一分责任感与使命感,力求对知识技能以外许多带有根本性质的精神追求形成明确的意识,从而具备一种对生命意义进行探索与追问的精神,一种以人文精神为背景的生存勇气和人格力量。那么,能够引导我们探索前行的一盏明灯,不就是闪烁着理想光芒的不朽的文学名著吗?

一个人乃至一个民族,从其对文学的亲疏态度,可以衡量出其文化素质的程度。文学应是从人类文化中升华出的理想的结晶,她"使人的心灵变得高尚,使人的勇气、荣誉感、希望、尊严、同情心、怜悯心和牺牲精神复活起来"(威廉·福克纳);无疑,只有文学才能从更高的层次上提升人的文化素质和整体素质,充实人的内心世界,焕发人的精神风貌,带给人们真善美。而亲近文学,特别是热爱祖国灿烂的文学以及文化,正是当代中国大学生加强文化修养,弘扬人文精神的有力脚步。

"越是民族的,就越是世界的",中国文学属于中国,也属于世界。和平是人类的共同愿望,交流与共享则是新世纪的潮流。

中国当代大学生的血液里流动着数千年的文化积淀,没有理由在让世界了解中国大学生聪明才智的同时,却无缘分享我们的骄傲——中国大学生不但能够读懂英语的莎士比亚,而且能让世界感动于中国文学的伟大。

  这是我们作为出版者的理想。我们原有一个世纪礼物的构想,是同大学生一起做一个"读书计划"。这一次将中国文学的最新荟萃配设高水平的英语译文,是其中推荐给新世纪大学生的第一批读物。盼望着您——我们无数知音中的5000名先来者,给我们鼓励,也给我们意见和批评。

编者

一九九九年五月三十日

只有文学才能从更高的层次上提升人的文化素质和整体素质,充实人的内心世界,焕发人的精神风貌,带给人们真善美。而亲近文学,特别是热爱祖国灿烂的文学以及文化,正是当代中国大学生加强文化修养,弘扬人文精神的有力脚步。

A Vision

It must have been after the Clear and Bright Festival,① for the crab-apple was coming into full bloom. Spring was late this year, of course, and butterflies still seemed fragile though the lusty bees from the very start found the whole wide world as delectable as honey. Swallows were having fun, too, pinning black letter T-s to the handful of fleecy white clouds in the sky. The willows, although there was no wind, kept their branches swaying softly to mock the hints of greenery all around. The fresh green of the fields, delicate and easily tired, crept up the hills growing fainter the higher it went, till near the top it was lost in patches of brown. The trees halfway up, even those not yet green, had a silky look about them, while the blue sky beyond the hills must have been warm, for geese were flying that way, honking, in formation. Shy epidendrums were hiding in clefts in the rock, their leaves smaller than their flowers.

The scent of the hills is best enjoyed with closed eyes to save the trouble of analysing its sources, for even last year's fallen leaves give off a good smell. The plaintive bleating of some kids in the distance just kept my pleasure within reasonable bounds. And one happened to stray my way. A little creature sprouting a beard

---

① This usually falls early in April.

微 神

　　清明已过了,大概是;海棠花不是都快开齐了吗?今年的节气自然是晚了一些,蝴蝶们还很弱;蜂儿可是一出世就那么挺拔,好像世界确是甜蜜可喜的。天上只有三四块不大也不笨重的白云,燕儿们给白云上钉小黑丁字玩呢。没有什么风,可是柳枝似乎故意的转摆,像逗弄着四外的绿意。田中的青绿轻轻的上了小山,因为娇弱怕累得慌,似乎是,越高绿色越浅了些;山顶上还是些黄多于绿的纹缕呢。山腰中的树,就是不绿的也显出柔嫩来,山后的蓝天也是暖和的,不然,雁们为何唱着向那边排着队去呢?石凹藏着些怪害羞的二月兰,叶儿还赶不上花朵大。

　　小山的香味只能闭着眼吸取,省得劳神去找香气的来源,你看,连去年的落叶都怪好闻的。那边有几只小白山羊,叫的声儿恰巧使欣喜不至过度,因而有些悲意。偶尔走过一只来,

英汉对照
English-Chinese
中国文学宝库
Gems of Chinese Literature
现代文学系列
Modern Literature

before its horns had grown, it stood foolishly in front of a rock for some seconds before trotting off again shaking its comical tail.

As I basked in the sun on the hillside, my mind a blank, pearls of poetry welled up unbidden in my heart to fall noiselessly into that sea of green in my breast, while faint smiles curved my lips and faded quickly away; but not a single line did I complete. The whole universe was poetry, and I no more than one small punctuation mark in a poem.

Basking there in utter content, I knew something of the rapture in a butterfly's wings. I hugged my knees, swaying this way and that in time to the willows' motion, and saw that each small gold-green leaf on their boughs was a tiny ear pricked up to catch the voice of spring. I looked up at the sky and blessed the white cloud at whose edge a swallow, nearly melting into the blue, seemed an infinitesimal black mote in that ocean of liquid light — my heart winged towards it.

Far away a path through the hills was like a brown line on a map of green provinces. Below sloped a wheat field, sweeping down the hillside until stopped by a dark green pine wood, and I hoped against hope that beyond the pines lay the sea. I stood up and climbed higher for a better view. No, there were trees over there — hard to make out just what they were — with low cottages among them. A sudden breeze carried over the faint crow of a cock.

That note of melancholy in a distant cock-crow in spring made me wonder if the scene before my eyes was reality or illusion, or perhaps a golden thread of sound between illusion and reality? For a second I had a vision of a blood-red comb; in my mind, in that

没长犄角就留下须的小动物，向一块大石发了会儿愣，又颠颠着俏式的小尾巴跑了。

我在山坡上晒太阳，一点思念也没有，可是自然而然的从心中滴下些诗的珠子，滴在胸中的绿海上，没有声响，只有些波纹走不到腮上便散了的微笑；可是始终也没成功一整句。一个诗的宇宙里，连我自己好似只是诗的什么地方的一个小符号。

越晒越轻松，我体会出蝶翅是怎样的欢欣。我搂着膝，和柳枝同一律动前后左右的微动，柳枝上每一黄绿的小叶都是听着春声的小耳勺儿。有时看看天空，啊，谢谢那块白云，它的边上还有个小燕呢，小得已经快和蓝天化在一处了，像万顷蓝光中的一粒黑痣，我的心灵像要往那儿飞似的。

远处山坡的小道，像地图上绿的省份里一条黄线。往下看，一大片麦田，地势越来越低，似乎是由山坡上往那边流动呢，直到一片暗绿的松树把它截住；很希望松林那边是个海湾。及至我立起来，往更高处走了几步，看看，不是；那边是些看不甚清的树，树中有些低矮的村舍；一阵小风吹来极细的一声鸡叫。

春晴的远处鸡声有些悲惨，使我不晓得眼前一切是真还是虚，它是梦与真实中间的一道用声音作的金线；我顿时似乎看见了个血红的

A Vision

village, or in the vicinity there was a cock — and I hoped it was snowy white.

I sat down again, or rather stretched out on the turf, my eyes opened just enough to catch the blue brilliance of the sky growing deeper and higher as it let fall on my pupils blue drops of light and warmth. And presently I closed my eyes to enjoy the sunshine and laughter within my own heart.

I was not asleep but close to the land of dreams, still able to hear distinctly the twittering and warbling of birds around me. Strangely enough, in that state between sleep and waking, the same scene — just where it is I do not know — always floats before me as I start dozing off. We may as well call it the borderland of dreams.

Not large, with neither hills nor sea, it is like a garden that has no definite limits, a rough triangle whose tips reach out into shifting darkness. The tip at which I invariably look first is a mass of gold and crimson flowers, with no sunlight, nothing but darkness, behind this blaze of colour; and the dark background intensifies the crimson and gold, just as red peonies painted in a black vase flame with almost fearful beauty. That dark background, I know, helps the crimson and gold to retain their brightness instead of diffusing it; for without sunshine the brightness cannot take flight but is held and imprinted on the ground. My eyes turn here first because this part conjures up a picture of the rest in the same way that by looking at the Western Hills you know where the Temple of Azure Clouds is hidden.

From the left tip curves a long slope of wild flowers like heather,

鸡冠；在心中，村舍中，或是哪儿，有只——希望是雪白的——公鸡。

我又坐下了；不，随便的躺下了。眼留着个小缝收取天上的蓝光，越看越深，越高；同时也往下落着光暖的蓝点，落在我那离心不远的眼睛上。不大一会儿，我便闭上了眼，看着心内的晴空与笑意。

我没睡去，我知道已离梦境不远，但是还听得清清楚楚小鸟的相唤与轻歌。说也奇怪，每逢到似睡非睡的时候，我才看见那块地方——不晓得一定是哪里，可是在入梦以前它老是那个样儿浮在眼前。就管它叫作梦的前方吧。

这块地方并没有多大，没有山，没有海。像一个花园，可又没有清楚的界限。差不多是个不甚规则的三角，三个尖端浸在流动的黑暗里。一角上——我永远先看见它——是一片金黄与大红的花，密密层层，没有阳光，一片红黄的后面便全是黑暗，可是黑的背景使红黄更加深厚，就好像大黑瓶上画着红牡丹，深厚得至于使美中有一点点恐怖。黑暗的背景，我明白了，使红黄的一片抱住了自己的彩色，不向四外走射一点；况且没有阳光，彩色不飞入空中，而完全贴染在地上。我老先看见这块，一看见它，其余的便不看也会知道的，正好像一看见香山，准知道碧云寺在哪儿藏着呢。

其余的两角，左边是一个斜长的土坡，满盖着灰紫的野花，在不漂亮中有些深厚的力量，或

英汉对照
English-Chinese
中国文学宝库
Gems of Chinese Literature
现代文学系列
Modern Literature

more virile than beautiful; and moonlight touching the grey tints with silver might well bring out the transcendence of poetry here; but it slips my mind whether there is a moon or not. At all events, far from disliking this heath, I delight in the frost-darkened purple which reminds me of a young mother in a dark purple gown. But the right-hand tip is the loveliest of all, for there stands a thatched cottage with a trellis before its door where pink rambler roses are a riot of pure blooms.

If I run my eyes from left to right, from the purple, the crimson and gold to the pale pink, it seems as if time has regressed from autumn to spring, as if nature's prime is not followed by decay but life ends with the two-fold glory of the scent and colour of roses.

In the middle of the triangle lies a meadow of dark green grass, soft, thick and moist, each blade thrusting up as if listening to distant rain. Not a breath of wind here, not an insect stirs. In this small world of ghostly beauty, only colours are alive.

In real life I have never seen a place like this. Yet it has a permanent existence on the threshold of my dreams. It may be descended — but who can say for certain? — from the deep green of England, the heather-clad moors of Scotland, the shadowy Black Forest of Germany. Again, take away the sunshine and there is a resemblance to the lush tropics; except that here are no snakes all colours of the rainbow, no birds of brilliant plumage. I know it, though, and that is enough for me.

I have visited it so often, it is like a picture in my heart, as real as the couplet:

者月光能使那灰的部分多一些银色显出点诗的灵空;但是我不记得在哪儿有个小月亮。无论怎样,我也不厌恶它。不,我爱这个似乎被霜弄暗了的紫色,像年轻的母亲穿着暗紫长袍。右边的一角是最漂亮的,一个小草房,门前有一架细蔓的月季,满开着单纯的花,全是浅粉的。

设若我的眼由左向右转,灰紫,红黄,浅粉,像是由秋看到初春,时节倒流;生命不但不是由盛而衰,反倒是以玫瑰作香色双艳的结束。

三角的中间是一片绿草,深绿,软厚,微湿;每一短叶都向上挺着,似乎是听着远处的雨声。没有一点风,没有一个飞动的小虫;一个鬼艳的小世界,活着的只有颜色。

在真实的经验中,我没见过这么个境界。可是它永远存在,在我的梦前。英格兰的深绿,苏格兰的紫草小山,德国黑林的幽晦,或者是它的祖先们,但是谁准知道呢。从赤道附近的浓艳中减去阳光,也有点像它。但是它又没有虹样的蛇与五彩的禽,算了吧,反正我认识它。

我看见它多少多少次了。它和"山高月小,

英汉对照
English-Chinese
中国文学宝库
Gems of Chinese Literature
现代文学系列
Modern Literature

High hills and the moon dwindles;
Low tide and rocks appear.

Yet I had never set foot inside that cottage, being either held spellbound by those colours or hurrying from that meadow into dreams of another kind. Like men who keep meeting we knew each other's names, but because we had never had a frank, intimate talk its innermost colour remained a mystery to me, as well as its secret music. I longed to see some sign of life there.

This time I decided to investigate.

At once, without even hearing my own footsteps, I found myself by the rose trellis. Since rambler roses are linked in my mind with the Dragon Boat Festival,[①] I hoped to find a vermilion Judge of Hell printed on dark yellow paper between two sprays of sweet artemisia. But, no! In fancy I heard the cry "Cherry ripe!" — that was all. The place was utterly still.

The door of the cottage was shut, ivory-white matting screened both windows and door, and the sunlight was too faint for flowers to cast shadows. Not a sound could be heard inside. This was surely the very well-spring of loneliness.

Gently pushing open the door, I was welcomed in by stillness and spotlessness — yes, they welcomed me. If outside was a world of ghosts, all here belonged to man — I hardly think these epithets too far-fetched.

A curtain divided the cottage into two rooms, one large and one

---

① In early summer.

水落石出",是我心中的一对画屏。可是我没到那个小房里去过。我不是被那些颜色吸引得不动一动,便是由它的草地上恍惚的走入另种色彩的梦境。它是我常遇到的朋友,彼此连姓名都晓得,只是没细细谈过心。我不晓得它的中心是什么颜色的,是含着一点什么神秘的音乐——真希望有点响动!

这次我决定了去探险。

一想,便到了月季花下,或也因为怕听我自己的足音?月季花对于我是有些端阳前后的暗示,我希望在哪儿贴着张深黄纸,印着个硃红的判官,在两束香艾的中间。没有。只在我心中听见了声"樱桃"的吆喝。这个地方是太静了。

小房子的门闭着。窗上门上都挡着牙白的帘儿,并没有花影,因为阳光不足。里边什么动静也没有,好像它是寂寞的发源地。轻轻的推开门,静娴与整洁双双的欢迎我进去,是,欢迎我,室中的一切是"人"的,假如外面景物是"鬼"的——希望我没用上过于强烈的字。

一大间,用幔帐截成一大一小的两间。幔

small. This curtain, too, was the colour of ivory and had tiny butterflies embroidered on it. The sole furniture in the outer room was a long, high table, a small oval table and a chair, all dark green and unvarnished. There was a light green cushion in the chair, a few books on the small table, and on the longer one a small pine in a pot as well as two old bronze mirrors, their patina a shade lighter than the pine.

Spread on the bed in the inner room was a green rug which hung nearly to the ground. Suspended at the head of the bed was a tiny basket of jasmine just beginning to wither. Next to an oblong rush mat on the floor lay a pair of small green slippers embroidered with white flowers.

My heart missed a beat. I had stumbled upon no intricate, splendid realm of poetry: the dominant note here was simple, everyday beauty. And this was no fantasy either, for I recognized those small green slippers embroidered with white flowers.

Most love stories are just as commonplace as spring rain or autumn frost. But ordinary people take delight in the poetry of these commonplace events, doubtless because so much else in the world is even more lacking in colour, heaven help them! I hope my tale may have some entertainment value.

We had one glorious time together, only one. Everything conspired to be perfect that day. The crab-apple tree in her courtyard was one mass of blossom like a pinky-white snowdrift, the delicate bamboo by the wall was putting out fresh shoots, the sky was a delicious blue, her parents were out and the big white cat was sound asleep under the flowers. When she heard me come, she darted

帐也是牙白的,上面绣着些小蝴蝶。外间只有一条长案,一个小椭圆桌儿,一把椅子,全是暗草色的,没有油饰过。椅上的小垫是浅绿的,桌上有几本书。案上有一盆小松,两方古铜镜,锈色比小松浅些。内间有一个小床,罩着一块快垂到地上的绿毯。床首悬着一个小篮,有些快干的茉莉花。地上铺着一块长方的蒲垫,垫的旁边放着双绣白花的小绿拖鞋。

我的心跳起来了!我决不是入了济慈的复杂而光灿的诗境;平淡朴美是此处的音调,也决不是辜勒律芝的幻境,因为我认识那只绣着白花的小绿拖鞋。

爱情的故事永远是平凡的,正如春雨秋霜那样平凡。可是平凡的人们偏爱在这平凡的事中找些诗意;那么,想必是世界上多数的事物是更缺乏色彩的;可怜的人们!希望我的故事也有些应有的趣味吧。

没有像那一回那么美的了。我说"那一回",因为在那一天那一会儿的一切都是美的。她家中的那株海棠花正开成一个大粉白的雪球;沿墙的细竹刚拔出新笋;天上一片娇晴;她的父母都没在家;大白猫在花下酣睡。听见我

英汉对照
English-Chinese
中国文学宝库
Gems of Chinese Literature
现代文学系列
Modern Literature

out like a swallow from under the eaves, not stopping to change her shoes, and her green slippers were like soft green leaves. She was radiant as the morning sun, her cheeks much rosier than usual, as if two fountains of liquid rouge had welled up through her dimples from a sweet red spring in her heart. In those days she wore her hair in a long plait.

When her parents were at home, she could only peep through the window or seize the chance to smile at me as I arrived. Today she was like a kitten that has found a playmate: her high spirits were a revelation to me. Side by side we walked into the house. We were just seventeen. Neither of us spoke, but two pairs of eyes were exchanging rapturous signals, leaving me no time today to admire the painting, *All the Birds Pay Homage to the Phoenix* done in meticulous style, for my eyes were on her green slippers. But though she tried to tuck her feet out of sight and blushed to the tips of her ears, she went on smiling. I meant to ask about her school work, whether any of their new kittens were wholly white; but the questions remained unspoken. There was so much to ask, but something had sealed my lips; and I knew this was true of her too for her white throat moved as if swallowing back some irrelevance, while she was too shy to say what was really worth saying.

She perched on a redwood stool beside the window, and shadows of crab-apple blossom stirred on her face. From time to time she glanced outside to make sure no one was coming, and the shadows of blossom on her face glowed red with joy. With both hands in turn she fidgeted with the edge of the stool, the picture of impatience, impatient with joy. At last she threw me a searching glance

来了,她像燕儿似的从帘下飞出来;没顾得换鞋,脚下一双小绿拖鞋像两片嫩绿的叶儿。她喜欢得像晨起的阳光,腮上的两片苹果比往常红着许多倍,似乎有两颗香红的心在脸上开了两个小井,溢着红润的胭脂泉。那时她还梳着长黑辫。

她父母在家的时候,她只能隔着窗儿望我一望,或是设法在我走去的时节,和我笑一笑。这一次,她就像一个小猫遇上了个好玩的伴儿;我一向不晓得她"能"这样的活泼。在一同往屋中走的工夫,她的肩挨上了我的。我们都才十七岁。我们都没说什么,可是四只眼彼此告诉我们是欣喜到万分。我最爱看她家壁上那张工笔百鸟朝凤;这次,我的眼匀不出工夫来。我看着那双小绿拖鞋;她往后收了收脚,连耳根儿都有点红了;可是仍然笑着。我想问她的功课,没问;想问新生的小猫有全白的没有,没问;心中的问题多了,只是口被一种什么力量给封起来,我知道她也是如此,因为看见她的白润的脖儿直微微的动,似乎要将些不相干的言语咽下去,而真值得一说的又不好意思说。

她在临窗的一个小红木凳上坐着,海棠花影在她半个脸上微动。有时候她微向窗外看看,大概是怕有人进来。及至看清没人,她脸上的花影都被欢悦给浸渍得红艳了。她的两手交换着轻轻的摸小凳的沿,显着不耐烦,可是欢喜的不耐烦。最后,她深深的看了我一眼,极不愿

英汉对照
English-Chinese
中国文学宝库
Gems of Chinese Literature
现代文学系列
Modern Literature

and said with most palpable reluctance: "You'd better go!" By then I was so lost to the world that I saw rather than heard what she was saying. Deep down in my heart, however, I guessed its gist, for something of the sort was nagging at my mind. I hated to go but knew that go I must. I held her eyes with mine. She faltered as if tempted to lower her head, then raised it bravely to meet my gaze, fearlessly fighting down her shyness. With one accord we hung our heads, with one accord raised them again to exchange long glances. We seemed to be seeing into each other's hearts.

Slowly at last I tore myself away, and there were tears in her eyes as she saw me outside the screen. When I reached the courtyard gate and turned my head, she was standing under the crab-apple blossom. I went away walking on air.

Another chance like that never came again.

Once there was a funeral in her house — not a death that distressed them unduly. I exchanged a few words with her under the lamp while she fidgeted with the button of her white mourning. We were so close, each could almost hear the other's blood racing, as you hear the young grain growing after rain. I uttered some brief commonplaces — a movement of the lips and tongue, that was all — our thoughts were far away.

Although we were twenty-two, this was before the May Fourth Movement. Segregation of the sexes was still the rule. After graduation they made me head of a primary school and that was the proudest day of my life because she wrote me a letter of congratulation. The letter — with plum blossom printed on it — had a postscript: "Don't reply." Nor did I dare. But I was afire to do all

意而又不得不说的说,"走吧"!我自己已忘了自己,只看见,不是听见,两个什么字由她的口中出来,可是在心的深处猜对那两个字的意思,因为我也有点那样的关切。我的心不愿动,我的脑知道非走不可。我的眼钉住了她的。她要低头,还没低下去,便又勇敢的抬起来,故意的,不怕的,羞而不肯羞的,迎着我的眼。直到不约而同的垂下头去,又不约而同的抬起来,又那么看。心似乎已碰着心。

我走,极慢的;她送我到帘外,眼上蒙了一层露水。我走到二门,回了回头,她已赶到海棠花下。我像一个羽毛似的飘荡出去。

以后,再没有这种机会。

有一次,她家中落了,并不使人十分悲伤的丧事。在灯光下我和她说了两句话。她穿着一身孝衣。手放在胸前,摆弄着孝衣的扣带。站得离我很近,几乎能彼此听得见脸上热力的激射,像雨后的木谷那样带着声儿生长。可是,只说了两句极没有意思的话——口与舌的一些动作:我们的心并没管它们。

我们都二十二岁了,可是五四运动还没降生呢。男女的交际还不是普通的事。我毕业后便作了小学的校长,平生最大的光荣,因为她给了我一封贺信。信笺的末尾——印着一枝梅花——她注了一行:不要回信。我也就没敢写回

in my power to improve that school: its success should be her answer. And in my dreams she clapped encouraging hands, hands lovely as jade.

To propose to her was out of the question. Too many senseless yet insuperable obstacles stood between us fierce and powerful as a tiger.

One consolation I had: no word of any engagement ever reached my ears thirsting for news of her. Better still, in my spare time I organized a night school and she did some teaching there. Just to see her from time to time was all I asked. But she avoided me — in her twenties she had lost the ingenuous high spirits of seventeen, acquiring in their place the dignity and mystery of a woman.

Two years later I went off to the South Seas. And the day that I called at her house to take my leave, she happened to be out.

I was abroad for several years, cut off from news of her. Unable to correspond directly and reluctant to make indirect inquiries, I had to be content with dreaming about her. Strange to say, I never dreamed of any other woman. They were unhappy as well as rapturous dreams: the fantasies of love have a flavour all their own. To me, she was still as she had been at seventeen: the same small round face, the same arch look in her clear eyes. She was not tall, but a sweet suppleness lent an indescribable grace to her walk; while to me her long black plait, seen from behind, was utterly bewitching. Though I remembered her with her hair up, I always dreamed of her with it in a long plait.

My first act, of course, on my return to China was to find out what had become of her. I could hardly credit my ears when I

信。可是我好像心中燃着一束火把,无所不尽其极的整顿学校。我拿办好了学校作给她的回信;她也在我的梦中给我鼓着得胜的掌——那一对连腕也是玉的手!

提婚是不能想的事。许多许多无意识而有力量的阻碍,像个专以力气自雄的恶虎,站在我们中间。

有一件足以自慰的,我那系着心的耳朵始终没听到她的定婚消息。还有件比这更好的,我兼任了一个平民学校的校长,她担任着一点功课。我只希望能时时见到她,不求别的。她呢,她知道怎么躲避我——已经是个二十多岁的大姑娘。她失去了十七八岁时的天真与活泼,可是增加了女子的尊严与神秘。

又过了二年,我上了南洋。到她家辞行的那天,她恰巧没在家。

在外国的几年中,我无从打听她的消息。直接通信是不可能的。间接的探问,又不好意思。只好在梦里相会了。说也奇怪,我在梦中的女性永远是"她"。梦境的不同使我有时悲泣,有时狂喜;恋的幻境里也自有一种味道。她,在我的心中,还是十七岁时的样子:小圆脸,眉眼清秀中带着一点媚意。身量不高! 处处都那么柔软,走路非常的轻巧。那一条长黑的发辫,造成最动心的一个背影。我也记得她梳起头来的样儿,但是我总梦见那带辫的背影。

回国后,自然先探听她的一切。一切消息

英汉对照
English-Chinese
中国文学宝库
Gems of Chinese Literature
现代文学系列
Modern Literature

heard she had become a prostitute.

Not even this fearful news could damp my ardour; in fact, I longed more than ever to see and help her. I called at her house but the family had moved. Nothing could be seen but the crab-apple tree over the wall. The house had been sold.

At last I found her. Her hair was short, combed back in a large green comb. The elbow-length sleeves of her long pink gown betrayed the fact that her arms had lost their softness, nor could heavy powder hide her wrinkles and crow's-feet. Her smile was still a joy to see, not that there was any genuine gaiety in it. If not for paint and powder, she would have looked like a woman just after childbirth. Not once did she meet my eyes, although her face showed no trace of embarrassment. She talked and laughed, but her heart was not really in it — she was merely making conversation. My tentative questions as to how she was managing were brushed aside as, lighting a cigarette, she exhaled smoke like an adept, leaning back with crossed legs to watch the smoke wreaths, the picture of empty-headed brashness. The tears that sprang to my eyes can hardly have passed unnoticed but she chose to ignore them, studying her finger-nails and smoothing back her hair as if this were all she lived for. My inquiries about her family went unanswered too. I had to take my leave. I gave her my address before parting, assuring her that I was at her service. She laughed indifferently and looked away, indicating that she did not mean to see me out. When she thought I had gone, although I was still rooted in the doorway, she turned and for a second our eyes met — but instantly she looked away again.

都像谣言,她已作了暗娼!

就是这种刺心的消息,也没减少我的情热;不,我反倒更想见她,更想帮助她。我到她家去。已不在那里住,我只由墙外看见那株海棠树的一部分。房子早已卖掉了。

到底我找到她了。她已剪了发,向后梳拢着,在项部有个大绿梳子。穿着一件粉红长袍,袖子仅到肘部,那双臂,已不是那么活软的了,脸上的粉很厚,脑门和眼角都有些折子。可是她还笑得很好看,虽然一点活泼的气象也没有了。设若把粉和油都去掉,她大概最好也只像个产后的病妇。她始终没正眼看我一次,虽然脸上并没有羞愧的样子,她也说也笑,只是心没在话与笑中,好像完全应酬我。我试着探问她些问题与经济状况,她不大愿意回答。她点着一支香烟,烟很灵通的从鼻孔出来。她左膝放在右膝上,仰着头看烟的升降变化,极无聊而又显着刚强。我的眼湿了,她不会看不见我的泪,可是她没有任何表示。她不住的看自己的手指甲,又轻轻的向后按头发,似乎她只是为它们活着呢。提到家中的人,她什么没告诉我。我只好走吧。临出来的时候,我把住址告诉给她——深愿她求我,或是命令我,作点事。她似乎根本没往心里听,一笑,眼看看别处,没有往外送我的意思。她以为我是出去了,其实我是立在门口没动,这么着,她一回头,我们对了眼光。只是那么一擦似的她转过头去。

英汉对照
English-Chinese
中国文学宝库
Gems of Chinese Literature
现代文学系列
Modern Literature

First love, the first flower of youth, is not something to be lightly thrown away. I asked a friend to take her some money. She kept it but made no acknowledgement.

My friends saw my unhappiness — my eyes gave me away — but their wives' well-meant offers to introduce girls to me won nothing but wry smiles or a shake of the head. I had to wait for her. First love keeps its charm like childhood treasures, whether rag dolls or coloured pebbles. Later on I confided in some of my closest friends, who considerately refrained from any harsh comments, simply hinting half-jokingly that I was a fool — the woman wasn't worth loving. This only made me more stubborn. She had opened the garden of love to me, and I must stay by her till the end of time. Pity is less romantic than love but kinder. Before long I sent a friend to her with a proposal of marriage. I dared not go in person. My friend returned to report that she had laughed wildly. No other answer — simply a fit of wild laughter. Was she laughing at my folly? Fair enough, there is something of folly in all who love. That would be gratifying. Or at herself because she was too close to tears? For anguish can result in wild laughter.

Folly emboldened me to seek her out and I prepared in advance what to say, rehearsing it several times. I must succeed, I told myself: to fail was forbidden. She was out and I went twice again without finding her. The fourth time, a cheap coffin was standing inside her door — she had died after an abortion.

I sent a basket of dewy roses with my heart's blood on their petals to her grave. That was the end of my first love and the start

初恋是青春的第一朵花,不能随便掷弃。我托人给她送了点钱去。留下了,并没有回话。

朋友们看出我的悲苦来,眉头是最会卖人的。他们善意的给我介绍女友,惨笑的摇首是我的回答。我得等着她。初恋像幼年的宝贝永远是最甜密的,不管那个宝贝是一个小布人,还是几块小石子。慢慢的,我开始和几个最知己的朋友谈论她,他们看在我的面上没说她什么,可是假装闹着玩似的暗刺我,他们看我太愚,也就是说她不配一恋。他们越这样,我越坚固。是她打开了我的爱的园门,我得和她走到山穷水尽。怜比爱少着些味道,可是更多着些人情。不久,我托友人向她说明,我愿意娶她。我自己没胆量去。友人回来,带回来她的几声狂笑。她没说别的,只狂笑了一阵。她是笑谁? 笑我的愚,很好,多情的人不是每每有些傻气吗? 这足以使人得意。笑她自己,那只是因为不好意思哭,过度的悲郁使人狂笑。

愚痴给我些力量,我决定自己去见她。要说的话都详细的编制好,演习了许多次,我告诉自己——只许胜,不许败。她没在家。又去了两次,都没见着。第四次去。屋门里停着小小的一口薄棺材,装着她。她是因打胎而死。

一篮最鲜的玫瑰,瓣上带着我心上的泪,放在她的灵前,结束了我的初恋,打开终生的虚空。为什么她落到这殷光景? 我不愿再打听。

英汉对照
English-Chinese
中国文学宝库
Gems of Chinese Literature
现代文学系列
Modern Literature

of a futile existence. I had no desire to find out what had brought her so low. In my heart, at any rate, she would never die.

I stared blankly at the small green slippers until a rustling made me look over my shoulder. The tiny butterflies embroidered on the curtain were fluttering over her head. There she was, as she had been at seventeen, graceful as a fairy who has just alighted on the earth. I stepped back, afraid to frighten her away, and as I recoiled she changed into the woman she had been at twenty-two. She stepped back in turn, and wrinkles appeared on her face. She started laughing wildly. I sank down on the narrow bed, then sprang up and ran over to her, whereupon she changed back in a flash to the girl of seventeen. These transformations in such a brief space made her seem unfettered by time. I sat down again, holding her in my arms, conscious that my cheeks had regained the ruddiness of fifteen years before. So we sat, listening to the pulsing of our blood. Some minutes slipped by before I found my voice to whisper into her ear:

"Do you live here alone?"

"It's not here I live, but here —" she pointed to my heart.

"You never forgot me, then?" I pressed her hand.

"When other men kissed me, I had a vision of you."

"Why let them kiss you?" I felt no jealousy as I asked this.

"There was love in my heart but my lips were at a loose end. Why didn't you come and kiss me?"

"Fear of offending your parents. And then I went to the South Seas, didn't I?"

反正她在我心中永远不死。

我正呆看着那小绿拖鞋,我觉得背后的幔帐动了一动。一回头,帐子上绣的小蝴蝶在她的头上飞动呢。她还是十七八时的模样,还是那么轻巧,像仙女飞降下来还没十分立稳那样立着。我往后退了一步,似乎是怕一往前凑就能把她吓跑。这一退的功夫,她变了,变成二十多岁的样子。她也往后退了,随退随着脸上加着皱纹。她狂笑起来。我坐在那个小床上。刚坐下,我又起来了,扑过她去,极快;她在这极短的时间内,又变回十七岁时的样子。在一秒钟里我看见她半生的变化,她像是不受时间的拘束。我坐在椅子上,她坐在我的怀中。我自己也恢复了十五六年前脸血的红色,我觉得出。我们就这样坐着,听着彼此心血的潮荡。不知有多么久。最后,我找到音声,唇贴着她的耳边,问:

"你独自住在这里?"

"我不住在这里;我住在这儿,"她指着我的心说。

"始终你没忘了我,那么?"我握紧了她的手。

"被别人吻的时候,我心中看着你!"

"可是你许别人吻你?"我并没有一点妒意。

"爱在心里,唇不会闲着;谁教你不来吻我呢?"

"我不是怕得罪你的父母吗? 不是我上了南洋吗?"

她点了点头,"怕使你失去一切,隔离使爱

She nodded. "You lost everything through fear; and in love separation leads to despair."

She told me what had happened. The year that I went abroad her mother died, so that she had a little more freedom. A spray of blossom above the wall is bound to attract the bees and men flocked round. I was still in her thoughts, but the flesh is less patient than love — not all love is as pure as the plum blossom. A young man who resembled me became her lover. Though he adored her she could not forget me; and he possessed her body but not her heart, for a physical resemblance could not take the place of true love. When he began to suspect this, she admitted that her heart was in the South Seas. Just about the time they separated, her father went bankrupt. Marriage was her only way out and she sold herself to a rich man to be able to provide for her father.

"Couldn't you make a living by teaching?" I asked.

"I could only have taught in a primary school — the pay wouldn't have been enough for my father's opium!"

We were both at a loss. I was thinking: Supposing I'd come back then, would I have been in a position to support her father? No, I'd just have had to watch her sell herself.

"I hid my love in my heart," she said, "and kept it alive by what I earned with my flesh. I dreaded the death of the body because I thought, wrongly, that would mean the end of love. Well, never mind that now. He was insanely jealous, always trailing after me whatever I did. Wherever I went, he followed. He couldn't catch me out, but he realized I didn't love him. His resentment developed into open abuse and violence, till he forced me to admit

的心慌了。"

她告诉了我,她死前的光景。在我出国的那一年,她的母亲死去。她比较得自由了一些。出墙的花枝自会招来蜂蝶,有人便追求她,她还想念着我,可是肉体往往比爱少些忍耐力,爱的花不都是梅花。她接受了一个青年的爱,因为他长得像我。他非常的爱她,可是她还忘不了我,肉体的获得不就是爱的满足,相似的音貌不能代替爱的真形。他疑心了,她承认了她的心是在南洋。他们俩断绝了关系。这时候,她父亲的财产全丢了。她非嫁人不可。她把自己卖给一个阔公子,为是供给她的父亲。

"你不会去教学挣钱?"我问。

"我只能教小学,那点薪水还不够父亲买烟吃的!"

我们俩都愣起来。我是想:假使我那时候回来,以我的经济能力说,能供给得起她的父亲吗？我还不是大睁白眼的看着她卖身？

"我把爱藏在心中,"她说,"拿肉体挣来的茶饭营养着他。我深恐肉体死了,爱便不存在,其实我是错了;先不用说这个吧。他非常的妒忌,永远跟着我,无论我是干什么,上哪儿去,他老随着我。他找不出我的破绽来,可是觉得出我是不爱他。慢慢的,他由讨厌变为公开的辱骂我,甚至于打我,他逼得我没法不承认我的心是另有所寄。忍无可忍也就顾不及饭碗问题

英汉对照
English-Chinese
中国文学宝库
Gems of Chinese Literature
现代文学系列
Modern Literature

A Vision

that there was another man. Things were so unbearable by then that I couldn't even stop to consider my rice-bowl. He threw me out with nothing but the clothes I stood in. My father was still looking to me for money and I had to live myself — I'd always been used to the best of everything. So I used carnal means to satisfy carnal desires, since my body was all the capital I had. Anyone could buy my smiles. I've a lovely smile: I used to practise it in front of the mirror. In the circumstances I preferred this type of retail sale to being under the thumb of one rich husband. Although plenty of lewd remarks were made behind me in the streets, at least I was free, and I rather preened myself sometimes when I met other women dowdily dressed. I had four abortions, but once the pain was over I could smile again.

"At first I had quite a reputation. Because I'd been a rich man's plaything and had some education. Men of the old school as well as the new all came to patronize me. I never stopped to think, never even tried to save. My one aim in life, all that mattered, was to be smart: tomorrow could take care of itself. Avoiding immediate unpleasantness left me too tired to worry about the future. But I couldn't keep it up. My father's opium ran away with my money and abortions were costly too. I'd never put anything by, and a bank balance doesn't mount up by itself. Soon my last shreds of foolish pride were gone and I stooped to the meanest ways of making money — plain stealing at times. If a man behind me jeered, I turned back to smile. Each abortion added two or three years to my age — the mirror doesn't lie. I had lost my looks but tried recklessly to make up for it by doing all I could to attract cus-

了。他把我赶出来,连一件长衫也没给我留。我呢,父亲照样和我要钱,我自己得吃得穿,而且我一向吃好的穿好的惯了。为满足肉体,还得利用肉体,身体是现成的本钱。凡给我钱的便买去我点筋肉的笑。我很会笑:我照着镜子练习那迷人的笑。环境的不同使人作退一步想,这样零卖,到是比终日叫那一个阔公子管着强一些。在街上,有多少人指着我的后影叹气,可是我到底是自由的,有时候我与些打扮得不漂亮的女子遇上,我也有些得意。我一共打过四次胎,但是创痛过去便又笑了。

"最初,我颇有一些名气,因为我既是作过富宅的玩物,又能识几个字,新派旧派的人都愿来照顾我。我没工夫去思想,甚至于不想积蓄一点钱,我完全为我的服装香粉活着。今天的漂亮是今天的生活,明天自有明天管照着自己,身体的疲倦,只管眼前的刺激,不顾将来。不久,这种生活也不能维持了。父亲的烟是无底的深坑。打胎需要花许多费。以前不想剩钱;钱自然不会自己剩下。我连一点无聊的傲气也不敢存了。我得极下贱的去找钱了,有时是明抢。有人指着我的后影叹气,我也回头向他笑一笑了。打一次胎增加两三岁。镜子是不欺人的,我已老丑了。疯狂足以补足衰老。我尽着肉体的所能伺候人们,不然,我没有生意。我敞着门睡着,我是大众的,不是我自己的。一天廿

英汉对照
English-Chinese
中国文学宝库
Gems of Chinese Literature
现代文学系列
Modern Literature

tomers. My doors were open even when I slept: my body was on sale at any hour of the day. I sank deeper and deeper into a sea of lust, dead to sober sanity, obsessed by money. That obsession with money took the place of thinking — calculations how to make an extra fifty cents. I never cried because crying makes a woman ugly. It was money, not myself I worried about."

She stopped for breath. Her gown was wet with my tears.

"Then you came back," she went on. "You were over thirty too. I remembered you as a student of seventeen. Your eyes weren't the same as when — how long ago is it? — you stared at my green slippers. Still, you yourself were intrinsically unchanged, whereas I'd died long ago. You could go on dreaming of your first love, but not I. I'd known all along that when you came back you would want me. But I'd lost myself and what had I to give you? While you were away I'd never denied to anyone that I loved you; but when you came back all I could do was laugh wildly. It seemed a cruel trick to play — not coming back till I had sunk so low. If you'd stayed away I could have gone on dreaming of the South Seas, gone on living in your heart. But, no, you must come back, so late —"

"Late doesn't have to mean too late," I interposed.

"No, it was too late. That's why I killed myself."

"No!"

"Yes, indeed. If I could live on in your heart, live on in a poem, it was the same to me whether I lived or died. I did it when I had my last abortion. With you near, I couldn't smile any more. Without smiling I couldn't make money. The only way out was to

四小时,什么时间也可以买我的身体。我消失在欲海里。在清醒的世界中我并不存在。我看着人们在我身上狂动,我的手指算计着钱数。我不思想,只是盘算——怎能多进五毛钱。我不哭,哭不好看。只为钱着急,不管我自己。"

她休息了一会儿,我的泪已滴湿她的衣襟。

"你回来了!"她继续着说,"你也三十多了;我记得你是十七岁的小学生。你的眼已不是那年——多少年了?——看我那双绿拖鞋的眼。可是,多少还是你自己,我,早已死了。你可以继续作那初恋的梦,我已无梦可作。我始终一点也不怀疑,我知道你要回来,必定要我。及至见着你,我自己已找不到我自己,拿什么给你呢?你没回来的时候,我永远不拒绝,不论是对谁说,我是爱你;你回来了,我只好狂笑。单等我落到这样,你才回来,这不是有意弄人?假如你永远不回来,我老有个南洋作我的梦景,你老有个我在你的心中,岂不很美?你偏偏的回来了,而且回来这样迟——"

"可是来迟了并不就是来不及了,"我插了一句。

"晚了就是来不及了。我杀了自己。"

"什么?"

"我杀了我自己。我命定的只能住在你心中,生存在一首诗里,生死有什么区别?在打胎的时候我自己下了手。有你在我左右,我没法子再笑。不笑,我怎么挣钱?只有一条路,名字叫死。你回来迟了,我别再死迟了:我再晚死一

die. You had come back too late, but I mustn't die too late. Any more delay and I had no hope of living on in your heart. I live here, here in your heart where there's no sunshine, no sound, nothing but colour. Colour lasts longer, colour paints pictures of our memories. These green slippers are a bit of colour that you and I would recognize anywhere."

"I remember your neat ankles too. Let me see them again!"

She smiled and shook her head.

I insisted, pulling down her stockings. Underneath were two white bones, no flesh on them.

"You must go now!" She shook me gently. "We can never meet again. I wanted to live in your heart, but this has finished it. I hope in your heart it will be always spring."

The sun was sinking west, a cold wind was rising, there were dark clouds in the east. All the joy had gone out of the spring while I was dreaming. I rose to my feet and stared at the dark green pines. A long, long time I stood there. In the distance a small procession was approaching, and presently a faint medley of sounds could be heard. As it drew near, the birds in the fields cried out in alarm and flew up on white wings towards my side of the hill. Raising a dust as they hurried along came a few musicians, a few mourners in white behind them, and last of all a coffin. Yes, there are dead to bury in spring too. A handful of paper money[1] was scattered like butterflies over the wheat field. The clouds in the east grew blacker, the green of the willows dark-

---

[1] Offered to the dead for use in the other world.

会儿,我便连住在你心中的希望也没有了。我住在这里,这里便是你的心。这里没有阳光,没有声响,只有一些颜色。颜色是更持久的,颜色画成咱们的记忆。看那双小鞋,绿的,是点颜色,你我永远认识它们。"

"但是我也记得那双脚。许我看看吗?"

她笑了,摇摇头。

我很坚决,我握住她的脚,扯下她的袜,露出没有肉的一只白脚骨。

"去吧"她推了我一把。"从此你我无缘再见了!我愿住在你的心中,现在不行了;我愿在你心中永远是青春。"

太阳已往西斜去;风大了些,也凉了些,东方有些黑云。春光在一个梦中惨淡了许多。我立起来,又看见那片暗绿的松树。立了不知有多久。远处来了些蠕动的小人,随着一些听不甚真的音乐。越来越近了,田中惊起许多白翅的鸟,哀鸣着向山这边飞。我看清了,一群人们匆匆的走,带起一些灰土。三五鼓手在前,几个白衣的在后,最后是一口棺材。春天也要埋人的。撒起一把纸钱,蝴蝶似的落在麦田上。东方的黑云更厚了,柳条的绿色加深了许多,绿得

英汉对照
English-Chinese
中国文学宝库
Gems of Chinese Literature
现代文学系列
Modern Literature

er, tragically dark. Sick at heart, I thought of that pair of small green slippers, like the leaves on some eternal tree dreaming of spring.

Translated by Gladys Yang

有些凄惨。心中茫然,只想起那双小绿拖鞋,像两片树叶在永生的树上作着春梦。

英汉对照
English-Chinese
中国文学宝库
Gems of Chinese Literature
现代文学系列
Modern Literature

Black Li and White Li

Though love was not the central theme of the misunderstanding which arose between the two brothers, I must begin my discussion there.

Black Li was five years older than White Li. They were both schoolmates of mine, though Black Li and I graduated from middle school the same year White Li began his studies there. Black Li and I were good friends, and since I visited their home frequently, I also got to know White Li quite well. In this day and age, five years makes a big difference. The two brothers' characters were as different as their nicknames: Black Li was old-fashioned; White Li was very modern. They didn't argue about this specifically, though their points of view differed radically on every subject under the sun. Black Li wasn't really black. He was called Black Li on account of a big black birthmark over his left eyebrow. His younger brother had no such marks, so he became White Li. Their classmates in middle school, who had given them these names, thought this was quite logical. Actually, both brothers' complexions were rather pale, and they looked very much alike.

They were both chasing the same woman — pardon me for not mentioning her name. She herself couldn't decide which of the brothers she loved more, though at the same time she wouldn't admit that she didn't love either of them. We were all very worried

黑白李

爱情不是他们哥儿俩这档子事的中心,可是我得由这儿说起。

黑李是哥,白李是弟,哥比弟大着五岁。俩人都是我的同学,虽然白李刚一入中学,黑李和我就毕业了。黑李是我的好友,因为常到他家去,所以对白李的事儿我也略知一二。五年是个长距离,在这个时代。这哥儿俩的不同正如他们的外号——黑,白。黑李要是古人,白李是现代的。他们俩并不因此打架吵嘴,可是对任何事的看法也不一致。黑李并不黑;只是在左眉上有个大黑痣。因此他是"黑李";弟弟没有那么个记号,所以是"白李";这在给他们送外号的中学生们看,是很逻辑的。其实他俩的脸都很白,而且长得极相似。

他俩都追她——恕不道出姓名了——她说不清到底该爱谁,又不肯说谁也不爱。于是大

英汉对照
English-Chinese
中国文学宝库
Gems of Chinese Literature
现代文学系列
Modern Literature

about them on account of this. Though we knew that neither of them was looking for a fight, we also knew that the game of love wasn't always played according to the rules of friendship.

Finally, Black Li surrendered.

I recall what happened very clearly. On a drizzly night in early summer, I went to have a chat with him in his home. He was sitting alone in his room with four fine porcelain tea bowls decorated with red fish standing on the table before him. We were very informal whenever we got together. I sat down and lit a cigarette while he played with his tea bowls. He turned them around, one by one, until the fish designs painted on them were all facing him. Once they were arranged in this manner he leaned back, examining them like a painter who had just completed a section of a new painting. Next he rearranged them so that the fish on the other side of the bowls were all lined up neatly in front of him. Once again, he leaned back to get a better look, and then turned and smiled at me. His smile was as innocent as a child's.

He was fond of playing this sort of game. He had no great talents, yet he dabbled in many areas. He never pretended to be an expert in any field, but he believed that everything he did contributed to moulding his temperament. There was no question about his being good natured. If he had a hobby to persue, such as repairing an old scroll painting, he could very easily while away an entire day at it .

Calling my name, he smiled and said, "I let Number Four have her." In terms of seniority in their family, White Li was number four, since an uncle on their father's side had two sons. "Brothers

家替他们弟兄捏着把汗。明知他俩不肯吵架,可是爱情这玩艺是不讲交情的。

可是,黑李让了。

我还记得清清楚楚:正是个初夏的晚间,落着点小雨,我去找他闲谈,他独自在屋里坐着呢,面前摆着四个红鱼细磁茶碗。我们俩是用不着客气的,我坐下吸烟,他摆弄那四个碗。转转这个,转转那个,把红鱼要一点不差的朝着他。摆好,身子往后仰一仰,像画家涂完一层色那么退后看看。然后,又逐一的转开,把另一面的鱼们摆齐。又往后仰身端详了一番,回过头来向我笑了笑,笑得非常天真。

他爱弄这些小把戏。对什么也不精通,可是什么也爱动一动。他并不假充行家,只信这可以养性。不错,他确是个好脾性的人。有点小玩艺,比如粘补旧画等等,他就平安的消磨半日。

叫了我一声,他又笑了笑,"我把她让给老四了,"按着大排行,白李是四爷,他们的伯父屋

英汉对照
English-Chinese
中国文学宝库
Gems of Chinese Literature
现代文学系列
Modern Literature

shouldn't become estranged on account of a woman."

"That's why they call you old-fashioned," I said with a chuckle.

"You're wrong, you can't teach an old bear new tricks. I couldn't handle a *menage a trois* anyway. So I said to her, no matter who she loves, I couldn't see her any more. You can't imagine how much better I felt after that."

"First time I've ever heard of a love affair like that."

"The first time? Then perhaps I shouldn't say any more. She can do as she pleases, but at least Number Four and I won't have any more arguments. If this sort of thing happened between us, I certainly hope one of us would give in the same way."

"Then there'd be peace on earth, right?"

We both laughed.

About ten days later, Black Li came to see me. I knew by now that whenever a grey shadow hovered over his forehead, there was something important on his mind. On occasions such as these, we'd always drink half a catty of Lotus brandy. I got the drinks ready quickly, since his forehead was looking unusually dim.

When he was drinking the second cup, his hands began trembling. It was hard for Black Li to conceal his feelings. If something was upsetting him, no matter how hard he tried to remain calm, it always showed on his face. He was such a kind and outgoing person.

"I went and had a talk with her," he said, smiling in a rather silly manner. But this was a genuine smile, since he was getting ready to pour out all his troubles to a close friend. If Black Li had no close friends, he wouldn't have survived for long.

中还有弟兄呢。"不能因为个女子失了兄弟们的和气。"

"所以你不是现代人,"我打着哈哈说。

"不是。老狗熊学不会新玩艺了。三角恋爱,不得劲儿。我和她说了,不管她是爱谁,我从此不再和她来往。觉得很痛快!"

"没看见过,这么讲恋爱的。"

"你没看见过?我还不讲了呢。干她的去,反正别和老四闹翻了。赶明儿咱俩要来这么一句话,希望不是你收兵,就是我让了。"

"于是天下就太平了?"

我们笑开了。

过了有十天吧,黑李找我来了。我会看,每逢他的脑门发暗,必定是有心事。每逢有心事,我俩必喝上半斤莲花白。我赶紧把酒预备好,因为他的脑门不大亮吗?

喝到第二盅上,他的手有点哆嗦。这个人的心里存不住事。遇上心事,他极想镇定,可是脸上还泄露出来。他太厚道。

"我刚从她那儿来,"他笑着,笑得无聊;可还是真的笑,因为要对个好友道出胸中的闷气。这个人若没有好朋友,是一天也活不了的。

英汉对照
English-Chinese
中国文学宝库
Gems of Chinese Literature
现代文学系列
Modern Literature

I didn't press him, and there was no need for us to hurry anyway. Our feelings could very easily fill in the little silences which occurred in our conversations. We glanced at each other and grinned. Our facial expressions and intuitive understanding of each other were more important than anything we might say. For this reason White Li always called us "two bumps on a log."

"Number Four got nice and upset with me," he said. I knew exactly what he meant by "nice": First, he didn't want to admit that they had an argument; and second, he didn't want to put all the blame on his younger brother, even though it was White Li who was in the wrong. The word "nice" was a complex expression of his unwillingness to say what was really on his mind. "It was all because of her. It's my fault, I don't know anything about feminine psychology. Remember the other day I told you that I had surrendered? I had no qualms about that whatsoever, but she took it very differently. She thought I was trying to humiliate her. You're right when you say I'm old-fashioned. For me, love is a matter of doing what's right. Little did I know that our lady friend's out to get the whole world chasing after her. Now she hates me. So what does she do to get her revenge? I rejected her, so she stops seeing Number Four. Number Four blew up in front of me. So today I went to apologize to her. If she had just cursed me and let off some steam, maybe she and Number Four could get back together again. Anyway, that's what I was hoping. But you know what? She didn't curse me at all. She said she wanted Number Four and I to be her friends. Of course that's impossible for me, though I didn't tell that to her directly. I came over here to talk to you about it.

我并不催促他;我俩说话用不着忙,感情都在话中间那些空子里流露出来呢。彼此对看着,一齐微笑,神气和默中的领悟,都比言语更有分量。要不怎么白李一见我俩喝酒就叫我们"一对糟蛋"呢。

"老四跟我好闹了一场,"他说,我明白这个"好"字——第一他不愿说兄弟间吵了架,第二不愿只说弟弟不对,即使弟弟真是不对。这个字带出不愿说而又不能不说的曲折。"因为她。我不好,太不明白女子心理。那天不是告诉你,我让了吗?我是居心无愧,然而她可出了花样。她以为我是特意羞辱她,你说对了,我不是现代人,我把恋爱看成该怎样就怎样的事,敢情人家女子愿意'大家'在后面追随着。她恨上了我。这么报复一下——我放弃了她,她断绝了老四。老四当然跟我闹了。所以今天又找她去,请罪。她骂我一顿,出出气,或者还能和老四言归于好。我这么希望。哼,她没骂我。她还叫我和老四都作她的朋友。这个,我不能干,我并没这么明对她讲,我上这儿跟你说说。我不干,她自

Problem is, if I don't do as she says, she'll ignore Number Four, and he'll start up with me all over again."

"A very difficult situation." I tacked this on for his benefit. A few moments passed. Then I said, "Why don't I go explain everything to Number Four?"

"That would be fine," he said, holding up his wine-cup, "but it might not do any good. Anyway, I'm finished with her. If Number Four wants to make an issue of it with me, I just won't say anything, that's all there is to it."

We shifted the topic of our conversation onto some other subjects. He told me he'd been reading about religion the last few days. I knew that his studying religion was purely a whim; Black Li wasn't the type to take up religion out of pessimism, or because he was undergoing some spiritual crisis.

Shortly after Black Li left, White Li came in. He rarely came to visit me, so I guessed that something important had happened. Though still a college student, White Li looked much more astute than his older brother. He gave you the immediate impression that he was capable of being a great leader. The things he said would either lead you down the very path he wanted you to follow or strap you to the guillotine. His manner was extremely direct, the very opposite of his brother. I was also quite direct with him, lest he call me a "bump on a log."

"Number Two came to see you of course." Black Li was the second oldest in their extended family. "And of course he's been telling you all about what's going on." Naturally, there was no

然也不再理老四。老四就得再跟我闹。"

"没办法!"我替他补上这一小句。待了会儿,"我找老四一趟,解释一下?"

"也好。"他端着酒盅愣了会儿,"也许没用。反正我不再和她来往。老四再跟我闹呢,我不言语就是了。"

我们俩又谈了些别的,他说这几天正研究宗教。我知道他的读书全凭兴之所至,决不因为谈到宗教而想他有点厌世,或是精神上有什么大的变动。

哥哥走,弟弟来了。白李不常上我这儿来,这大概是有事。他在大学还没毕业,可是看起来比黑李精明着许多。他这个人,叫你一看,你就觉得他应当到处作领袖。每一句话,他不是领导着你走上他所指出的路子,便是把你绑在断头台上。他没有客气话,和他哥正相反。

我对他也不便太客气了,省得他说我是糟蛋。

"老二当然来过了?"他问;李是大排行行二。"也当然跟你谈到我们的事?"我自然不便

need for me to reply in a hurry, since he said "of course" twice. But before I even had a chance to open my mouth, he went on, "You know, I just did it to make a point."

I told him I didn't know that.

"You think I'm really after that woman?" He smiled at me with Black Li's smile, except that Black Li's smiles were never so disdainful. "The only reason I got involved with her at all was to cause trouble for Number Two; otherwise, why would I want to waste my time with her? Aren't all relations between men and women based purely on animal desire? What do I need her for then? Number Two believes that animal desire is sacred, so he went out of his way to kowtow to her. Now that she's rejected him, he thinks it's my turn to kowtow to her. I'm sorry, that's not my style." He laughed loudly.

I didn't smile, nor did I dare interrupt him. I listened carefully to what he had to say and paid even closer attention to his facial expression. Black Li and White Li's faces were similar in every respect, except for the fact that Black Li had none of his younger brother's arrogance. For this reason, one moment I felt I was talking to a very close friend, and the next as if I were sitting across from a complete stranger. This was quite discomfiting; the face before me was familiar, but the expression was very strange.

"You see, I didn't even kowtow to her once. At the proper moment, I kissed her. She really liked that, a whole lot more than all that kowtowing. But that's not the main point. What I mean is, do you think Number Two and I ought to go on living together?"

I couldn't answer this question immediately.

急于回答,因为有两个"当然"在这里。果然,没等我回答,他说了下去:"你知道,我是借题发挥?"

我不知道。

"你以为我真要那个女玩艺?"他笑了,笑得和他哥哥一样,只是黑李的向来不带着这不屑于对我笑的劲儿。"我专为和老二捣乱,才和她来往;不然,谁有工夫招呼她?男与女的关系,从根儿上说,还不是兽欲的关系?为这个,我何必非她不行?老二以为这个兽欲的关联应当叫作神圣的,所以他郑重的向她磕头,及至磕了一鼻子灰,又以为我也应当去磕,对不起,我没那个瘾!"他哈哈的笑起来。

我没笑,也不敢插嘴。我很留心听他的话,更注意看他的脸。脸上处处像他哥哥,可是那股神气又完全不像他的哥哥。这个,使我忽而觉得是和一个顶熟识的人说话,忽而又像和个生人对坐着。我有点不舒坦 看着个熟识的面貌,而找不到那点看惯了的神气。

"你看,我不磕头;得机会就吻她一下。她喜欢这个,至少比受几个头更过瘾。不过,这不是正笔。正文是这个,你想我应当老和二爷在一块儿吗?"

我当时回答不出。

英汉对照
English-Chinese
中国文学宝库
Gems of Chinese Literature
现代文学系列
Modern Literature

47

He smiled — probably he was thinking to himself how I was just a "bump on a log." "I've got my own life to live, my own plans; the same is true for him. The best thing would be for both of us to go our own ways, don't you think?"

"Yes. What are your plans then?" It was no easy task coming up with this question; I already felt extremely awkward.

"This is no time to talk about my plans. Once we divide our family property and start living apart, you'll find out what my plans are."

"You started an argument with Number Two just because you want to move out? Is that the point you're getting to?" Now I was being clever.

He nodded with a smile but said nothing, knowing I probably had more to say. I continued, "Why didn't you discuss it with him peacefully instead of having an argument?"

"Do you think he's capable of understanding me? You may be able to hold a reasonable dialogue with him, but not me. As soon as I mention living apart to him, he starts crying. Then it's the same old thing — 'What did Mother say before she died? Didn't she tell us we should always be good to each other?' He brings that up every time, as if the dead were supposed to run the lives of the living. Not only that, if I mention dividing up the estate, he'll disagree, I swear to you, and tell me how he wants to sign everything over to me. But I don't want to take advantage of him like that. He always treats me like a little brother. He thinks he can control other people's behaviour. He pretends to understand me, but actually he's just a big anachronism. The present belongs to me; why do I

他又笑了笑——大概心中是叫我糟蛋呢。"我有我的前途,我的计划;他有他的。顶好是各走各的路,是不是?"

"是;你有什么计划?"我好容易想起这么一句;不然便太僵得慌了。

"计划,先不告诉你。得先分家,以后你就明白我的计划了。"

"因为要分居,所以和老二吵;借题发挥?"我觉得自己很聪明似的。

他笑着点了点头;没说什么,好像准知道我还有一句呢。我确是有一句:"为什么不明说,而要吵呢?"

"他能明白我吗?你能和他一答一和的说,我不行。我一说分家,他立刻就得落泪。然后,又是那一套——母亲去世的时候,说什么来着?不是说咱俩老得和美吗?他必定说这一套,好像活人得叫死人管着似的。还有一层,一听说分家,他管保不肯,而愿把家产都给了我,找个想占便宜,他老拿我当作"弟弟",老拿自己的感情限定住别人的举止,老假装他明白我,其实他是个时代落伍者。这个时代是我的,用不着他

英汉对照
English-Chinese
中国文学宝库
Gems of Chinese Literature
现代文学系列
Modern Literature

49

need him to tell me what to do?" His expression suddenly became very serious.

Looking at his face, I gradually began to see things in a different light. White Li was a proud young man who looked down on us two "bumps on a log." All he really wanted was to stand on his own two feet. I also realized that if the two of them tried to talk over their differences, they'd get carried away for hours discussing the whole range of fraternal obligations. If White Li didn't bring this up, Black Li certainly would. A quick argument was preferable to all of this, lest their conflict drag out indefinitely. White Li wanted a clean break, after which each of them could go their own way. Furthermore, if they held a proper discussion on the matter, Black Li would never respond in a straightforward manner. If White Li kicked up a storm first and Black Li offered a lot of resistance, Black Li would appear to be trying to appropriate White Li's share of the estate. At this point I suddenly felt enlightened.

"So you want me to go and talk to Number Two about it, right?"

"That's right. This way we can avoid a big argument." He smiled again. "Of course you shouldn't put him on the spot. We're still brothers." It seemed he felt very uncomfortable with the word "brothers."

I agreed to do as he said.

"The more insistent you are the better. I propose that he and I have nothing to do with each other for the next twenty years." He paused for a moment, forcing a grin. "You can tell him that if he wants to forget about me, he should get married and have a nice fat baby as soon as possible. In twenty years, I'll be old-fashioned

来操心管我。"他的脸上忽然的很严重了。

看着他的脸,我心中慢慢的起了变化——白李不仅是看不起"两糟蛋"的狂傲少年了,他确是要树立住自己,我也明白过来,他要是和黑李慢慢的商量,必定要费许多动感情的话,要讲许多弟兄间的情义;即使他不讲,黑李总要讲的。与其这样,还不如吵,省得拖泥带水,他要一刀两断,各自奔前程。再说,慢慢的商议,老二决不肯干脆的答应。老四先吵嚷出来,老二若还不干,便是显着要霸占弟弟的财产了。猜到这里,我心中忽然一亮:

"你是不是叫我对老二去说?"

"一点不错。省得再吵。"他又笑了。"不愿叫老二太难堪了,究竟是弟兄。"似乎他很不喜说这末后的两个字——弟兄。

我答应了给他办。

"把话说得越坚决越好。二十年内,我俩不能作弟兄。"他停了一会儿,嘴角上挤出点笑来。"也给老二想了,顶好赶快结婚,生个胖娃娃就容易把弟弟忘了。二十年后,我当然也落

英汉对照
English-Chinese
中国文学宝库
Gems of Chinese Literature
现代文学系列
Modern Literature

myself. If I'm still alive then, I'll come home and play uncle. Make sure you tell him that when he's courting his future wife, he should kiss more and kowtow less; he should spend his energy chasing her rather than kneeling down before her." He stood up, paused for a moment, and then said, "Thank you." It was evident that these last two words were intended for me, but also that he really didn't want to bear the responsibility for having said them.

I discussed this matter nearly every day with Black Li. Every time I went to visit him he had the Lotus wine ready. We'd eat, drink and talk a lot together, but never came up with any conclusions. This went on for at least two weeks. He understood and appreciated everything I said and even expressed the hope that his younger brother would go out in the world and make a name for himself. But his last words always were: "How can I get along without him?"

"What could Number Four's plans possibly be?" He asked himself this question pacing back and forth in his room. His black birthmark sunk into the creases on his forehead and seemed to have shrunk somewhat. "What are his plans? Why don't you ask him. If you could find out, I could stop worrying so much."

"He won't tell me." I must have told him that at least fifty times.

"That's dangerous though. He's my only brother. Let him come and argue it out with me; there's nothing wrong with two brothers having an argument. He was never this way with me before. We only started disagreeing with each other very recently. It must be

伍了,那时候,假如还活着的话,好回家作叔叔。不过,告诉他,讲恋爱的时候要多吻少磕头,要死追,别死跪着。"他立起来,又想了想,"谢谢你呀。"他叫我明明的觉出来,这一句是特意为我说的,他并不负要说的责任。

为这件事,我天天找黑李去。天天他给我预备好莲花白。吃完喝完说完,无结果而散。至少有半个月的工夫是这样。我说的,他都明白,而且愿意老四去创练创练。可是临完的一句老是"舍不得老四呀!"

"老四的计划? 计划?"他走过来,走过去,这么念道。眉上的黑痣夹陷在脑门的皱纹里,看着好似缩小了些。"什么计划呢? 你问问他,问明白我就放心了。"

"他不说,"我已经这样回答过五十多次了。

"不说便是有危险性! 我只有这么一个弟弟! 叫他跟我吵吧,吵也是好的。从前他不这样,就是近来和我吵。大概还是为那个女的!

英汉对照
English-Chinese
中国文学宝库
Gems of Chinese Literature
现代文学系列
Modern Literature

on account of that woman. He wants me to get married? I didn't get married, and looked what happened. I'll get married then! What could his plans possibly be? Really! He wants to divide up the family property? Let him take whatever he wants. I probably offended him in some way. Though I never wanted to start a fight with him, I know I have my own opinions on things. So what are his plans then? He can do as he pleases. Why do we have to divide up the estate?"

Once he started on this topic, you could be sure he would drone on for more than an hour. His hobbies increased in number day by day: divination by tossing coins or using the Eight Trigrams, analysing Chinese charaters, reading about religion.... But none of these hobbies helped him to figure out what Number Four's plans were; on the contrary, they only increased his anxiety. This is not to say that he appeared any more nervous than usual. Actually, he was his usual maudlin self. It seemed as if his actions could never keep up with his emotions. No matter how agitated he was inside, he always moved slowly; he seemed to be playing with his life as if it were a toy.

I told him that Number Four's plans involved his future career and had nothing to do with the present. But he only shook his head.

In this manner, more than a month went by.

"You know," I said, appealing to reason, "Number Four isn't pressing me, so it must be that he has some long range plans. He's not about to run off and do anything big right now."

He just shook his head again.

劝我结婚？没结婚就闹成这样，还结婚！什么计划呢？真！分家？他爱要什么拿什么好了。大概是我得罪了他，我虽不跟他吵，我知道我也有我的主张。什么计划呢？他要怎样就怎样好了，何必分家……"

这样来回磨，一磨就是一点多钟。他的小玩艺也一天比一天增多：占课，打卦，测字，研究宗教……什么也没能帮助他推测出老四的计划，只添了不少小恐怖。这可并不是说，他显着怎样的慌张。不，他依旧是那么婆婆慢慢的。他的举止动作好像老追不上他的感情，无论心中怎着急，他的动作是慢的，慢得仿佛是拿生命当作玩艺儿似的逗弄着。

我说老四的计划是指着将来的事业而言，不是现在有什么具体的办法。他摇头。

就这么耽延着，差不多又过了一个多月。

"你看，"我抓住了点理，"老四也不催我，显然他说的是长久之计，不是马上要干什么。"

他还是摇头。

As time passed, the number of stories about him increased. One Sunday morning I happened to see him entering a church, where I assumed he was looking for a friend. I waited for him outside, but he didn't come out. I had to go somewhere, and as I walked away I thought about how the recent events in his life must have been upsetting for him — his broken love affair; his falling out with his brother; and perhaps there were more things I didn't know about. But two things alone seemed to be too much for him to bear. His actions revealed that life was just a game for him, but this was because he was so preoccupied with the most trivial matters. It made him uncomfortable if the patterns on tea bowls were out of line. Similarly, he arranged things neatly in his mind to soothe his conscience. Perhaps by going to church and praying he could put his mind at rest. While his conscience had been provided to him by the wise sages of yore, at the same time he didn't reject all modern things and modern thinking. As a result, his own "way of thinking" was never quite as coherent as "the way things really were," making it difficult for him to know how to act properly. He was probably in love with her, but he had to reject her for his brother's sake; he certainly never mentioned falling out of love with her to me. He often said, "Let's take a ride in an airplane." Then he'd laugh, but it wasn't really him laughing, it was "the flesh and bones he'd inherited from his parents" that were laughing.

One afternoon I went to see him. It was our custom to begin talking about Number Four immediately — at least this had been the pattern over the last month or so. But that day he looked like an entirely different person. His eyes were bright and he had an

时间越长,他的故事越多。有一个礼拜天的早晨,我看见他进了礼拜堂。也许是看朋友,我想。在外面等了他会儿。他没出来。不便再等了,我一边走一边想:老李必是受了大的刺激——失恋,弟兄不和,或者还有别的。只就我知道的这两件事说,大概他已经支持不下去。他的动作仿佛是拿生命当作小玩艺,那正是因他对任何小事都要慎重的考虑。茶碗上的花纹摆不齐都觉得不舒服。那一件小事也得在他心中摆好,摆得使良心上舒服。上礼拜堂去祷告,为是坚定良心。良心是古圣先贤给他制备好了的,可是他又不愿将一切新事新精神一笔抹杀。结果,他"想"怎样老不如"已是"怎样来得现成,他不知怎样才好。他大概是真爱她,可是为弟弟不能不放弃她,而且失恋是说不出口的。他常对我说,"咱们也坐一回飞机。"说完,他一笑,不是他笑呢,是"身体发肤,受之父母"笑呢。

过了响午,我去找他。按说一见面就得谈老四,在过去的一个多月都是这样。这次他变了花样,眼睛很亮,脸上有点极静适的笑意,好

英汉对照
English-Chinese
中国文学宝库
Gems of Chinese Literature
现代文学系列
Modern Literature

57

expression of great contentment on his face. It was as if he'd just purchased a fine edition of a rare book.

I began the conversation. "What's the good news?"

He nodded, smiling. "Very interesting!" He always said this after experiencing something for the first time. If someone told him an old ghost story, you could be sure he would respond with "Very interesting!" He wouldn't argue with you about whether ghosts existed or not since he believed in the supernatural. "Who knows, there must be stranger things in the world than that," he would say. In his mind, anything was possible. Thus he accepted new things quite readily, but without understanding them very thoroughly. It wasn't that he lacked the desire to understand things. However, on those occasions when he should have used his brain, he used his emotions.

"The principle is the same," he said, "people should make sacrifices for others."

"Didn't you sacrifice your girlfriend for him already?" I was trying to remain rational.

"That doesn't count. That was a passive separation; I wasn't giving up anything that belonged to me. I've spent the last two weeks reading the Four Gospels, and I've made up my mind. I ought to support Number Four; it's wrong for me to try to stop him from moving out. Think about it for a moment. If it's only a matter of dividing up our estate, why can't he just come and talk to me about it?"

"He's afraid you'll disagree with him," I said.

"No. The last few days, I've been thinking about it. He must

像是又买着一册善本的旧书。

"看见你了,"我先发了言。

他点了点头,又笑了一下,"也很有意思!"

什么老事情被他头次遇上,他总是说这句。对他讲个闹鬼的笑话,也是"很有意思"!他不和人家辩论鬼的有无,他信那个故事,"说不定世上还有比这更奇怪的事。"据他看,什么事都是可能的。因此,他接受的容易,可就没有什么精到的见解。他不是不想多明白些,但是每每在该用脑子的时候,他用了感情。

"道理都是一样的,"他说,"总是劝人为别人牺牲。"

"你不是已经牺牲了个爱人?"我愿多说些事实。

"那不算,那是消极的割舍,并非由自己身上拿出点什么来。这十来天,我已经读完'四福音书'。我也想好了,我应当分担老四的事,不应当只不准他离开我。你想想吧,设若真是专为分家产,为什么不来跟我说明?"

"他怕你不干,"我回答。

"不是!这几天我用心想过了,他必是真有

英汉对照
English-Chinese
中国文学宝库
Gems of Chinese Literature
现代文学系列
Modern Literature

have something specific in mind, probably something very dangerous, but he wants to make a clean break with me so that I won't get implicated if he gets in trouble. You think he's just young and impulsive? He acts that way just to fool us. He's actually going out of his way for my benefit, since he doesn't want me to suffer unjustly on account of anything he does. He wants to make sure I'm safe first, so he can do whatever he wants on his own with a clear conscience. I'm sure that's it. But I can't let him go now; I've got to make sacrifices for him too. Right before Mother died, she...." He stopped there, knowing I'd heard it all before.

I never thought he would take it so far, and I still didn't believe everything he said. Perhaps under the influence of religion he was giving vent to some previously hidden emotions.

I decided to speak to White Li about it on the very slim chance that Black Li was right. Though I didn't believe that what he said was true, I couldn't afford to take any chances.

I looked everywhere for White Li, but he was nowhere to be found. There was no trace of him on the campus, in the dormitories, in the library, on the tennis courts or in any of the little restaurants he frequented. No one I asked had seen him for days. White Li was like that. If Black Li went away for a few days, he would have notified all of his friends. But White Li would disappear like a puff of smoke. I came up with a possible solution: I asked "her" if she knew anything about his whereabouts.

Since I spent so much time with Black Li, she already knew who I was. But she hadn't seen White Li for a long time either. She

个计划，而且是有危险性的。所以他要一刀两断，以免连累了我。你以为他年青，一冲子性？他正是利用这个骗咱们；他实在是体谅我，不肯使我受屈。把我放在安全的地方，他好独作独当的去干。必定是这样！我不能撒手他，我得为他牺牲！母亲临去世的时候——"他没往下说，因为知道我已听熟了那一套。

我真没想到这一层。可是还不深信他的话；焉知他不是受了点宗教的刺激而要充分的发泄感情呢？

我决定去找白李，万一黑李猜得不错呢！是，我不深信他的话，可也不敢耍玄虚。

怎样找也找不到白李。学校，宿舍，图书馆，网球场，小饭铺，都看到了，没有他的影儿。和人们打听，都说好几天没见着他。这又是白李之所以为白李；黑李要是离家几天，连好朋友们他也要通知一声。白李就这么人不知鬼不觉的不见了。我急出一个主意来——上"她"那里打听打听。

她也认识我，因为我常和黑李在一块儿。她也好几天没见着白李。她似乎很不满意李家

seemed to be quite disappointed in both of them, especially Black Li. When I asked her specifically about White Li, she directed the conversation back to Black Li. I could see that she cared a lot about — or perhaps even loved — Black Li. She seemed to want to capture Black Li and preserve him like a specimen. If she could find someone better than him, she would let Black Li go; in the event she failed, she'd probably marry him after all. Since I was only guessing, I chose not to play matchmaker for the two of them. On principle I should have done that, but I was much too fond of Black Li and believed that he deserved to marry nothing less than an angel.

By the time I left her place, my heart was pounding. Where was White Li? I couldn't tell Black Li about it, since as soon as he found out he'd put a notice in the newspaper and stay up all night divining with his coins and poring over his characters. But if I didn't tell him, I wouldn't be able to think about anything else. Why couldn't I just forget about the whole thing? No, that wouldn't work either.

From outside his study, I could hear Black Li humming. He only hummed when he was very happy about something. He hummed on a more or less regular basis when he recited poetry or sang those famous lines, "deep in the boudoir, there lies a piece of flawless jade," though this was not what he was humming now. Listening carefully, I discovered he was reciting the Psalms over and over. He didn't have a very musical ear, so all music sounded the same to him. Likewise, everything he sang came out sounding the same. In any case, I could tell that he was extremely happy now. What

兄弟,特别是对黑李。我和她打听白李,她偏跟我谈论黑李。我看出来,她确是注意——假如不是爱——黑李。大概她是要圈住黑李,作个标本。有比他强的呢,就把他免了职;始终找不到比他高明的呢,最后也许就跟了他。这么一想,虽然只是一想,我就没乘这个机会给他和她再撮合一下;按理说应当这么办,可是我太爱老李,总觉得他值得娶个天上的仙女。

从她那里出来,我心中打开了鼓。白李上哪儿去了呢?不能告诉黑李!一叫他知道了,他能立刻登报找弟弟,而且要在半夜里起来占课测字。可是,不说吧,我心中又痒痒。干脆不找他去?又不行。

走到他的书房外边,听见他在里面哼唧呢。他不高兴的时候不哼唧着玩。可是他平日哼唧,不是诗便是那句代表一切歌曲的"深闺内,端的是玉无瑕",这次的哼唧不是这些。我细听了听,他是练习圣诗呢。他没有音乐的耳朵,无论什么,到他耳中都是一个味儿。他唱出的时候,自然也还是一个味儿。无论怎样吧,反正我知道他现在是很高兴。为什么事高兴呢?

英汉对照
English-Chinese
中国文学宝库
Gems of Chinese Literature
现代文学系列
Modern Literature

brought this about?

The moment I walked in, he put down his book of Psalms. He looked ecstatic. "You're here at just the right time. I was just about to go and see you. Number Four just left. He asked me to give him a thousand dollars. He didn't mention dividing the estate, not even once."

It was evident that he hadn't asked his brother why he needed the money, otherwise he wouldn't have been in such a good mood. He probably had begged his brother to keep living with him, and promised him not to meddle in his affairs. It seemed now that even if White Li had a dangerous mission to accomplish, as long as they didn't split up the family estate, Black Li would have nothing to be afraid about. I could see this quite clearly.

"Praying really works," he said quite seriously. "I've been praying for the last few days, and it turned out that Number Four didn't bring up that old business. Even if he throws away the money I gave him, at least I still have a brother."

I suggested we drink our customary pot of Lotus wine, but he smiled and shook his head. "Go ahead, I'll have something to eat instead. I'm giving up drinking."

I didn't drink either, nor did I tell him how I'd searched everywhere for White Li. Now that White Li was back, why bring it up again? I mentioned "her" to him, but he didn't say a word, and only smiled.

We had very little to say about White Li's relationship with "her," so he told me some Bible stories. While listening to him, I thought there was something a little strange about the way Black Li

我进到屋中,他赶紧放下手中的圣诗集,非常的快活:"来得正好,正想找你去呢!老四刚走。跟我要了一千块钱去。没提分家的事,没提!"

显然他是没问弟弟,那笔钱是干什么用。要不然他不能这么痛快。他必是只求弟弟和他同居,不再管弟弟的行动;好像即使弟弟有带危险的计划,自要不分家,便也没什么可怕的了。我看明白了这点。

"祷告确是有效,"他郑重的说。"这几天我天天祷告,果然老四就不提那回事了。即使他把钱都扔了,反正我还落下个弟弟!"

我提议喝我们照例的一壶莲花白。他笑着摇摇头:"你喝吧,我陪着吃菜,我戒了酒。"

我也就没喝,也没敢告诉他,我怎么各处去找老四。老四既然回来了,何必再说?可是我又提起"她"来。他连搭茬儿也没接,只笑了笑。

对于老四和"她",似乎全没什么可说的了。他给我讲了些圣经上的故事。我一面听着,一面心中嘀咕——老李对弟弟与爱人所取的态度

英汉对照
English-Chinese
中国文学宝库
Gems of Chinese Literature
现代文学系列
Modern Literature

behaved towards his brother and his girlfriend, though I couldn't put my finger on it. I felt very uneasy about this and continued to feel this way when I got home.

Four or five days passed, but this matter remained on my mind. One evening, Wang Five came to see me. Wang, the Li's ricksha puller, had been working for them for four years.

Wang Five was straightforward and reliable. A man in his early thirties, he had a prominent scar on his head. It was said that this was the result of a donkey bite when he was a child. Wang's only weakness was that he enjoyed a drink once in a while.

He'd drunk a bit too much on the night he visited me, which made the scar on his head appear somewhat redder than usual.

"Wang Five, what brings you here this evening?" I was on good terms with him; whenever I left the Li's home late at night, they always got him to take me home, and I always gave him a little money to buy drinks with.

"I've come to see you," he said, taking a seat.

I knew he'd come to tell me something. "I just made a pot of tea. Would you like some?"

"That would be very nice. I'll pour it myself. I'm really thirsty."

I offered him a cigarette and started off the conversation by asking him, "What's on your mind?"

"Ah.... I just finished off two pots of wine, but there's something I can't get off my mind. It's something I really shouldn't be talking about at all." He took a long drag on his cigarette.

似乎有点不大对;可是我说不出所以然来。我心中不十分安定,一直到回在家中还是这样。

又过了四五天,这点事还在我心中悬着。有一天晚上,王五来了。他是在李家拉车,已经有四年了。

王五是个诚实可靠的人,三十多岁,头上有块疤——据说是小时候被驴给啃了一口。除了有时候爱喝口酒,他没有别的毛病。

他又喝多了点,头上的疤都有点发红。

"干吗来了,王五?"我和他的交情不错,每逢我由李家回来得晚些,也总张罗把我拉回来,我自然也老给他点酒钱。

"来看看你,"说着便坐下了。

我知道他是来告诉我点什么。"刚沏上的茶,来碗?"

"那敢情好;我自己倒;还真有点渴。"

我给了他支烟卷,给他提了个头儿:"有什么事吧?"

"哼,又喝了两壶,心里痒痒;本来是不应当说的事!"他用力吸了口烟。

"要是李家的事,你对我说了准保没错。"

英汉对照
English-Chinese
中国文学宝库
Gems of Chinese Literature
现代文学系列
Modern Literature

67

"If it's anything to do with the Lis, it's perfectly alright for you to tell me."

"That's what I was thinking too." He paused for a moment, but due to the effects of the wine could not remain silent for long. "I've been working for the Lis for a total of four years and thirty-five days. I'm in a very difficult position now. Second Master treats me very kindly and all, but Fourth Master, well, he's my friend. So it's hard for me to know what to do. I can't tell Second Master's such a nice guy. If I told Second Master, I would be unworthy of Fourth Master's trust — he's my friend. But when I try not to think about it I get all confused inside. In principle, you know, I ought to be on Fourth Master's side. Second Master's a nice guy, there's no doubt about it. But in the end he's my boss. No matter how nice he is, he's still my boss. There's no way we can treat each other as brothers. He's good to me. For instance, on really hot days, when I'm pulling Second Master around, he'll always find some place along the way to stop for a little while to buy a box of matches or take a look at a book stall. Why does he do that? So I can rest and catch my breath. That's what I mean when I say he's a good boss. And since he's good to me, I've got to treat him with respect too. Like they say, one good turn deserves another. You learn that when you pull a ricksha for a few years."

I offered him another bowl of tea as a way of demonstrating I wasn't ignorant of the proper etiquette. When he finished his tea, he pointed to his chest with his cigarette. "Here, it's right here where I feel for Fourth Master. Why is that? Because Fourth Master is young and doesn't treat me like a ricksha puller. Those two

"我也这么想,"他又停顿了会儿,可是被酒气催着,似乎不能不说,"我在李家四年零三十五天了!现在叫我很难。二爷待我不错,四爷呢,简直是我的朋友。所以不好办。四爷的事,不准告诉二爷;二爷又是那么傻好的人。对二爷说吧,又对不起四爷——我的朋友。心里别提多么为难了!论理说呢,我应当向着四爷。二爷是个好人,不错;可究竟是个主人。多么好的主人也还是主人,不能肩膀齐为弟兄。他真待我不错,比如说吧,在这老热天,我拉二爷出去,他总设法在半道上耽搁会儿,什么买包洋火呀,什么看看书摊呀,为什么?为是叫我歇歇,喘喘气。要不怎说,他是好主人呢,他好,咱也得敬重他,这叫作以好换好。久在街上混,还能不懂这个?"

我又让了他碗茶,显出我不是不懂"外面"的人。他喝完,用烟卷指着胸口说:"这儿,咱这儿可是爱四爷。怎么呢?四爷年青,不拿我当个拉车的看。他们哥儿俩的劲儿——心里的劲

英汉对照
English-Chinese
中国文学宝库
Gems of Chinese Literature
现代文学系列
Modern Literature

69

guys — I mean their personalities — are very different. On hot days, Second Master always gives me time to rest, but that would never occur to Fourth Master. No matter how hot it is he's always telling me to run like the wind. But when Fourth Master and I sit around talking, he'll say, 'Who says that some people have to be ricksha pullers?' He's talking about how unfair things are for us — I mean all the ricksha pullers in the world. Second Master treats me well, but he doesn't give a damn about the rest of us ricksha men. You see what I mean? Second Master is narrow-minded while Fourth Master looks at the bigger picture. Fourth Master doesn't give a damn about my legs, but he cares about my heart. Second Master cares about the little things, he takes pity on my legs — but he doesn't give a damn about this here." He pointed to his heart again.

I knew he had more to say, but I was really afraid that tongue-loosening effects of the wine he drank would be diluted by the strong tea, so I encouraged him a little, "Go on, Wang. Tell me everything. I'm not an old lady who's going to give all your secrets away."

He rubbed his scar and lowered his head for a few moments of contemplation. Then he pulled his chair up close to mine and lowered his voice. "Have you heard they've almost finished installing the new streetcar line? When that starts operating, we ricksha pullers are done for. I'm not worried about myself; I'm talking about everybody." He looked up at me.

I nodded to him.

"Fourth Master knows all about it; we're close friends, right? He

儿——不一样。二爷吧,一看天气热就多叫我歇会儿,四爷就不管这一套,多么热的天也得拉着他飞跑。可是四爷和我聊起来的时候,他就说,凭什么人应当拉着人呢?他是为我们拉车的——天下的拉车的都算在一块儿——抱不平。二爷对'我'不错,可想不到大家伙儿。所以你看,二爷来的小,四爷来的大。四爷不管我的腿,可是管我的心;二爷是家长里短,可怜我的腿,可不管这儿。"他又指了指心口。

我晓得他还有的谈呢,直怕他的酒气被酽茶给解去,所以又紧他一板:"往下说呀,王五!都说了吧,反正我还能拉老婆舌头,把你搁里!"

他摸了摸头上的疤,低头想了会儿。然后把椅子往前拉了拉,声音放得很低:"你知道,电车道快修完了?电车一开,我们拉车的全玩完!这可不是为我自个儿发愁,是为大家伙儿。"他看了我一眼。

我点了点头。

"四爷明白这个;要不怎么我俩是朋友呢。

英汉对照
English-Chinese
中国文学宝库
Gems of Chinese Literature
现代文学系列
Modern Literature

said to me, 'Wang, you've got to find a way out.' I said, 'Fourth Master, I've got an idea. We'll destroy them!' He said, 'Wang, that's the right idea, we'll destroy them!' So we worked it all out then and there. I can't tell you the details. This is what I came here to tell you." He lowered his voice again. "There's someone following Fourth Master around. It doesn't necessarily have anything to do with the streetcar business, but it's bad having someone tailing you all the time. The worst thing is, if I tell Second Master, how can I face Fourth Master? But if I don't tell him, he might get dragged in for no reason at all. I don't know what to do ."

After seeing Wang Five out, I thought it all over carefully.

Black Li surmised correctly that White Li was involved in something dangerous. In addition to wrecking trolley cars, he probably had something more formidable in mind. Thus his desire to move away from his brother was for the purpose of avoiding implicating him. He was not afraid of sacrificing his own life, or the lives of others, but he was unwilling to sacrifice his brother unless there were a good reason for it — such an act would come to no avail. And with the action against the streetcar company about to take place, he had no time to worry about Black Li anyway.

Where was I to turn? Warning Black Li would only stir up a wave of warm feelings in him for his brother. Speaking to White Li was not only useless; it would incriminate Wang Five as well.

The situation grew tenser day by day. The streetcar company announced the opening of the new line. I couldn't wait any longer. I had to go and tell Black Li.

四爷说:王五,想个办法呀! 我说:四爷,我就有一个主意,揍! 四爷说:王五,这就对了,揍! 一来二去,我们可就商量好了。这我不能告诉你。我要说的是这个,"他把声音放得很低了,"我看见了,侦探跟上了四爷! 未必然是为这件事,可是叫侦探跟着总不妥当。这就来到坐蜡的地方了:我要告诉二爷吧,对不起四爷;不告诉吧,又怕把二爷也饶在里面。简直的没法儿!"

把王五支走,我自己琢磨开了。

黑李猜的不错,白李确是有个带危险性的计划。计划大概不一定就是打电车,他必定还有厉害的呢。所以要分家,省得把哥哥拉扯在内。他当然是不怕牺牲,也不怕牺牲别人,可是还不肯一声不发的牺牲了哥哥——把黑李牺牲了并无济于事。电车的事来到眼前,连哥哥也顾不得了。

我怎办呢? 警告黑李是适足以激起他的爱弟弟的热情。劝白李,不但没用,而且把王五搁在里边。

事情越来越紧了,电车公司已宣布出开车的日子。我不能再耗着了,得告诉黑李去。

英汉对照
English-Chinese
中国文学宝库
Gems of Chinese Literature
现代文学系列
Modern Literature

He wasn't home, but Wang Five was still there.

"Where's Number Two?"

"He went out."

"You didn't take him?"

"He hasn't taken the ricksha for a long time."

From the expression on his face, I knew the answer to my question: "Wang, did you tell him?"

Wang Five's scar turned a bright purple. "I drank too much. I couldn't help it."

"What did he say?"

"He started crying."

"What did he say?"

"He asked me one question: 'Wang, what are you going to do?' I said, 'I'll do whatever Fourth Master says.' All he said was, 'OK.' He goes out every day now, but he never rides in the ricksha."

I waited there for three hours. After sunset, he finally came back.

"What's up?" These two words summed up everything I wanted to know.

He smiled. "Not much." I nvever expected him to answer me this way. There was no need for me to ask him any more questions, since I knew his mind was already made up. I felt I needed a drink, but it's no fun drinking alone. I decided to go. Before leaving, I said to him, "Why don't the two of us go away for a couple of days."

"Let's discuss that in a few days, shall we?" That was all he

他没在家,可是王五没出去。

"二爷呢?"

"出去了。"

"没坐车。"

"好几天了,天天出去不坐车。"

由王五的神气,我猜着了:"王五,你告诉了他?"

王五头上的疤都紫了:"又多喝了两盅,不由的就说了。"

"他呢?"

"他直要落泪。"

"说什么来着?"

"问了我一句——老五,你怎样? 我说,王五听四爷的。他说了声,好。别的没说,天天出去,也不坐车。"

我足足的等了三点钟,天已大黑,他绕回来。

"怎样?"我用这两个字问到了一切。

他笑了笑,"不怎样。"

决没想到他这么回答我。我无须再问了,他已决定了办法。我觉得非喝点酒不可,但是独自有什么味呢。我只好走吧。临别的时候,我提了句:"跟我出去玩几天,好不好?"

英汉对照
English-Chinese
中国文学宝库
Gems of Chinese Literature
现代文学系列
Modern Literature

said.

Passionate men are capable of acting with great indifference. I never imagined him treating me this way.

The night before the opening of the trolley line, I went to his house again, but he wasn't in. I waited until midnight, but he didn't come back. He was probably trying to avoid me.

Wang Five came in and smiled at me. "Tomorrow's the big day!"

"Where's Number Two?"

"I haven't seen him. After you left the other day, he used some strange chemical and burned off the black birthmark over his eyebrow. Then he just sat there staring at himself in the mirror."

It was all over now. Without his black birthmark, there was no more Black Li. I didn't have to wait for him any longer. When I walked out, Wang Five called to me, "If anything happens to me tomorrow," he said, scratching his scar, "take care of my mother for me."

About five o'clock the next afternoon Wang Five rushed into my room. His pants were soaked through with sweat. "We smashed all the trolley cars to bits." After that he said nothing and just sat there panting for several minutes. When he recovered his breath, he picked up the teapot and took a long drink directly from the spout.

"We destroyed everything! No one left till they brought in the cavalry troops. They took Little Ma Six away, I saw it with my own eyes. If only we had guns! But all we had was bricks. Little Ma Six is done for."

"过两天再说吧。"他没说别的。

感情到了最热的时候是会最冷的。想不到他会这样对待我。

电车开车的头天晚上,我又去看他。他没在家,直等到半夜,他还没回来。大概是故意的躲我。

王五回来了,向我笑了笑,"明天!"

"二爷呢?"

"不知道。那天你走后,他用了不知什么东西,把眉毛上的黑丐子烧去了,对着镜子直出神。"

完了,没了黑痣,便是没有了黑李。不必再等他了。

我已经走出大门,王五把我叫住:"明天我要是——"他摸了摸头上的疤,"你可照应着点我的老娘!"

约摸五点多钟吧,王五跑进来,跑得连裤子都湿了。"全——揍了!"他也说不出话来。直喘了不知有多少工夫,他才缓过气来,抄起茶壶对着嘴喝了一气。"啊!全揍了!马队冲下来,我们才散。小马六叫他们拿了去,看得真真的。我们吃亏没有家伙,专仗着砖头哪行!小马六

英汉对照
English-Chinese
中国文学宝库
Gems of Chinese Literature
现代文学系列
Modern Literature

"What about Number Four?"

"I didn't see him at all." He bit his lower lip and thought for a moment. "There was a hell of a lot of excitement there. If they caught anyone else, I guess Fourth Master would have to be among them. He was one of the people in charge. Don't forget though, Fourth Master's no fool, even though he's very young. Little Ma Six is done for, but I'm not so sure about Fourth Master."

"You didn't see Number Two?"

"He didn't come home last night." He thought for a moment. "I'm going to lay low here for a couple of days."

"That's fine."

The next day, the papers carried the following news:

> The ringleader of a bunch of violent hooligans who destroyed the trolley cars, a Mr Li, was arrested on the spot. A student and five ricksha pullers were taken into custody as well.

Wang Five could only recognize one word in the headline: the surname Li. "Fourth Master is done for! Fourth Master is done for!" He lowered his head and pretended to be scratching his scar, while his tears dropped onto the newspaper.

The news spread quickly through the city — Li and Little Ma Six were going to be paraded through the streets and shot.

The cruel sun beat down on the cobblestone streets, heating them to the point where you could feel the heat through your shoes,

要玩完"。

"四爷呢?"我问。

"没看见。"他咬着嘴唇想了想,"哼,事闹得不小!要是拿的话呀,准保是拿四爷。他是头目。可也别说,四爷并不傻,别看他青年。小马六要玩完,四爷也许不能。"

"也没看见二爷?"

"他昨天就没回家。"他又想了想,"我得在这儿藏两天。"

"那行。"

第二天早晨,报纸上登出——砸车暴徒首领李——当场被获,一同被获的还有一个学生,五个车夫。

王五看着纸上那些字只认得一个"李"字,"四爷玩完了!四爷玩完了!"低着头假装抓那块疤,泪落在报上。

消息传遍了全城,枪毙李——和小马六,游街示众。

毒花花的太阳,把路上的石子晒得烫脚,街

yet the streets were lined with huge crowds of spectators. The two men were seated in a large open wagon with their hands tied behind their backs. They were guarded on either side by policemen in khaki uniforms and soldiers dressed in grey. As the wagon drew near, the two blades of their bayonets reflected the sunlight with a chilling brilliance. The wooden placards announcing their crimes could be seen swaying back and forth above their heads. The man seated in front had his eyes closed; his forehead was dotted with beads of sweat and his lips were moving as if he were mouthing a prayer. The wagon was very close, and I watched him sway past me. I broke down and cried, stopping only after he had gone past. I followed the wagon all the way to the execution ground. Not once did he raise his head.

His eyebrows were knitted; his mouth hung open. The blood spurted forth from his chest, as if he were praying the moment he died. I took his body away.

Two months later, I ran into White Li in Shanghai. If I hadn't called to him, he probably would have walked right past me. "Number Four!" I called out to him.

"Huhh?" He appeared startled. "Hey, is that you? Sounded just like Number Two."

Maybe the way I called to him reminded him of Black Li's voice, but this was totally unintentional on my part. Or maybe it was Black Li himself, alive somewhere inside me, who called out on my behalf.

White Li seemed to have aged, and looked more like his older brother than ever. We said very little to each other. He didn't

上可是还挤满了人。一个敞车上坐着两个人,手在背后捆着。土黄制服的巡警,灰色制服的兵,前后押着,刀光在阳光下发着冷气。车越走越近了,两个白招子随着车轻轻的颤动。前面坐着的那个,闭着眼,额上有点汗,嘴唇微动,像是祷告呢。车离我不远,他在我眼前坐着摆动过去。我的泪迷住了我的心。等车过去半天,我才醒了过来,一直跟着车走到行刑场。他一路上连头也没抬一次。

他的眉皱着点,嘴微张着,胸上汪着血,好像死的时候正在祷告。我收了他的尸。

过了两个月,我在上海遇见了白李,要不是我招呼他,他一定就跑过去了。

"老四!"我喊了他一声。

"啊?"他似乎受了一惊。"呕,你?我当是老二复活了呢。"

大概我叫得很像黑李的声调,并非有意的,或者是在我心中活着的黑李替我叫了一声。

白李显着老了一些,更像他的哥哥了。我

英汉对照
English-Chinese
中国文学宝库
Gems of Chinese Literature
现代文学系列
Modern Literature

have much to say to me anyway.

I remember two things he did say though:

"Number Two must have gone to heaven; that's a perfect place for him. But I'm still here smashing the gates of hell."

Translated by Don J. Cohn

们俩并没说多少话,他好似不大愿意和我多谈。只记得他的这么两句:

"老二大概是进了天堂,他在那里顶合适了;我还在这儿砸地狱的门呢。"

英汉对照
English-Chinese
中国文学宝库
Gems of Chinese Literature
现代文学系列
Modern Literature

The Eyeglasses

Although Song Xiushen was studying science, there was nothing scientific about the way he conducted his life. He firmly believed that all restaurant flies had been disinfected; thus when he ordered cold noodles with sesame sauce he made no effort to shoo them away. He had a pair of near-sighted eyes, and a pair of near-sighted glasses to match them, though he only used the latter for reading. According to conventional wisdom, wearing glasses made one's sight worse; he was sure of this. Thus he wore his glasses as infrequently as possible. For instance, whenever he went for a stroll downtown or attended an athletic event, he held his glasses in his hands. If this prevented him from seeing what was going on, or caused him chronic dizziness, well, he deserved it!

One day he was on his way to school. He kept very close to the city wall to avoid running into people, though he would occasionally collide with a dog. Today, he'd wrapped his glasses in the folds of two thick scientific magazines. He knew this was somewhat risky, and therefore stopped every few steps to make sure his glasses were still there. If he lost them, he'd be totally helpless in class. And since he wasn't rich, purchasing a new pair might drive him into bankruptcy. He usually put his glasses case in one of his pockets, but today his pockets were occupied by notebooks, handkerchiefs, pencils, erasers, two small bottles and the remains of a

眼 镜

　　宋修身虽然是学着科学,可是在日常生活上,不管什么科学科举的那一套。他相信饭馆里苍蝇都是消过毒的,所以吃芝麻酱拌面的时候不劳手挥目送的瞎讲究。他有对儿近视眼,也有对儿近视镜。可是他除非读书的时候不戴上它们。据老说法:越戴镜子眼越坏。他信这个。得不戴就不戴,譬如走路逛街,或参观运动会的时候,他的镜子是在手里拿着。即使什么也看不见,而且脑袋常常的发晕,那也活该。

　　他正往学校里走。溜着墙根,省得碰着人;不过有时候踩着狗腿。这回,眼镜盒子是卷在两本厚科学杂志里。他准知道这个办法不保险,所以走几步,站住摸一摸。把镜子丢了,上堂听课才叫抓瞎。况且自己的财力又不充足,买对眼镜说不定就会破产。本打算把盒子放在袋里,可是身上各处的口袋都没有空地方:笔记本,手绢,铅笔,橡皮,两个小瓶,一块吃剩下的

英汉对照
English-Chinese
中国文学宝库
Gems of Chinese Literature
现代文学系列
Modern Literature

The Eyeglasses

half-eaten bun. Carrying his glasses in this way required only a little extra care; and in any case, if he dropped them, he'd be sure to hear them when they hit the ground.

Turning a corner, he ran into one of his classmates. Since it was his classmate who had called to him, it would have been difficult for him not to respond. They stood there talking for a few minutes. A car approached, and he instinctively drew his hands out of the way. Actually, this movement was unnecessary, but his poor eyesight made him extra cautious, and he pressed his nose to the wall. After the car and the friend left, he started running, since he was afraid of being late. But when he got to school, he discovered that his glasses case was missing. Beads of sweat formed on his forehead. He rushed back to look for it, but it was nowhere to be found. A few ricksha pullers had parked their vehicles by the corner of the wall where he'd stopped to talk. He asked them about his glasses, but none of them had seen them — perhaps they were all near-sighted too. He headed back to school, but all he had to show was two hands covered with dirt. He had never been so frustrated in his entire life! He removed the uneaten portion of his bun from his pocket and threw it angrily against the school entrance. If only he had fewer things in his pockets! If only he hadn't run into his friend! If only he hadn't flinched to avoid that car which was being driven so recklessly! Was all of this coincidental? If so, it was enough to drive anyone batty. One of the ricksha men must have lied to his face. What a world this was! He walked by here every day. When he lost something, shouldn't they at least tell him about it, rather than pick it up and put it in their pocket? What

烧饼,都占住了地盘。还是这么拿着吧,小心一点好了;好在盒子即使掉在地上也会有响声的。

一拐弯,碰上了个同学。人家招呼他,他自然不好不答应。站住说了几句。来了辆汽车,他本能的往里手一躲,本来没有躲的必要,可是眼力不济,得特别的留神,于是把鼻子按在墙上。汽车和朋友都过去了,他紧赶了几步,怕是迟到。走到了校门,一摸,眼镜盒子没啦!登时头上见了汗。抹回头去找,哪里有个影儿。拐弯的地方,老放着几辆洋车。问拉车的,他们都没看见,好像他们也都是近视眼似的。又往回找到校门,只摸了两手的土。心里算是别扭透了!掏出那块干烧饼狠命的摔在校门上,假如口袋里没这些零碎?假如不是遇上那个臭同学?假如不躲那辆闯丧的汽车?巧!越巧心里越堵得慌!一定是被车夫拾了去,瞪着眼不给,什么世界!天天走熟了的路,掉了东西会连告诉一声都不告诉,而捡起放在自己的袋里?一

英汉对照
English-Chinese
中国文学宝库
Gems of Chinese Literature
现代文学系列
Modern Literature

use was a pair of near-sighted glasses to them anyway?

Song Xiushen's glasses fell when he had pressed his nose against the wall. Wang Four, one of the ricksha pullers, had noticed this.

Wang Four was about to say something, but when he realized who it was — that strange boy who walked along the wall everyday and never took a ricksha — he held back the words that were on the tip of his tongue. After the car turned the corner, he picked up the case and stuck it in his pocket.

He didn't dare take it out and examine it in front of the other ricksha pullers. Rather, he sat contentedly in the seat of his ricksha with a broad smile across his lips.

When he saw Song Xiushen come back all sweaty and nervous, his heart went out to him, and he was about to return the glasses case to him. But since none of the other ricksha pullers admitted to having seen it, this would have been embarrassing to him — like spitting something up after having swallowed it. There was probably nothing in it for him anyhow, since he doubted the boy would offer him a reward. If he gave it back for nothing, he'd be the laughing stock of the ricksha pullers: "You took it and didn't say anything; you thought we were going to steal it from you?" "You think you're so generous, don't you, handing it back to him for nothing?" It was easier to deny having seen it in the first place. It was his now, that's all that mattered. Students are richer than ricksha pullers anyway.

After Song Xiushen went back to school, Wang Four prepared to leave and said rather self-consciously, "No need to hang around

对近视眼镜有什么用?

宋修身的鼻子按在墙上的时候,眼镜盒子落在墙根。车夫王四看见了。

王四本想告诉一声,可是一看是"他",一年到头老溜墙根,没坐过一回车。话到了嘴边,又回去了。汽车刚拐过去,他顺手捡起盒子,放在腰中。

当着别的车夫,不便细看,可是心中不由的很痛快,坐在车上舒舒服服的微笑。

他看见宋修身回来了,满头是汗,怪可怜的。很想拿出来还给他。可是别人都说没看见,自己要是招认了,吃了又吐,怪不好意思的。况且给他也是白给,他还能给点报酬?白叫他拿去,而且还得叫朋友们奚落一场——喝,拾了东西连一声都不出,怕我们抢你的?喝,拾了又白给了人家,真大方?莫若也说没看见。拾了就是拾了,活该。学生反正比拉车的阔。

宋修身往回走,王四拉起车来,搭讪着说,

英汉对照
English-Chinese
中国文学宝库
Gems of Chinese Literature
现代文学系列
Modern Literature

The Eyeglasses

here any longer; I'll head east for a while." At the same time, he said to himself, "Even if I don't get a single customer today, I ought to be able to sell these glasses along with the case for about two dollars." He found a quiet place, parked his ricksha and sat down to examine his find.

The case was in such bad condition that the match seller would probably trade him only one box of matches for it. The cloth cover had been rubbed off entirely, leaving a greasy surface impregnated with something sticky like persimmon juice. The glasses' thick black frames were in better condition, though. Wang Four had never liked glasses with thin wire frames. Whenever he saw someone wearing them, he would avoid asking them if they wanted a ricksha. He flicked the earpieces with his finger. They didn't look like iron, nor did they appear to be made of wood; maybe they were tortoise-shell! His heart skipped a beat!

The lenses were filthy, and bulged out in their centers. They were ground in a series of concentric circles, each of which was outlined in a ring of greasy dust. This accumulation was thicker on the outer circles than on the inner. A broken matchstick lay in the bottom of the case. Wang Four struck it and tossed it on the ground. He then removed a shaggy cloth duster from his ricksha. Breathing on the lenses, he began to polish them with the cloth strips of his duster. After repeating this operation four times, the lenses began to take on the appearance of real lenses; he then applied a coating of saliva and completed the cleaning. He tried them on, but they didn't fit; the frames were far too small for his head. Song Xiushen was small in stature and had a small head. "Nobody

"别这儿耗着啦,东边去搁会儿。"心里可是说,"今儿个咱算票不了啦,连盒子带镜子还不卖个块儿八七的?"到了个僻静地方,放下车,把盒子掏出来。

好破的盒子,大概换洋火也就是换上一小包。盒子上面的布全磨没了,倒好,油汪汪的,上边还好像粘着点柿子汁儿。打开,眼镜框子还不坏,挺粗挺黑——王四就是不喜欢细铁丝似的那路镜框,看见戴稀软活软的镜框的人,他连"车"也不问一声。用手弹了弹耳插子,不像是铁的,可也不是木头的——许是玳瑁的!他心中一跳。

镜子真脏,往外凸着,上面净是一圈一圈的纹,腻着一圈圈的土,越到镜边上越厚。镜子底下还压着半根火柴。他把火柴划着,扔在地上。从车厢里拿出小破蓝布掸子来。给镜子哈了两口气,开始用掸子布擦。连哈了四次气,镜子才有个样儿;又沾了一回吐沫,才完全擦干净。自己戴了戴,不行,架子太小,戴不上;宋修身本是个小头小脸的人。"卖不出去,连自己戴着玩都

英汉对照
English-Chinese
中国文学宝库
Gems of Chinese Literature
现代文学系列
Modern Literature

wants to buy them, and I can't even wear them as a joke!" Wang Four was disappointed, though he rationalized as follows: "It doesn't look right for a ricksha puller to wear glasses anyway. Why don't I just try to sell them?"

He picked up the shafts of his ricksha and went around until he found a junk seller. "Hey! You want to buy these?"

"No!" The junk seller, a man with a red nose and yellow eyes, didn't even look at them, even though his stock of goods included many pairs of glasses, and even some old-fashioned embroidered glasses cases.

Not wanting to pick a fight with this man, Wang Four went away without even saying, "Aren't you a polite son of a bitch!"

He soon came upon another junk dealer who was carrying his wares in two baskets suspended at the end of a pole. "Hey, you want to buy these? They've got real tortoise-shell frames."

"First time I've seen tortoise-shell like that," the junk dealer said, glancing at the frames. "How much you want for them?"

"What'll you give me?" Wang Four handed him the glasses.

"Twenty cents."

"What?" Wang Four grabbed them back.

"What's a darned good price! Plain lenses and far-sighted glasses go pretty quickly. But those are near-sighted lenses. Those frames are made out of celluloid. They'll probably break just sitting in my baskets. Then I'd be out twenty cents."

Wang Four was discouraged, but he couldn't sell at such a low price. Twenty cents? If he'd known that, he would have given the glasses back to the boy.

不行!"王四未免有点失望。可是继而一想:拉车戴眼镜,不大像样儿;再说,怎能卖不出去呢?

拉着车,找着一个破货摊。"喏,卖给你这个。"

"不要。"摆摊的人——一个红鼻子黄眼的家伙——连看也没看,虽然他的摊上有许多眼镜,而且有老式绣花的镜套子呢。

王四不想打架,连"妈的真和气!"都没说出声来。

又遇上个挑筐买卖破烂的,"喏,卖给你这个,玳瑁框子!"

"没见过这样的玳瑁!"挑筐的看了一眼,"干脆要多少钱?"

"干脆你给多少?"王四把镜子递过去。

"二十子儿。"

"什么?"王四把镜子抢回来。

"给的不少。平光好卖,老花镜也好卖;这是近视镜。框子是化学的,说个定挑来挑去就弄碎了;白赔二十枚。"

王四的心凉了,可是还不肯卖;二十子?早知道还送给那个溜墙根的学生呢!

英汉对照
English-Chinese
中国文学宝库
Gems of Chinese Literature
现代文学系列
Modern Literature

93

The Eyeglasses

He decided then to return them to their rightful owner the next day. That way, he at least had a chance of earning a few dimes' reward.

The next morning, Wang Four parked his ricksha at the corner of the wall. The school bell rang, but the near-sighted boy didn't appear. By ten o'clock there was still no sign of him. He picked up a passenger and made it back by noon. The students were going home for lunch, but the near-sighted boy was nowhere to be seen.

Song Xiushen didn't go to school that day.

The day before, when he had lost his glasses, he went to class as usual. Though he sat in the front of the classroom, he couldn't even make out what the teacher wrote on the blackboard. The fuzzier the words became, the more he strained his eyes, and by the end of the class he had a splitting headache. The second class that day was mathematics. Pressing his nose to the paper, he worked through several problems, but he was all itchy inside and his head was burning. He felt lost. Mathematics had always been his favorite subject, but today the sight of all those numbers only made him nervous. The formulas he knew so well were now accompanied by something new in his mind; his glasses, an automobile and a ricksha puller. This new combination of elements transformed his favorite subject into the most intolerable grind. He felt very confined in the classroom and longed to escape to some wide open space where he could shout at the top of his lungs. Today, things he had been loath to think about before — such as the meaning of life — totally occupied his mind. No matter how uesless an old pair of near-sighted glasses was, the ricksha puller had

不卖了,他决定第二天把镜子送归原主;也许倒能得几毛钱的报酬。

第二天早晨,王四把车放在拐弯的地方。学校打了钟,溜墙根的近视眼还没来。一直等到十点多,还是没他的影儿。拉了趟买卖,约摸有十二点多了,又特意放回来。学生下了课,只是不见那个近视眼。

宋修身没来上课。

眼镜丢了以后,他来到教堂里。虽然坐在前面,黑板上的字还是模糊不清。越看不清,越用力看;下了课,他的脑袋直抽着疼。他越发心里堵得慌。第二堂是算术习题。他把眼差不多贴在纸上,算了两三个题,他的心口直发痒,脑门非常的热。他好像把自己丢失了。平日最欢喜算术,现在他看着那些字码心里起急。心中熟记的那些公式,都加上了点新东西——眼镜,汽车,车夫。公式和懊恼搀杂在一块,把最喜爱的一门功课变成了最讨厌的一些气人的东西。他不能再安坐在课室里,他想跑到空旷的地方去嚷一顿才痛快。平日所不爱想的事,例如生命观等,这时候都在心中冒出来。一个破近视镜,拾去有什么用?可是竟自拾去!经济的压

英汉对照
English-Chinese
中国文学宝库
Gems of Chinese Literature
现代文学系列
Modern Literature

95

taken them. If someone is poor, even a single stick of firewood is a good thing; in the end, then, he couldn't very well blame the ricksha puller for what he did. He rationalized it this way, but he was still very upset. He wouldn't be able to finish today's homework assignment, and tomorrow there would be more headaches. He certainly couldn't afford a new pair of glasses. At the beginning of the semester, his family had given him about seventy dollars, but there were still two more months of meals to pay for. The wheat harvest at home had been a good one, but they couldn't sell what they grew. He thought about how his father and brother slaved away day in and day out; yet they were still unable to sell what they reaped.

He never had the time — nor the need — to think about such things before, but today they settled down in his mind next to those mathematical formulas. He could think of no way out. This was the first time he had ever experienced such despair. It was as if all those aspects of his life which had been stable up to now had vanished along with his glasses. Everything appeared hazy and unresolved before him. He was reluctant to quit school, but continuing his studies seemed totally meaningless.

The next hour passed like an eternity. When the bell rang, there was something peculiar about it. It sounded as if it were ordering everyone to go out into the wild and shout at the top of their lungs. He walked out of the classroom; a strong sense of resentment led him out of the school courtyard. He failed to attend the third class that morning, nor did he ask to be excused. He was no longer aware that there was such a thing as a third class, or that he should have asked for permission to be excused.

迫,白拾一根劈柴也是好的。不怨那个车夫。虽然想到这个,心中究竟是难过。今天的功课交不上。明天当然还是头疼。配镜子去,作不到。学期开始的时候,只由家中拿来七十几块钱,下俩月的饭费还没有着落。家中打的粮不少,可是卖不出去。想到了父亲,哥哥,一天到头受苦受累,粮可是卖不出去。平日他没工夫想这些问题,也不肯想这些问题;今天,算术的公式好像给它们匀出来点地方。他想不出一个办法,他头一次觉得生命没着落,好像一切稳定的东西都随着眼镜丢了,眼前事事模糊不清。他不想退学,也想不出继续求学的意义。

长极了的一点钟,好容易才过去。下课的钟声好像不和平日一样,好像有点特别的声调,是一种把大家都叫到野地去喊叫的口令。他出了教室,有一股怨气引着他走出校门;第三堂不上了,也没去请假。他就没想到还有什么第三堂,什么请假的规则。

英汉对照
English-Chinese
中国文学宝库
Gems of Chinese Literature
现代文学系列
Modern Literature

The Eyeglasses

As he walked along the wall, his mind was in a fog. When he got to the corner, he suddenly recalled his glasses. Several ricksha pullers were there chatting, but just as he was about to ask them about his glasses again, he changed his mind; lowering his head, he walked right by them.

The next day, he didn't go to school.

Wang Four didn't wait any longer for the near-sighted boy. For the rest of the day, he couldn't take his mind off the glove compartment of his ricksha, where he'd put the old glasses case for safe keeping. For some strange reason, he just couldn't stop thinking about it.

Just as he was about to put his ricksha away for the day, Little Zhao turned up. Little Zhao's family ran a small grocery shop, but he himself took no part in it. His father was eager for him to work in the shop, but he knew that if he did he would only end up stealing from the till; hired clerks were much more reliable. Whenever Little Zhao's father went out on a social call or to a temple to burn incense, he always wore a pair of non-prescription glasses with plain lenses, which he had picked up at a little stand in the street for about eighty cents. Big shop owners and cashiers always wore glasses with plain lenses when attending the theatre or temple fairs as a means of displaying their position on the social ladder. Similarly, owners of small shops felt it necessary to keep up with their wealthier counterparts.

Little Zhao was in no particular hurry for his father to pass away, nor would his death matter very much to him. If his father did die,

溜着墙根,他什么也没想,又像想着点什么。到了拐弯的地方,他想起眼镜。几个车夫在那儿说话呢,他想再过去问问他们,可是低着头走了过去。

第二天,他没去上课。

王四没有等到那个近视眼。一天的工夫,心老在车箱里——那里有那个破眼镜盒子。不知道为什么老忘不了它。

将要收车的时候,小赵来了。小赵家里开着个小杂货铺,可是他不大管铺子里的事。他的父亲很希望他能管点事,可是叫他管事他就偷钱;儿子还不如伙计可靠呢。小赵的父亲每逢行个人情,或到庙里烧香,必定戴上过光的眼镜——八毛钱在小摊儿上买的。大铺户的掌柜和先生们都戴过光的眼镜,以便在戏馆中,庙会上,表示身分。所以小铺掌柜也不能落伍。小赵并不希望他父亲一病身亡,虽然死了也并没大关系。假如父亲马上死了,他想不出怎样表

however, the only way he could show the world that he was the new proprietor of the shop was to wear a pair of glasses with plain lenses. Though the glasses cost only eighty cents, their true value was inestimable. Shopkeepers who had established businesses wore them as a sign that their pockets were always full of money.

He spent a lot of time with Wang Four and the other ricksha pullers. Whenever he succeeded in extricating some spare change from the shop, he'd gamble with the ricksha men or entertain himself in a low class brothel. The ricksha men called him "Little Zhao," though he became "Young Manager" whenever his face turned red in the excitement of a good game. Actually, it was only at such climactic moments that he became conscious of his elevated position in society. At all other times, he was free of all pretensions, and treated Wang Four and the other ricksha pullers like best friends.

"Let's play a round. I'll be banker." Little Zhao held up a fistful of dirty red ten-cent notes for all to see, took out a cigarette and lit it.

Wang Four removed a half-smoked cigarette from behind his ear and lit it from Little Zhao's match.

They were all squatting down behind the parked rickshas.

Before very long, all of Wang Four's coppers found a new owner. The muscles in his forehead were visibly tense. He was eager to recoup his losses. "Hey, Redeyes, lend me a few coppers, will you?"

Redeyes bet all the coppers in his hand on five numbers. Since he was cleaned out himself, naturally he felt no need to respond,

示出他变成了正式的掌柜,除非他也戴上平光的眼镜。八毛钱买的眼镜,价值不限于八毛。那是掌柜立业,袋中老带着几块现洋的象征。

他常和王四们在一块儿。每逢由小铺摸出几毛来,他便和王四们押个宝,或者有时候也去逛个土窑子。车夫们都管他叫"小赵",除非赌急红了脸才称呼他"少掌柜",而在这种争斗的时节,他自己也开始觉到身分。平日,他没有什么脾气,对王四们都很"自己"。

"押押?我的庄?"小赵叫他们看了看手中的红而脏的毛票,然后掏出烟卷,吸着。

王四从耳朵上取下半截烟,就着小赵的火儿吸着。

大家都蹲在车后面。

不大一会儿,王四那点铜子全另找到了主人。他脑袋上的筋全不服气的涨起来。想往回捞一捞——"喀,红眼,借给我几个子儿!"

红眼把手中的铜子都押上,押了五道;手中既空,自然不便再回答什么,挤着红眼专等看骰子。

英汉对照
English-Chinese
中国文学宝库
Gems of Chinese Literature
现代文学系列
Modern Literature

so he squinted with his red eyes in the direction of the dice.

Wang Four was in a quandary. He stood up angrily and looked around to see if there were any policemen nearby. Though he had lost all his money, if a policeman grabbed him, he still wouldn't be able to get away.

Little Zhao was ahead quite a bit now, and asked if anyone wanted to continue playing. They all responded in the affirmative, though Little Zhao was going to have to lend them each some capital to gamble with. With his filthy hands, Little Zhao picked up the coins and ten-cent notes he'd won and stuffed it all into his pocket. "Don't be sissies. You all want to play, don't you? Put your money where your mouths are!"

They were all getting ready to call Little Zhao "Young Manager," when Li Six, who sold baked sweet potatoes, arrived. "Everyone take one, courtesy of Manager Zhao!" Little Zhao treated them all to sweet potatoes. "You're a good man, Little Zhao!" They all crowded around the sweet potato seller's portable oven. Wang Four chose one for himself, and gulped it down in big bites accompanied by deep breaths.

When he finished eating, Wang Four said, "Little Zhao, I have something for you." He removed the glasses from the back of his ricksha. "The case is in pretty bad shape, but wait till you see what's inside."

The moment Little Zhao set eyes on the glasses, the word "Manager" lit up inside his head. He tossed the remainder of his potato on the ground, adding a stray dog to his list of guests. What a fine pair of glasses, even better looking than his father's! He tried them

王四想不出招儿来。赌气子立起来,向四外看了看,看有巡警往这里来没有。虽然自己是输了,可是巡警要抓的话,他也跑不了。

小赵赢了,问大家还接着干不。大家还愿意干,可是小赵得借给他们资本。小赵满手是土,把铜子和毛票一齐放在腰里:"别套着烂,要干,拿钱。"

大家快要称呼他"少掌柜"了。卖烧白薯的李六过来了。"每人一块,赵掌柜的给钱!"小赵要请众朋友。"这还不离,小赵!"大家围上了白薯挑子。王四也弄了块,深呼吸的吃着。

吃完白薯,王四想起来了:"小赵,给你这个。"从车箱里把眼镜找出来:"别看盒子破,里面有好玩艺儿。"

小赵一见眼镜,"掌柜的"在心中放大起来;把没吃完的白薯扔在地上,请了野狗的客。果然是体面的镜子,比父亲的还好。戴上试试。

英汉对照
English-Chinese
中国文学宝库
Gems of Chinese Literature
现代文学系列
Modern Literature

The Eyeglasses

on. "Hey, these are near-sighted glasses; they make me dizzy."

"You'll get used to them," Wang Four said with a chuckle.

"Get used to them? I'll have to get near-sighted first!" Little Zhao thought that was too high a price to pay, but he really liked glasses. He put them back on and started to walk around. When he took them off and looked at his friends, they all approved of the way they looked on him.

Wang Four said, "Very stylish!"

"But they make me dizzy," Little Zhao said, but he was still reluctant to part with them.

"You'll get used to them." Wang Four thought this was the best thing he could say in this situation.

Little Zhao tried them on again and looked up at the sky. "It's no good, they still make me dizzy."

"Take them anyway, just take them." Wang Four was being as ingratiating as he possibly could. "They're a gift for you; I can't use them. You take them; in two years, if your eyes start going bad, they'll be just right for you."

"You're giving these to me?" Little Zhao asked. "Really? Shit, it'll cost me half a dollar to buy a new case for them."

"Yes, they're for you. I can't do anything with them. I'd only get about two dollars if I sold them." Wang Four was acting even more ingratiating.

"Let me see what I have here." Little Zhao took out all of his ten-cent notes and paid Li Six for the sweet potatoes. "I've only got 60 cents left. Goddammit, I'm only up twenty cents."

"You still have a pocketful of coppers," someone reminded

不行,"这是近视镜,戴上发晕!"

"戴惯就好了,"王四笑着说。

"戴惯?为戴它,还得变成近视眼?"小赵觉得不上算,可是又真爱眼镜。试着走了几步。然后,摘下来,看看大家。大家都觉得上镜子确是体面。王四领着头说:

"真有个样儿!"

"就是发晕呢!"小赵还不肯撒手它。

"戴惯就好了!"王四觉得只有这一句还像话。

小赵又戴上镜子,看了看天。"不行,还是发晕!"

"你拿着吧,拿着吧。"王四透着很"自己"。"送给你的,我拿着没用。拿着吧,等过二年,你的眼神不这么足了,再戴也就合适了。"

"送给我的?"小赵钉了一句。"真的?操!换个盒子还得好几毛!"

"真送给你,我拿着没用;卖,也不过卖个块儿八七的!"王四更显着"自己"了。

"等我数数,"小赵把毛票都掏出来,给了李六白薯钱。"还有六毛,才他妈的赢了两毛!"

"你还有铜子呢!"有人提醒他一声。

英汉对照
English-Chinese
中国文学宝库
Gems of Chinese Literature
现代文学系列
Modern Literature

105

him.

"Couldn't be more than a dime's worth." Though he didn't take them out and count them, no one believed him. Little Zhao wasn't upset because he had won so little money; he was actually quite satisfied with himself since he usually lost when he gambled. Losing a few dimes meant less to him than the embarrassment of being called a "turkey." But today he had won his reputation back, even though he only won about thirty cents, including the coppers — maybe more, since those coppers were quite heavy. "Wang Four, I can't accept these as a gift. Here, I've got sixty cents altogether. You take half and I take half, that's only fair."

Wang Four hadn't expected to get so much, but since Little Zhao was being so generous, he pressed him for a little more: "How about throwing in a few coppers as well. That was easy money for you anyway."

"Whoa! That's my lucky money. I better keep that, since we're going to play tomorrow, right?" Little Zhao believed that if he showed up the next day, he'd be sure to win again. The last few days, the dice had been rolling in his favor.

"Alright, thirty cents it is. Thirty cents for such a fine pair of glasses." Wang Four took the money and put it in one of his inner pockets.

"Didn't you say you wanted to give them to me as a gift? Son of a bitch!"

"Alright, alright! Good friends shouldn't argue over such small amounts."

Little Zhao put the glasses back in their case and made ready to

"至多也就有一毛来钱的铜子，"小赵可是没往外掏它们，大家也不就深信他的话。小赵可是并不因为赢得少而不高兴；他的确很欢喜。往常，他每押必输。输几毛原不算什么，不过被大家拿他当"大头"，有些难堪。今天总算恢复了名誉，虽然连铜子算上才三毛来钱——也许是三毛多，铜子的分量怪沉的吗。"王四，我也不白要你的。看见没？有六毛。你三毛，我三毛；像回事儿不像？"

王四没想到能给三毛。他既然开通，不妨再挤一下："把铜子再掏出点来，反正是赢去的。"

"吹！吉祥钱，腰里带着好。明儿个还得跟你们干呢！"小赵觉得明天再来，一定还要赢的。这两天运气必是不坏。

"好啦，三毛。三毛买那么好的镜子！"王四把票子接过来。放在贴肉的小兜里。

"你不是说送给我吗？这小子！"

"好啦，好啦，朋友们过得多，不在乎这个。"

小赵把眼镜放在盒子里，走开。"明儿再

leave. "See you all tomorrow!" He took a few steps and opened the case to take another look. When he turned around to look, he saw that none of the ricksha men were watching him, so he put the glasses on. Though everything went blurry in front of him, he didn't want to take them off now; he'd get used to them sooner or later. Wang Four was right. There was nothing more frustrating than owning a pair of glasses and not being able to wear them, especially since all shop managers had to wear glasses. With a pair of glasses, a watch and a gold inlay in one of his front teeth, he'd have no trouble winning the heart of Little Pheonix, who lived in Nangangzi.

As Little Zhao turned the corner, a loud horn sounded in his ears. Since he couldn't see where the car was coming from, he quickly removed his glasses....

After that, neither the near-sighted boy who walked along the city wall, Little Zhao nor Wang Four were seen in the vicinity of the school. Li Six announced, "Wang Four's been hanging around the southern part of the city recently."

Translated by Don J. Cohn

干!"走了几步,又把盒子打开。回头看了看,拉车的们并没把眼看着他。把镜子又戴上,眼前成了模糊的一片。可是不肯马上摘下来——戴惯就好了。他觉得王四的话有理。有眼镜不戴,心中难过。况且掌柜们都必须戴镜子的。眼镜,手表,再安上一个金门牙:南岗子的小凤要不跟我才怪呢!

刚一拐弯,猛的听见一声喇叭。他看不清,不知往哪面儿躲。他急于摘镜子……

学校附近,这些日子了,不见了溜墙根的近视学生,不见了小赵,不见了王四。"王四这些日子老在南城搁车,"李六告诉大家。

Brother You Takes Office

Brother You set out to take office.

When he came in sight of the building where he would be working, he slowed down. It wasn't very large. He knew the place. He had visited nearly all the offices, gambling houses and opium dens in the city. He remembered this place — when the door was open you could see the Mountain of the Thousand Buddhas. Naturally at the moment he had no interest in the Mountain of the Thousand Buddhas; his duties would be heavy! But he showed no agitation. He'd knocked about for years, he knew how to make his feelings. You walked slower still.

Fat, fortyish, heavy brows, a sallow clean-shaven face. A grey serge gown, wide sleeves, black satin shoes. He moved sedately, with never a glance at the Mountain of the Thousand Buddhas. Maybe I should have come in a car, he thought. No, what for? His men were all his own kind. Everyone knew each other. Why put on a show? Besides, his was an important job. Why throw his weight around? It wasn't as if he had anything to worry about. Black satin shoes, grey serge gown — just right for a man of his position. You strolled slowly, calm and composed. No need to wear a military uniform. A "hard guy" was stuck in his belt beneath his gown. You smiled to himself.

No signboard hung outside the two-room office but, like You's

上 任

尤老二去上任。

看见办公的地方,他放慢了步。那个地方不大,他晓得。城里有大小公所和赌局烟馆,差不多他都进去过。他记得这个地方——开开门就能看见千佛山。现在他自然没心情去想千佛山;他的责任不轻呢!他可是没透出慌张来;走南闯北的多年了,他拿得住劲,走得更慢了。胖胖的,四十多岁,重眉毛,黄净子脸。灰哔叽夹袍,肥袖口;青缎双脸鞋。稳稳的走,没看千佛山;倒想着:似乎应当坐车来。不必,几个伙计都是自家人,谁还不知道谁;大可以不必讲排场。况且自己的责任不轻,干吗招摇呢。这并不完全是怕;青缎鞋,灰哔叽袍,恰合身分,慢慢的走,也显着稳。没有穿军衣的必要。腰里可藏着把硬的。自己笑了笑。

办公处没有什么牌匾:和尤老二一样,里边

英汉对照
English-Chinese
中国文学宝库
Gems of Chinese Literature
现代文学系列
Modern Literature

clothing, there were hard guys inside. The door was open. His four men were seated on stools, smoking, their heads down. No one was looking at the Mountain of the Thousand Buddhas. On a large table by the wall were several teacups. On the floor, a new iron kettle was surrounded by cigarette butts. One was still burning. As the men rose to greet him, You again thought about the car. Assuming office this way really was a little cheap. But his old friends stood very ceremoniously. Although everyone was smiling warmly, there was respect in their manner. They didn't look down on him because he hadn't arrived in a car. When you came to think of it, the inspector and his office operated secretly. The less attention they attacted, the better. Of course, his men knew this. You felt somewhat easier.

After pausing before the large table and smiling at the men, he went into the inner room. Its furnishings consisted of a desk and two chairs. On the wall was a calendar, decorated with the blood of a departed bedbug. The office is a bit too bare, You mused. But he couldn't think of what to add.

Zhao brought in a cup of tea with a piece of twig floating in it. You didn't speak to him. Rubbing his forehead, You got an idea. Ah, that's right, he needed a wash basin. But he didn't tell Zhao to buy one. He had to think this over carefully. The money for the office expenses was in his hands. Should he use it, or keep it all for himself? His salary was a hundred and twenty dollars. The expense account gave him eighty more. On a job where you risked your life, another eighty wasn't too much. But weren't his men also risking their lives? And they were old friends. You had eaten and

有硬家伙。只是两间小屋。门开着呢,四位伙计在凳子上坐着,都低着头吸烟,没有看千佛山的。靠墙的八仙桌上有几个茶杯,地上放着把新洋铁壶,壶的四围爬着好几个香烟头儿,有一个还冒着烟。尤老二看见他们立起来,又想起车来,到底这样上任显着"秃"一点。可是,老朋友们都立得很规矩。虽然大家是笑着,可是在亲热中含着敬意。他们没因为他没坐车而看不起他。说起来呢,稽察长和稽察是作暗活的,越不惹耳目越好。他们自然晓得这个。他舒服了些。

尤老二在八仙桌前面立了会儿,向大家笑了笑,走进里屋去。里屋只有一条长桌,两把椅子,墙上钉着个月分牌,月分牌的上面有一条臭虫血。办公室太空了些,尤老二想;可又想不出添置什么。赵伙计送进一杯茶来,飘着根茶叶棍儿。尤老二和赵伙计全没的说,尤老二擦了下脑门。啊,想起来了:得有个洗脸盆,他可是没告诉赵伙计去买。他得细细的想一下:办公费都在他自己手里呢,是应当公开的用,还是自己一把死拿?自己的薪水是一百二,办公费八十。卖命的事,把八十全拿着不算多。可是伙计们难道不是卖命?况且是老朋友们?多少年

英汉对照
English-Chinese
中国文学宝库
Gems of Chinese Literature
现代文学系列
Modern Literature

drunk with them for years. When they lived in the earthen cave dwelling, hadn't they all slept on the same platform bed? No, he couldn't keep the whole expense account for himself.

Zhao went out. When Zhao was leader of his own band, had he ever privately pocketed money? You blushed. From the next room, Liu glanced at him through the open door. Although over fifty, Liu had come to work as one of his men. But three years ago, Liu had fifty rapid fire rifles under his command. No, he couldn't keep all the expense money. But in that case, what was the use of being boss? Share the eighty with the others? Of course they too had been leaders, but only of bandit gangs in the mountains. Although You kept in constant touch with them, he had never formally become a bandit. There was a difference. They, to put it bluntly, were crooks who had given up crime to join the forces of law and order. He was an official. An official had his own way of doing things. Very well, then, he'd run his office in an official manner — the eighty dollars would be reserved for his personal use. But he still needed that wash basin, and a couple of towels, too.

There were also certain things he ought to do. For instance, an inspector ought to read the newspaper, or lecture his men. The newspaper he had to have. Whether he read it or not didn't matter. Just spreading it on his desk would make an impression. As for lecturing people, he was no novice at that. He had been a corporal in the army, and a member of the tax commission. Yes, he'd have to lecture his men, otherwise it wouldn't seem like a real office-taking. Anyhow, these fellows had all been up in the hills, and at various times they'd been in the army. If he didn't give

不是一处吃,一处喝;睡土窑子不是一同住大炕?不能独吞。赵伙计走出去,老赵当头目的时候,可曾独吞过钱?尤老二的脸红起来。刘伙计在外屋溜了他一眼。老刘,五十多了,倒当起伙计来,三年前手里还有过五十枝快枪!不能独吞。可是,难道白当头目?八十块大家分?再说,他们当头目是在山上。尤老二虽然跟他们不断的打联络,可是没正式上过山。这就有个分别了。他们,说句不好听的,是黑面上的;他是官。作官有作官的规矩。他们是弃暗投明,那么,就得官事官办。八十元办公费应当他自己拿着。可是,洗脸盆是要买的;还得来两条手巾。

除了洗脸盆该买,还似乎得作点别的。比如说,稽察长看看报纸,或是对伙计们训话。应当有份报纸,看不看的,摆着也够样儿。训话,他不是外行。他当过排长,作过税卡委员;是的,他得训话,不然,简直不像上任的样儿。况且,伙计们都是住过山的,有时候也当过兵;不

them a couple of stingers, they wouldn't respect him.

Zhao had left the room. Liu kept coughing. He definitely had to lecture them. He'd teach them how to behave. You cleared his throat and stood up. He wanted to wash his face. But he still had no basin and towel. He sat down again. He'd lecture them. What should he say? Hadn't he made everything clear when he asked them to help? Hadn't he said exactly the same thing to Zhao and Liu and Wang and Chu? "Give me a hand, old friend. When there's food on You's table, nobody goes hungry. We're brothers!" And he'd said it more than once. Why repeat it?

As for their duties, they were all quite clear. It was simply a case of set a thief to catch a thief. Every one of them knew it, though it wasn't a good idea to put it into words.

The main thing was to look out for himself, to protect his own neck. If he really tried to make good on this job and arrested a few of his underworld friends, Liu and the others might let their pistols off in his direction. It was best for him to keep one eye closed. He couldn't start off with a big flourish. They'd all be meeting again some day. But could You say this? How could he lecture them? Get a load of the eyes of that Liu — those lids wouldn't close even when he was dead. The help the men were giving You was a form of bandit loyalty. He couldn't get rid of the code of the hills in one sweep. True, the police commissioner had put him on this job to nab bandits. But they were all his friends. Intimate friends. A tough problem!

You took off his grey serge gown, then went out and smiled at his men.

给他们几句漂亮的,怎能叫他们佩服。老赵出去了。老刘直咳嗽。必定得训话,叫他们得规矩着点。尤老二咳了声,立起来,想擦把脸;还是没有洗脸盆与手巾。他又坐下。训话,说什么呢?不是约他们帮忙的时候已经说明白了吗,对老赵老刘老王老褚不都说的是那一套么?"多年的朋友,捧我尤老二一场。我尤老二有饭吃,大家伙儿就饿不着;自己弟兄!"这说过不止一遍了,能再说么?至于大家的工作,谁还不明白——反正还不是用黑面上的人拿黑面上的人。这只能心照,不便实对实的点破。自己的饭碗要紧,脑袋也要紧。要真打算立功的话,拿几个黑道上的朋友开刀,说不定老刘们就会把盒子炮往里放。睁一眼闭一眼是必要的,不能斩尽杀绝;大家日后还得见面。这些话能明说么?怎么训话呢?看老刘那对眼睛,似乎死了也闭不上。帮忙是义气,真把山上的规矩一笔勾个净,作不到。不错,司令派尤老二是为拿反动分子。可是反动分子都是朋友呢。谁还不知道谁吃几碗干饭?难!

尤老二把灰哔叽袍脱了,出来向大家笑了笑。

英汉对照
English-Chinese
中国文学宝库
Gems of Chinese Literature
现代文学系列
Modern Literature

"Inspector," Liu hailed him. Contempt was plain in his eyes. "How about assigning us some work?" he said.

You nodded. He'd show them. "I'm going to write a list. I have to make a report to Commissioner Li. As I told you brothers the other day, our job is to help Commissioner Li nab bandits. The commissioner called me in and said, 'You, you've got to help me, I don't know the layout here.' How could I refuse? He's an old friend too. I can do it, I thought. Why? Because I thought of you fellows. I know the setup pretty well, and you know it right down to the ground. Working together, we can put it over. 'Commissioner,' I said, 'leave it to me.' Since he did me the honour of offering me the job, I couldn't be ungrateful enough to refuse. Brothers, whatever Commissioner Li gets, there's a share for me. Whatever I get, you're in it too. I've got it all figured out. Now I'm going to write this list — who does what. After we've talked it over, I'll hand it in, then we'll get started. We'll do it all official and proper. Right?" You asked with a laugh.

No one replied. Chu blinked. Although there wasn't any awkward silence, You couldn't very well say any more. He'd have to prepare his list, write it out with a pomp that would crush Liu and his pals. After all, You recalled, wasn't he the one who wrote the ransom note the year Chu kidnapped that rich young Wang? Yes, he'd certainly wriggle that writing brush. But where was his brush and ink slab? These men couldn't get anything done!

"Say, Zhao...." You thought he'd send Zhao to buy the writing brush. But then he checked himself. Why Zhao? You had to be discriminating where money was involved. This wasn't up in the

"稽察长！"老刘的眼里有一万个"看不起尤老二"，"分派分派吧。"

尤老二点点头。他得给他们一手看。"等我开个单子，咱们的事儿得报告给李司令。昨儿个，前两天，不是我向诸位弟兄研究过？咱们是帮助李司令拿反动派。我不是说过：李司令把我叫了去，说，老二，我地面上生啊，老二你得来帮帮忙。我不好意思推辞，跟李司令也是多年的朋友。我这么一想，有办法。怎么说呢，我想起你们来。我在地面上熟哇。你们可知底呢。咱们一合把，还有什么不行的事。司令，我就说了，交给我了，司令既肯赏饭吃，尤老二还能给脸不兜着？弟兄们，有李司令就有尤老二，有尤老二就有你们。这我早已研究过了，我开个单子，谁管哪里，谁管哪里，合计好了，往上一报，然后再动手，这像官事，是不是？"尤老二笑着问大家。

老刘们都没言语。老褚挤了挤眼。可是谁也没感到僵得慌。尤老二不便再说什么，他得去开单子。拿笔刷刷的一写，他想，就得把老刘们吓背过气去。那年老褚绑王公子的票，不是求尤老二写的通知书？是的，他得刷刷的写一气。可是笔墨砚呢？这几个伙计简直没办法！"老赵，"尤老二想叫老赵买笔去。可是没说出来。为什么买东西单叫老赵呢？一来到钱上，叫谁去买东西都得有个分寸。这不是山上，

hills where they did things any old way. This was official business. Who should do the buying, who should deliver letters — these jobs had to be assigned right. It wasn't easy. The man who bought things got a rake-off from the store. You didn't earn anything delivering letters. Who should be stuck with the messenger job?

"Ah ... nothing ... nothing," he told Zhao. He wouldn't buy the writing brush just yet. He'd have to give the matter more thought. You was rather disturbed. He never imagined being an inspector was so troublesome. It wasn't such a wonderful job. Yet it might not be too bad, particularly if he could keep the eighty dollars expense money. But he couldn't do that. His men had all been bandits. If he held on to the money too tightly, their pistols might pump him full of "black dates." That wouldn't be so funny.

It was a tricky situation. An official with bandits for his assistants. What kind of an official was that? Yet he couldn't operate without them. Could he nab crooks by himself? A fat chance! He patted the pistol in his belt.

"Brothers, have you got your hardware?"

Everyone nodded.

Are the bastards mute! What was the idea? Was it scorn, or fear? Just nodding, that was no way for a friend to behave. If they had anything to say, they ought to say it. Look at that Liu, his face all grim and solemn. You laughed again. He wasn't being quite officious enough. But he couldn't be too officious with this crowd. Maybe they'd like it better if he swore at them. But he didn't dare. He wasn't a real bandit. You felt as if he were standing with his feet in two different boats. He hated himself for not

可以马马虎虎。这是官事,谁该买东西去,谁该送信去,都应当分配好了。可是这就不容易,买东西有扣头,送信是白跑腿;谁活该白跑腿呢?"啊,没什么,老赵!"先等等买笔吧,想想再说。尤老二心里有点不自在。没想到作稽察长这么啰嗦。差事不算很甜;也说不上苦来,假若八十元办公费都归自己的话。可是不能都归自己,伙计们都住过山;手儿一紧,还真许个尝黑枣,是玩的吗?这玩艺儿不好办,作着官而带着土匪,算哪道官呢?不带土匪又真不行,专凭尤老二自己去拿反动分子?拿个屁!尤老二摸了摸腰里的家伙:"哥儿们,硬的都带着哪?"

大家一齐点了点头。

"妈的怎么都哑吧了?"尤老二心里说。是什么意思呢?是不佩服咱尤老二呢,还是怕呢?点点头,不像自己朋友,不像;有话说呀。看老刘!一脸的官司。尤老二又笑了笑。有点不够官派,大概跟这群家伙还不能讲官派。骂他们一顿也许就骂欢喜了?不敢骂,他不是地道土匪。他知道他是脚踩两支船。他恨自己不是地

英汉对照
English-Chinese
中国文学宝库
Gems of Chinese Literature
现代文学系列
Modern Literature

being a genuine bandit. At the same time, he felt he was high-class. If he weren't, would he have been made an official? Lighting a cigarette, he pondered. He'd have to feed this bunch. He could hang on to the office expense money, but he'd have to spend a bit on food.

"Let's go, brothers, to the Wufu Restaurant!" You went to put on his grey serge gown.

Zhou's face cracked into wrinkles, like an overripe pumpkin. Two smile lines appeared in Liu's fifty-year-old stony cheeks. Wang and Chu also revived. Moisture had evidently returned to everyone's throat. Those who couldn't find anything to say, licked their lips.

At the restaurant, they were all great friends again. They didn't stand on ceremony. For their joint feast this one proposed a jellied fresh ham, that one wanted a mixed roast with sea-slugs. Liu suggested grilled whole chicken — two of them. When they were half full, they started to talk business. Liu, of course, spoke first, since he was by far the eldest. His stony cheeks were red with feasting. He took another drink of liquor, another bite of the ham, another drag on his cigarette.

"Inspector," he began. His eyes swept the other. "Opium pedlars, pimps — we can take them easy. But with bandits, we've got to be careful. Are we going to sell our brothers for a small heap of silver dollars?"

Drink had given You courage. "That's no way to talk, Brother Liu. Commissioner Li appointed us to catch bandits. There are too many of them around. If we don't nab some, fast, Commissioner

道土匪,同时又觉得他到底高明,不高明能作官么？点上根烟,想主意,得喂喂这群家伙。办公费可以不撒手;得花点饭钱。

"走哇,弟兄们,五福馆!"尤老二去穿灰哔叽夹袍。

老赵的倭瓜脸裂了纹,好似是熟透了。老刘五十多年制成的石头腮梆笑出两道缝。老王老褚也都复活了,仿佛是。大家的嗓子里全有了津液,找不着话说也舔舔嘴唇。

到了五福馆,大家确是自己朋友了,不客气:有的要水晶肘,有的要全家福,老刘甚至于想吃锅㸆鸡,而且要双上。吃到半饱,大家觉得该研究了。老刘当然先发言,他的岁数顶大。石头腮梆上红起两块,他喝了口酒,夹了块肘子,吸了口烟。"稽察长!"他扫了大家一眼:"烟土,暗门子,咱们都能手到擒来。那反——反什么？可得小心！咱们是干什么的？伤了义气,叫合㸃看。不是一共才这么一小堆洋钱吗？"

尤老二被酒劲催开了胆量:"不是这么说,刘大哥！李司令派咱们哥几个,就为拿反动派。反动派太多了,不赶紧下手,李司令就不稳;他

英汉对照
English-Chinese
中国文学宝库
Gems of Chinese Literature
现代文学系列
Modern Literature

Li may lose his job. If he goes, where will that leave us?"

"Suppose we do nab some, knock a couple off?" A strong liquor breath accompanied the smoke Zhao exhaled. "Sure, we've got guns, but so have they. Anyhow we're not going to keep these jobs for ever. It's not that I'm scared."

"Whoever's scared is a son of a bitch," was the analysis Chu drew.

"A stinking son of a bitch," Zhao confirmed. And he added, "Nobody's scared, and everybody's willing to give Commissioner Li a hand. Fraternity — that's the problem. It's true you've helped us, Brother You, and you've been around more than we, but you've never been up in the hills."

"Don't I know what the code is?" You gazed off into space and laughed coldly.

"Who says you don't?" countered gourd-mouthed Wang.

"It's this way, brothers." You decided to needle them. "If we're friends, you'll stick with me. If you don't want to stick with me," again he laughed off into space, "that's all right too."

"Inspector." Once more it was Liu. His eyes were piercing. "If you really want us to go at it, we will. But don't forget this. We're just your assistants, you're the head man. Any comebacks will go direct to you. You're a friend, so I'm talking straight. If you want us to nab guys, that's a cinch. Nothing to it."

The lovely sea-slugs You had consumed turned to ice in his stomach. This was just what he was afraid of. His men would do the work and he would report the victories. But when the bandits started dishing out black dates, he would be first on the list!

吹了,还有咱们?"

"比如咱们下了手,"老赵的酒气随着烟喷出老远,"毙上几个,咱们有枪,难道人家就没有?还有一说呢,咱们能老吃这碗饭吗?这不是怕。"

"谁怕谁是丫头养的!"老褚马上研究出来。

"丫头妮养的!"老赵接了过来:"不是怕,也不是不帮李司令的忙。义气,这是义气!好尤二哥的话,你虽然帮过我们,公面私面你也比我们见的广,可是你没上过山。"

"我不懂?"尤老二眼看空中,冷笑了声。

"谁说你不懂来着?"葫芦嘴的王小四顿出一句来。

"是这么着,哥儿们,"尤老二想烹他们一下:"捧我尤老二呢,交情;不捧呢。"又向空中一笑,"也没什么。"

"稽察长,"又是老刘,这小子的眼睛老瞪着:"真干也行呀,可有一样,我们是伙计,你是头目;毒儿可全归到你身上去。自己朋友,丑话先说明白了。叫我们去掏人,那容易,没什么。"

尤老二胃中的海参全冰凉了。他就怕的是这个。伙计办下来的,他去报功;反动派要是请吃黑枣,可也先请他!

英汉对照
English-Chinese
中国文学宝库
Gems of Chinese Literature
现代文学系列
Modern Literature

He mustn't worry in advance. He'd take things as they came. Eating black dates was uncomfortable, but reporting success and being rewarded was very sweet. He had been around for years. He knew no matter what you did, you had to strike first. When you played, you played for keeps! You was over forty. If he didn't get much out of this himself, at least he could leave a little something for his son. He wasn't going to be like Liu and the others. Always guarding their heads but leaving their backsides sticking out. Doing dirty work all their lives but ending up without even a burial plot to lie in when they died. He was shrewd, he could plan. He wouldn't listen to Liu. You decided to go ahead. He'd play along with Commissioner Li. If he cracked a couple of cases, he might even be transferred to headquarters. Who could tell? With a car to ride around in wherever he went. He couldn't always walk to take office!

The concluding soup expanded spirits and stomachs together. Everyone grew much more cordial. Although You was still quite firm, his tone mellowed:

"You've got to help me, brothers. Pick someone with no connections and bring him in. It'll serve him right. We've got to put on some kind of a show. We're all carrying hardware. How will it look if we just nab a few pimps? All right, then. This is how we'll do it. First find some small fry. Nab the kind that can't cause any trouble, then we'll see. When we finish that, we'll come back here for another feed, what do you say? That cold ham wasn't bad."

"It's autumn, it's getting cool. We ought to have hot roast pork

但是他不能先害怕,事得走着瞧。吃黑枣不大舒服,可是报功得赏却有劲呢。尤老二混过这么些年了,哪宗事不是先下手的为强?要干就得玩真的!四十多了,不为自己,还不为儿子留下点吗儿?都像老刘们还行,顾脑袋不顾屁股,干一辈子黑活,连坟地都没有。尤老二是虚子,会研究,不能只听老刘的。他决定干。他得捧李司令。弄下几案来,说不定还会调到司令部去呢。出来也坐坐汽车什么的!尤老二不能老开着正步上任!

汤使人的胃与气一齐宽畅。三仙汤上来,大家缓和了许多。尤老二虽然还很坚决,可是话软和了些:"伙计们,还得捧我尤老二呀,找没什么蹦儿的弄吧——活该他倒霉,咱们多少露一手。你说,腰里带着硬的,净弄些个暗门子,算哪道呢?好啦!咱们就这么办,先找小的,不刺手的办,以后再说。办下来,咱们还是这儿,水晶肘还不坏,是不是?"

"秋天了,以后该吃红焖肘子了。"王小四不

英汉对照
English-Chinese
中国文学宝库
Gems of Chinese Literature
现代文学系列
Modern Literature

from now on." Wang didn't talk much, but when he said something it was to the point.

You decided to keep Wang with him in the office and send the other three out to investigate. No need to write a list. When they came back he'd make a report. Yes, he'd have to buy a writing brush and an ink slab, and also a wash basin. He'd buy it himself so there'd be no question of favouritism. What he needed was a secretary, but he had forgotten to mention this to Commissioner Li. For the time being, he'd do his own writing. He'd ask for a secretary after they'd cracked their first case. There was no rush. You was a man who kept both feet on the ground. People said Erdie's son could write. You would give him a start in the world. He'd make Erdie's son his secretary. Good. For his first day in office he wasn't doing badly.

Chatting with Wang on the way back, he forgot all about the brush and the ink slab. The office wasn't a bit like a real office. Still, it was just as well. All that business about writing with a great flourish was only something in his mind. When it came to actually writing, he didn't know many words. They always seemed to escape him whenever he wanted to put them down on paper. It was just as well that he had no brush and ink slab.

But what should he do with his time? He ought to have a newspaper, even if it was only to look at the pictures. He couldn't just keep gabbing with Wang. Although they were old friends, he was an official and Wang was an underling. You had to think of his dignity. He had already stood in the doorway. He couldn't drink any more tea. He had looked twice through the pages of the

大说话,一说可就说到根上。

尤老二决定留王小四陪着他办公,其余的人全出去采访。不必开单子了,等他们采访回来再作报告。是的,他得去买笔墨砚,和洗脸盆。他自己去买省得有偏有向。应当来个书记,可是忘了和李司令说。暂时先自己写吧,等办下案来再要求添书记;不要太心急,尤老二有根。二爷的儿子,听说,会写字,提拔他一下吧。将来添书记必用二爷的儿子,好啦,头一天上任,总算不含糊。

只顾在路上和王小四瞎扯,笔墨砚到底还是没有买。办公室简直不像办公室。可是也好:刷刷的写一气,只是心里这么想;字这种玩艺刷刷的来的时候,说真的,并不多;要写那个,那个偏偏不在家。没笔墨砚也好。办什么呢,可是? 应当来份报纸,哪怕是看看广告的图呢。不能老和王小四瞎扯,虽然是老朋友,到底现在是官长与伙计,总得有个分寸。门口已经站过了,茶已喝足,月份牌已翻过了两遍。再没有事

英汉对照
English-Chinese
中国文学宝库
Gems of Chinese Literature
现代文学系列
Modern Literature

calendar. There was nothing else for him to do. You thought over his family finances. Their condition was hopeful. Salary a hundred and twenty, plus eighty dollars expense money — even if he didn't take it all. He could count on at least a hundred and fifty a month. Gradually, he could save up for a little house.

Damn —! Dog Shang did just one job with warlord Zhang Zongchang and they raked in a hundred thousand! There was never anything like it. Never. They were the kind of bandits Commissioner Li was after. Who could be as careful with his money as Dog Shang? With money in your hands, you went dizzy. Take himself for instance. You had picked up twenty or thirty thousand when he was working in the tax office. And now where was it? No wonder men went crooked. He was used to eating and drinking and playing around. Live on bran muffins again? He couldn't stand it. Nobody could stand it.

Yes, to tell the truth, they all — including You — were waiting for Marshal Zhang's return. Naturally. Damn —! Ding the Third alone was storing two trunks full of military notes[①] which Zhang had printed. If Zhang came back, Ding would be a rich man with those trunks!

How could You talk about arresting bandits? They were all old friends. But on a salary of a hundred and twenty, plus eighty in expense money, what else could he do? He had to! Damn! Get on with it. Who could worry about so much? Every man for himself.

---

① At that time China was ruled by various big warlords, who issued notes which they used as money in the areas under their control.

可干。盘算盘算家事,还有希望。薪水一百二,办公费八十——即使不能全数落下——每月一百五可靠。慢慢的得买所小房。妈的商二狗,跟张宗昌走了一趟,干落十万!没那个事了,没了。反动派还不就是他们么?哪能都像商二狗,资资本本的看着?谁不是钱到手就迷了头?就拿自己说吧,在税卡子上不是也弄了两三万吗?都哪儿去了?难怪反动呀,吃喝玩乐的惯了,再天天啃窝窝头?受不了,谁也受不了!是的,他们——凭良心说,连尤老二自己——都盼着张督办回来,当然的。妈的,丁三立一个人就存着两箱军用票呢!张要是回来,打开箱子,老丁马上是财主!拿反动派,说不下去,都是老朋友。可是月薪一百二,办公费八十,没法儿。得拿!妈的脑袋吊了碗大的疤,谁能顾得了许多!

英汉对照
English-Chinese
中国文学宝库
Gems of Chinese Literature
现代文学系列
Modern Literature

Whose fault was it that Marshal Zhang couldn't come back? Nab them! Shoot a couple! You had never been up in the hills. He wouldn't be betraying any of his own gang.

It was after four, and still no sign of Liu and the other two. Had they really gone to pry into nests, or were they just fooling around? He'd have to set office hours. Everyone must be back by four-thirty to report. What kind of an office would it be like, if they never showed up? Without them he couldn't operate. With them, they were a headache. Damn —!

He wouldn't wait for them any longer than five. He started work at eight, at five he quit. His men could go out whenever they liked. It wasn't unusual for arrests to be made in the middle of the night. But the inspector couldn't always be waiting around for his assistants. He ought to tell them, but it was rather hard to say. What was so hard about it? Wasn't he the boss? He immediately notified Wang. Wang grunted. What did that mean?

"It's five o'clock!" You glanced at the Mountain of the Thousand Buddhas. The sun was gilding its summit. In the sunlight the autumn grass still had a bit of green. "Look after things, Wang. See you tomorrow at eight."

Wang's gourd-shaped mouth was closed in a tight line.

The next morning You deliberately came a half hour late. He had to hold back. Suppose he arrived before his men? How embarrassing.

But the men were all there, seated on stools, smoking, their heads down. You felt like punching them. What clods! When he entered, they rose as they had the day before, but very slowly, as

各自奔前程,谁叫张大帅一时回不来呢。拿,毙几个! 尤老二没上过山,多少跟他们不是一伙。

四点多了,老刘们都没回来。这三个家伙是真踩窝子去了,还是玩去了? 得定个办公时间,四点半都得回来报告。假如他们干铲儿不回来,像什么公事? 没他们是不行,有他们是个累赘,真他妈的。到五点可不能再等;八点上班,五点关门;伙计们可以随时出去,半夜里拿人是常有的事;长官可不能老伺候着。得告诉他们,不大好开口。有什么不好开口,尤老二你不是头么? 马上告诉王小四。王小四哼了一声。什么意思呢?

"五点了,"尤老二看了千佛山一眼,太阳光儿在山头上放着金丝,金光下的秋草还有点绿色。"老王你照应着,明儿八点见。"

王小四的葫芦嘴闭了个严。

第二天早晨,尤老二故意的晚去了半点钟,拿着点劲儿。万一他到了,而伙计们没来,岂不是又得为难?

伙计们却都到了,还是都低着头坐在板凳上吸烟呢。尤老二想揪过一个来揍一顿,一群死鬼! 他进了门,他们照旧又都立起来,立起来

英汉对照
English-Chinese
中国文学宝库
Gems of Chinese Literature
现代文学系列
Modern Literature

133

if they all had athlete's foot. You smiled at them, though he felt more like swearing. It would be awkward if he did. He had to act big. Who told him to become a leader of men? He had to act shrewd. You gave a grandiose laugh. Casual, unconcerned.

"Ah, Liu, do any business?" Natural, pleasant, humorous. You mentally praised himself.

"There was business," Liu, grim-visaged, bored into You with his eyes. "But we didn't do any."

"Why not?" You laughed.

"We didn't have to. They'll be coming in themselves soon."

"Oh!" You tried to laugh again, but no sound emerged. "What about you?" he asked Zhao and Chu.

The two just shook their heads.

"Shall we go out again today?" queried Liu.

"Ah, wait a while," You walked towards his room. "Let me think." He turned his head back and looked. The men were again seated, their eyes on the cigarette butts. They weren't saying a word. Clods.

You sat down in his office. He was puzzled. They'll be coming in themselves? He couldn't ask Liu what that meant. He couldn't admit they had him stumped. They'd lose respect. But what did it mean — they'll be coming in themselves? He'd just have to wait and see.

Should he send Liu and the others out on their rounds today? That had to be decided immediately. "Hey, Chu, get going. Keep your eyes open, do you hear?" You waited for them all to laugh. That would show they appreciated his carefree humour. No one

的很慢,仿佛都害着脚气。尤老二反倒笑了;破口骂才合适,可是究竟不好意思。他得宽宏大量,谁叫轮到自己当头目人呢。他得拿出虚子劲儿,唏唏哈哈,满不在乎。

"嗨,老刘,有活儿吗?"多么自然,和气,够味儿;尤老二心中夸赞着自己的话。

"活儿有,"老刘瞪着眼,还是一脸的官司:"没办。"

"怎么不办呢?"尤老二笑着。

"不用办,待会了他们自己来。"

"呕!"尤老二打算再笑,没笑出来。"你们呢?"他问老赵和老褚。

两人一齐摇了摇头。

"今天还出去吗?"老刘问。

"啊,等等,"尤老二进了里屋,"我想想看。"回头看了一眼,他们又都坐下了,眼看着烟头,一声不发,一群死鬼。

坐下,尤老二心里打开了鼓——他们自己来? 不能细问老刘,硬输给他们,不能叫伙计小看了。什么意思呢,他们自己来? 不能和老刘研究,等着就是了。还打发老刘们出去不呢? 这得马上决定:"嗨,老褚! 你走你的,睁着点眼,听见没有?"他等着大家笑,大家一笑便是欣

laughed.

"Liu, you'd better wait. Didn't you say they were coming to see me? You and I will keep them company. We're all old friends." He didn't send Wang and Zhao out either. The more men he had around the more secure he'd feel. But suppose they wanted to go out themselves? He couldn't stop them. You had to act reserved on a job like this. If they asked him, then he'd speak. But Wang and Zhao didn't say anything, so that was all right.

It was on the tip of his tongue to ask, "How many of them are coming?" but he swallowed back the words. Didn't he have three assistants with him, all packing guns? If they came in a big gang, well, he'd just have to close his eyes. He'd act according to the situation. Damn —!

He still had no newspaper. What kind of an office was this anyhow! The official had to sit around waiting for bandits. It was really too much. Why not telephone Commissioner Li to send down a company of soldiers, nab the bandits as they came in, then shoot the whole lot! No, better not be too hasty. Better wait and see. Nine thirty.

"Hey, Liu, when are they coming?"

"Soon, inspecter." Was there a mocking note in Liu's voice?

"Go out and get me a paper." You simply had to have his newspaper.

When it was brought, he turned to the local news section. He pretended to chuckle at something he saw. He'd read it learnedly aloud. But there were too many words he didn't recognize. Like the name of that cafe hostess there. What the devil was it?

赏他的胆量与幽默;大家没笑。"老刘,你等等再走。他们不是找我来吗?咱俩得陪陪他们。都是老朋友。"他没往下分派,老王老赵还是不走好,人多好凑胆子。可是他们要出去呢,也不便拦阻;干这行儿还能不耍玄虚么?等他们问上来再讲。老王老赵都没出声,还算好。"他们来几个?"话到嘴边上又咽了回去。反正尤老二这儿有三个伙计呢,全有硬家伙。他们要是来一群呢,那只好闭眼。走到哪儿说哪儿,肏!

还没报纸!哪像办公的样!况且长官得等着反动派,太难了。给司令部个电话,派一队来,来一个拿一个,全毙!不行,别太急了,看看再讲。九点半了,"嗨,老刘,什么时候来呀?"

"也快,稽察长!"老刘这小子有点故意的看哈哈笑。

"报!叫卖报的!"尤老二非看报不可了。

买了份大早报,尤老二找本地新闻,出着声儿笨。非啃啃的念,念不上句来。他妈的女招待的姓别扭,不认识。别扭!啃啃,软一下,女招待的姓!

"They're here, inspector." Liu was quite formal.

You was calm. Setting aside the irritating cafe hostess, he said softly, "Come in." He felt for the pistol in his belt.

A whole crowd entered, headed by Big Yang. Following him was Fancy Brow, another hulking brute. Walking between them, Monkey Four looked particularly small. Sixth Horse, Big-mouth Cao and White Zhang Fei also walked into the room.

"Brother You," they hailed him cordially.

He had to admit he knew them. You stood up and smiled.

Everybody talked at the same time. There was such a clamour no one could hear himself think.

"Big Yang, you tell him." Gradually everyone's interest focussed on one point. They urged one another: "Listen to Big Yang!"

Frowning, Big Yang leaned forward and rested his hands on the desk. His mouth virtually against You's nose, he said, "We've come to congratulate you, Brother You."

"Listen!" White Zhang Fei gave Monkey Four a poke in the back.

"Congratulations are congratulations, but you ought to give us a treat. Actually, we should be treating you, but the last few days we're a little short of this." Big Yang's index finger and thumb pinched together in a circle like a silver dollar. "So you'll have to treat us."

"Anything I can do, brothers —" You began.

Big Yang rolled right on. "You don't have to invite us to a restaurant. That's not necessary. We want this." Again his thumb

"稽察长!他们来了。"老刘特别的规矩。

尤老二不慌,放下姓别扭的女招待,轻轻的。"进来!"摸了摸腰中的傢伙。

进来了一串。为首的是大个儿杨;紧跟着花眉毛,也是大傻个儿;猴四被俩大个子夹在中间,特别显着小;马六,曹大嘴,白张飞,都跟进来。

"尤老二!"大家一齐叫了声。

尤老二得承认他认识这一群,站起来笑着。

大家都说话,话便挤到了一处。嚷嚷了半天,全忘记了自己说的是什么。

"杨大个儿,你一个人说;嗨,听大个儿说!"大家的意见渐归一致,彼此的劝告:"听大个儿的!"

杨大个儿——或是大个儿杨,全是一样的——拧了拧眉毛,弯下点腰,手按在桌上,嘴几乎顶住尤老二的鼻子:"尤老二,我们给你来贺喜!"

"听着!"白张飞给猴四背上一拳。

"贺喜可是贺喜,你得请请我们。按说我们得请你,可是哥儿们这几天都短这个,"食指和拇指成了圈形。"所以呀,你得请我们。"

"好哥儿们的话啦,"尤老二接了过去。

"尤老二,"大个儿杨又接回去。"倒用不着你下帖,请吃馆子,用不着。我们要这个,"食指

英汉对照
English-Chinese
中国文学宝库
Gems of Chinese Literature
现代文学系列
Modern Literature

139

Brother You Takes Office

and index finger formed a circle. "We want money for train tickets."

"Train tickets?" said You.

"That's right." Big Yang nodded thoughtfully. "You see, brother, you're now in charge of this district. How can we keep on operating here? We're all friends. You come, we go. There can't be any squabbles between us. You do your official job. We'll go back to the hills. You pay the fare. No hard words. We part friends. We'll be meeting again some day." Big Yang turned to his cronies. "Isn't that the idea?"

"Right. It's just that," cried Monkey Four. "Now let's hear from Brother You."

This was something You had never expected. He hadn't thought that it would be so easy. But he certainly hadn't expected it would be so hard either. These six wanted train fares. Suppose another sixty, or another six hundred, came in, all wanting him to pay their fares? Besides, Commissioner Li had appointed him to arrest them. If You gave them all fares, spoke to them gently, and sent them off one by one, how would it look? And where would the money come from? He could hardly ask Li for it. Should he spend his hundred and twenty dollars salary, plus eighty dollars expense money?

The trouble was these birds were giving him a lot of face. Not a hard word out of them. "You come, we go." Short and sweet. Spoken like a real friend. It was easy enough, if a man was willing to lay out the money. With a smiling face, You invited them to have some tea. He couldn't make up his mind. He didn't dare

和拇指成了圈形。"你请我们坐车就结了。"

"请坐车?"尤老二问。

"请坐车!"大个儿有心事似的点点头。"你看,尤老二,你既然管了地面,我们弟兄还能作活儿吗?都是朋友。你来,我们滚。你来,我们滚;咱们不能抓破了脸。你作你的官,我们上我们的山。路费,你的事。好说好散,日后咱们还见面呢。"大个儿杨回头问大家:"是这么说不是?"

"对,就是这几句;听尤老二的了!"猴四把话先抢到。

尤老二没想到过这个。事情容易,没想到能这么容易。可是,谁也没想到能这么难。现在这群是六个,都请坐车;再来六十个,六百个呢,也都请坐车?再说,李司令是叫抓他们;若是都送车费,好话说着,一位一位的送走,算什么办法呢?钱从那儿来呢?这大概不能向李司令要吧?就凭自己的一百二薪水,八十块办公,送大家走?可是说回来,这群傢伙确是讲面子,一声难听的没有:"你来,我们滚。"多么干脆,多么自己。事情又真容易,假如有人肯出钱的话。他笑着,让大家喝水,心中拿不定主意。他不敢

英汉对照
English-Chinese
中国文学宝库
Gems of Chinese Literature
现代文学系列
Modern Literature

offend them. They might talk nicely, but they also could be very rough. If they said they'd go, they'd definitely go. But they wouldn't leave unless You gave them the fares. It would make an awful dent in his expense money. And he'd have to pretend to be happy about it, too. They wouldn't stand for any tough talk.

"How much, friends?" he asked casually.

"Ten dollars apiece," said Big Yang, speaking for all.

"It's just the train fare. Once we're up in the hills, we'll manage fine," Monkey Four added.

"We'll leave this afternoon, friend. When we say a thing we mean it," said Big-mouth Cao.

You couldn't be so decisive. Ten dollars apiece meant sixty dollars! Three-fourths of his eighty dollars expense money!

White Zhang Fei got a bit impatient. "Fork over the sixty dollars and we'll be moving along. It's either you or us. With you here, we've got to leave. Isn't that the answer? If you give us the money, we'll go. If you don't — but why talk about that? We understand each other. Real men don't beat about the bush. Brother You, I'm holding out my hand for that train fare."

"Right, we're all holding out our hands. We'll pay it back later. Our friendship hasn't been just for a day," said Big Yang. The others also chimed in. Although their words were different, the meaning was the same.

You could no longer delay. He took out the wallet next to the pistol in his belt and counted out sixty dollars. "Here you are, brothers." He didn't smile.

"Thanks, brother," chorused Big Yang and his gang. Monkey

得罪他们,他们会说好的,也有真厉害的。他们说滚,必定滚;可是,不给钱可滚不了。他的八十块办公费要连根烂。他还得装作愿意拿的样子,他们不吃硬的。

"得多少?朋友们!"他满不在乎似的问。

"一人十拉块钱吧。"大个儿杨代表大家回答。

"就是个车钱,到山上就好办了。"猴四补充上。

"今天后响就走,朋友,说到哪儿办到哪儿!"曹大嘴说。

尤老二不能脆快,一人十块就是六十呀!八十办公费,去了四分之三!

"尤老二,"白张飞有点不耐烦,"干脆拍出六十块来,咱们再见。有我们没你,有你没我们,这不痛快。你拿钱,我们滚。你——不用说了,咱们心照。好汉不必费话,三言两语。尤二毌,咱老张手背向下,和你讨个车钱!"

"好了,我们哥儿们全手背朝下了,日后再补付,哥儿们不是一天半天的交情!"杨大个儿领头,大家随着;虽然词句不大一样,意思可是相同。

尤老二不能再说别的了,从"腰里硬"里掏出皮夹来,点了六张十块的:"哥儿们!"他没笑出来。

杨大个儿们一齐叫了声"哥儿们"。猴四把

英汉对照
English-Chinese
中国文学宝库
Gems of Chinese Literature
现代文学系列
Modern Literature

143

Four rolled up the bills and stuffed them into his waist-band. "We'll be seeing you, brother," he said. The bandits left. In the outer room they nodded at Liu and the others. "Come up and see us in the hills." You's men smiled and escorted them to the door.

You was miserable. If he had known this was going to happen he would have sent for soldiers and had those six birds arrested. But maybe this way of handling it was better. He'd be running into them in the future. Sixty dollars gone. A few more visits like this and his hundred and twenty dollars of salary would also vanish. What kind of an inspector was he? An inspector who gets squeezed by bandits. He was like a mute who's eaten wormwood — it was more bitter than he could say. Had Liu been trying to be helpful, or was he just kidding around? He ought to ask him! Not only hadn't Liu captured any bandits — he had invited them to the office. Was that any way to do things?

Still, maybe he shouldn't be too strict with Liu. He might go back to the hills. You had to have him. He couldn't afford to offend anyone. What a life. If he had brought a couple of green hands along when he took office, when those bandits came he'd have had to eat black dates. Those sixty dollars bought him his life. If you looked at it that way, it was worth it.

You had no choice. What's done was done. He was only afraid that another gang might show up tomorrow asking for railway fares. He couldn't tell this to his men. He had to smile, show that You was big-hearted to his friends, as if sixty dollars or a hundred were nothing at all. But if he kept handing money out at this rate what would the inspector have to eat? The northwest wind? A fine thing!

票子捲巴捲巴塞在腰里:"再见了,哥儿们!"大家走出来,和老刘们点了头:"多咱山上见哪?"老刘们都笑了笑,送出门外。

尤老二心里难过的发空。早知道,调兵把六个傢伙全扣住!可是,也许这么善办更好;日后还要见面呀。六十块可出去了呢;假如再来这么几当儿,连一百二的薪水赔上也不够!作哪道稽察长呢?稽察长叫反动派给炸了酱,哑吧吃黄连有苦说不出!老刘是好意呢,还是玩坏?得问问他!不拿土匪,而把土匪叫来,什么官事呢?还不能跟老刘太紧了,他也会上山。不用他还不行呢;得罪了谁也不成,这年头。假若自己一上任就带几个生手,哼,还许登时就吃了黑枣儿;六十块钱买条命,前后一合算,也还值得。尤老二没办法,过去的不用再提,就怕明儿个又来,要路费的!不能对老刘们说这个,自己得笑,得让他们看清楚:尤老二对朋友不含糊,六十就六十,一百就一百,不含糊;可是六十就六十,一百就一百,自己吃什么呢,稽察长喝西北风,那才有根!

英汉对照
English-Chinese
中国文学宝库
Gems of Chinese Literature
现代文学系列
Modern Literature

Again he picked up the newapaper, but he'd lost interest. He had no interest in anything. Like a fool he'd given away sixty dollars. It was really sickening. He ought to be ashamed — being afraid for his life. It was as if his life didn't belong to him — he had to buy it. Damn — ! He had to admire Monkey Four and the others. They dared come to the inspector's office and demand train fares. Weren't they afraid of being nabbed? No, the devils. But he, You had lost face. Not only hadn't he arrested them, he hadn't even dared to speak a harsh word. What a disgrace. Next time would be different. He wouldn't act so soft again. It wasn't worth going soft just to remain an inspector. An inspector had to arrest people. There were no two ways about it. Blast that cafe hostess. What *was* her name?

Chu had returned. At least he ought to come in and report. The inspector couldn't very well run out and question him. In the next room Chu and Liu talked and talked. He would wait. He'd see whether Chu came in or not. Who could reason with bandits?

Finally Chu entered. "Brother ... er ... inspector. There's a gang holed up north of the city. Want to go see them?"

"Where are they?" You couldn't be afraid again. Sixty dollars gone already. If he had to die, then he'd die. He'd go even if they were gods.

"On the lake shore."

"Take your gun. Let's go." You didn't hesitate. He'd clean out that nest. No one would get any more railway fare out of him.

"Just us two?" Chu certainly could be infuriating.

"What kind of talk is that? Tell me the address and I'll go

尤老二又拿起报纸来,没劲!什么都没劲,六十块这么窝窝囊囊的出去,真没劲。看重了命,就得看不起自己;命好像不是自己的,得用钱买,他妈的!总得佩服猴四们,真敢来和稽察长要路费!就不怕登时被捉吗?竟自不怕,邪!丢人的是尤老二,不用说拿他们呀,连句硬张话都没敢说,好泄气!以后再说,再不能这么软!为当稽察长把自己弄软了,那才合不着。稽察长就得拿人,没第二句话!女招待的姓真别扭,老褚回来了。

老褚反正得进来报告,稽察长还能赶上去问么?老褚和老赵聊上了;等着,看他进来不!土匪们,没有道理可讲。

老褚进来了:"尤——稽察长,报告!城北窝着一群朋——啊,什么来着?动——动子!去看看?"

"在哪儿?"尤老二不能再怕;六十块被敲出去,以后命就是命了,人爷哪儿也敢去。

"湖边上,"老褚知道地方。

"带傢伙,老褚,走!"尤老二不含糊。坐窝儿掏!不用打算再叫稽察长出路费。

"就咱俩去了?"老褚真会激人哪。

"告诉我地方,自己去也行,什么话呢!"尤

英汉对照
English-Chinese
中国文学宝库
Gems of Chinese Literature
现代文学系列
Modern Literature

myself." If he didn't act bold, his assistants wouldn't know what sort of man the inspector was. Just handing out train fares, not cracking a single case. How could he face the commissioner? What was he being paid a salary of a hundred and twenty a month for?

Silently, Chu poured himself a bowl of tea. He seemed to be getting ready to go along. Ignoring him, You stalked out. Chu followed. That was more like it. You felt a little braver. Of course two on this job were much better than one. If they ran into trouble they could talk it over.

By the lakeside was a lane about the size of a nostril. In it was a small inn. You was very familiar with this area. Of course he recognized the inn. He needed only one look to see that it was a nest of thieves. He should have brought more men along. You, he said to himself, you've wasted your years of experience. When you lost your temper, your brains went with it. Why didn't you bring more men? Who told you to get mad at them?

Since he'd come, he'd have to see it through. He'd show his men — although he'd never been up in the hills, he had plenty of guts. If he could haul a couple of crooks out of this place, the next time he spoke his words would carry a lot more weight. He'd try his luck. Maybe he was a goner. Who could tell?

"Chu, will you guard the door or shall I?"

"There they are," said Chu, pointing inside. "No need to guard the door. None of them want to run."

Another farce. Yes, they would talk about fraternity. Damn —! You looked in. Several toughs were sitting in a small hallway: Coloured Butterfly, Nose Six, Burly Song, Young Desheng, and

老二拚了,不玩命,他们也不晓得稽察长多少钱一斤!好吗,净开路费,一案办不下来,怎么对李司令呢?一百二的薪水!

老褚没言语,灌了碗茶,预备着走的样儿,尤老二带理不理的走出来,老褚后面跟着,尤老二觉得顺了点气,也硬了点胆子来。说真的,到底俩人比一个挡事的多,遇到事多少可以研究研究。

湖边上有个鼻子眼大小的胡同,里边会有个小店,尤老二的地面多熟,竟自会不知道这家小店,看着就像贼窝!忘了多带伙计!尤老二,他叫着自己,白创练了这么多年,还是气浮哇!怎么不多带人呢?为什么和伙计们斗气呢?

可是,既来之则安之,走哇!也得给伙计们一手瞧瞧,咱尤老二没住过山哪,也不含糊!咱要是掏出那么一个半个的来,再说话可就灵验多了,看运气吧;也许是玩玩,谁知道呢,"老褚,你堵门是我堵门?"

"这不是他们?"老褚往门里一指,"用不着堵,谁也不想跑。"

又是活局子!对,他们讲义气,他妈的!尤老二往门里打了一眼,几个傢伙全在小过道里坐着呢,花蝴蝶,鼻子六儿,宋占魁,小得胜,还

英汉对照
English-Chinese
中国文学宝库
Gems of Chinese Literature
现代文学系列
Modern Literature

149

two others he hadn't seen before. Finished. Again old friends.'

"Come in, Brother You. We haven't even dared go to congratulate you. Come in and meet the gang. Dog Zhang, Jewels Xu, this is Brother You. Old friends. Our own brother." Greetings exchanged, the gangsters chatted animatedly.

"Have a seat, brother." Young Desheng — his pa, Old Desheng, had just been executed in Henan Province — was particularly courteous.

You hated himself. Why couldn't he think of what to say? In the end it was Chu who found just the right words.

"Brothers, the inspector has come personally. Speak up if you have anything on your mind."

The inspector smiled and nodded.

"Then we'll talk frankly," said Nose Six. "Brother Song, take Brother You and show him."

"This way, Brother You." Burly Song jerked his thumb towards the rear and went into a small room.

You followed. There was no danger. He was sure of that. He couldn't risk his life even if he wanted to. How irritating. The little room was pitch dark. Its earthen floor stank of mildew. Against the wall was a small wooden bed strewn with straw. Burly Song pulled the bed away from the wall and squatted in the corner. Removing two or three moist bricks, he extracted several pistols and threw them on the bed.

"That's the lot." Burly Song smiled and wiped his hands on his tunic. "Things are too hot around here. If we carry those, we can't even get on a train. That's our problem. We didn't know you were

有俩不认识的;完了,又是熟人!

"进来,尤老二,我们连给你贺喜都不敢去!来吧,看看我们这群!过来见见,张狗子,徐元宝;尤老二。老朋友,自己弟兄。"大家东一句西一句,扯的非常亲热。

"坐下吧,尤老二,"小得胜——爸爸老得胜刚在河南正了法——特别的客气。

尤老二恨自己,怎么找不到话说呢?倒是老褚漂亮:"弟兄们,稽察长亲自来了,有话就说吧。"

稽察长笑着点了点头。

"那么,咱们就说干脆的,"鼻子六儿扯了过来:"宋大哥,带尤二哥看看吧!"

"尤二哥,这边!"宋占魁用大姆指往肩后一挑,进了间小屋。

尤老二跟过去,准没危险,他看出来。要玩命都玩不成;别扭不别扭? 小屋里漆黑,地上潮得出味儿。靠墙有个小床,铺着点草。宋占魁把床拉出来,蹲在屋角,把湿碌碌的砖起了两三块,掏出几杆小傢伙来,全扔在了床上。

"就是这一堆!"宋占魁笑了笑,在襟上擦擦手:"风太紧,带着这个,我们连火车也上不去!弟兄们就算困在这儿了。老褚来,我们才知道

英汉对照
English-Chinese
中国文学宝库
Gems of Chinese Literature
现代文学系列
Modern Literature

in charge till Brother Chu dropped in. Now we have a way out. We'll turn this pile over to you. You give us a little railway fare and have Chu put us on the train. That's how it's got to be. We're asking you this favour."

You wanted to vomit. The stench of the mildew was seeping into his brain. Holding his nose, he said, "Why give them to me?" As they went back to the hallway, he added: "I can't keep that stuff for you."

"But if we take them with us, we can't leave. The heat's on," Burly Song explained earnestly.

"If I take them, I can hand them over to the authorities. I'm not turning in any men. At least if I've got some weapons to show, that will be something. You've got to think of it from my angle. Right?" You was enraged to hear himself speak like this. Much too soft.

"That's up to you, Brother You."

He had been hoping they would refuse.

"Whatever you say, brother. Of course you know we need guns in our line of work. Would we give them up if we had any other way out? Do whatever you like with them. All we want is to hit the road right now. Without your help we can't get away. Have Brother Chu put us on the train."

The bandits were giving orders to the inspector. Their own brother. You had nothing to say. He had no ideas, no energy. He had ideas, but they didn't work. He had a position, but he couldn't use it. The truth was out. He scratched his head. He couldn't turn in those weapons. But could he refuse to take them?

你上去了,我们可就有了办法。这一堆交给你,你给点车钱,叫老褚送我们上火车,行也得行,不行也得行,弟兄们求到你这儿了!"

尤老二要吐!潮气直钻脑子,他捂上了鼻子,"交给我算怎么回事呢?"他退到屋门那溜儿,"我不能给你们看着傢伙!"

"可我们带不了走呢,太紧!"宋占魁非常的恳切。

"我拿去也可以,可是得报官;拿不着人,报点傢伙也是好的!也得给我想想啊,是不是?"尤老二自己听着自己的话都生气,太软了,尤老二!

"尤老二,你随便吧!"

尤老二本希望说僵了哇。

"随便吧,尤老二你知道,干我们这行的但分有法,能扔傢伙不能?你怎办怎好,我们只求马上跑出去,没有你,我们走不了;叫老褚送我们上车。"

土匪对稽察长下了命令,自己弟兄!尤老二没有可说,没主意,没劲。主意有哇,用不上!身分是有哇,用不上!他显露了原形,直抓头皮,拿了傢伙敢报官吗?况且,敢不拿着吗?

He'd have to give the gang railway fares and look after their guns to boot. What kind of official business was that? The only alternative was to refuse the weapons and not give them any money either. Let them do as they pleased. But did he dare? Arresting them was even more unthinkable. A dead body could be pushed off the lake bank at any time. You didn't want to end up in a watery grave.

"Brother You," Burly Song was extremely sincere, "it's hard for you. Anyone who says different is a son of a bitch. But we can't help it. Take the hardware, give us a couple of dollars, and we'll say no more. The words are in our hearts."

"How much?" You gave a sickly smile.

"Six sixes are thirty-six. The man's a bastard who asks for a dollar more. Thirty-six dollars."

"But I don't want those guns."

"That's up to you. Anyhow, we can't take them along. If we're nabbed, at most we'll get six months. But if they catch us with that hardware on us, it's black dates or something very much like it. That's the truth. We're not scared — we brothers don't have to boast — but when you ought to be careful, you'd better be careful. Well then brother, thirty-six dollars, and we'll be seeing you again." Burly Song turned up his palm.

Thirty-six dollars changed hands. The inspector had no choice. "What are we going to do with these guns, Chu?"

"Brother Chu," called the gangsters, "take us to the train."

"Brother You," they were very polite, "thanks a lot."

"Thanks" was all You got. So many guns in one bundle would be too heavy to carry. He divided them with Chu, and each tucked

嘿,送了车费,临完得给他们看傢伙,哪道公事呢? 尤老二只有一条路:不拿那些傢伙也不送车钱,随他们去。可是,敢吗? 下手拿他们,更不用想,湖岸上随时可以扔下一个半个的死尸;尤老二不愿意来个水葬。

"尤老二,"宋大哥非常的诚恳:"狗玩的不知道你为难;我们可也真没法,傢伙你收着,给我们俩钱,后话不说,心照!"

"要多少?"尤老二笑得真伤心。

"六六三十六,多要一块是杂宗! 三十六块大洋!"

"傢伙我可不管。"

"随便,反正我们带不了走。空身走,捉住不过是半年;带着硬的,不吃黑枣也差不多! 实话! 怕不怕,咱们自己哥儿们用不着吹腾;该小心也得小心。好了,二哥,三十六块,后会有期!"宋大哥伸了手。

二十八块过了手,稽察长没办法,"老褚,这些傢伙怎办?"

"拿回去再说吧,"老褚很有根。

"老褚,"他们叫,"送我们上车!"

"尤二哥,"他们很客气,"谢谢啦!"

尤二哥只落了个"谢谢"。把傢伙全拢起来,没法拿,只好和老褚分着插在腰间。多威

英汉对照
English-Chinese
中国文学宝库
Gems of Chinese Literature
现代文学系列
Modern Literature

several in his belt. How awesome. A belt full of pistols. But You couldn't fire a single one. These fellows all trusted him. That's why they gave him their guns. It never occurred to them that he might turn them down. How could he even think of arresting them. They had guts. He had to admire them. By now, he had spent sixteen dollars more than his eighty dollars office expense money. What else could he do? He'd probably lose his hundred and twenty dollars salary too.

You's lunch was tasteless to him that day, though he drank two big tumblers of liquor. What was the use of talking? He was a dud. He had let Commissioner Li down. You was not without a sense of dignity. He thought it over. One more fiasco and the only course left would be to resign. But what a disgrace — to resign. And where else could he find a job paying a hundred and twenty a month these days? Commissioner Li certainly wouldn't give him another appointment. Not only hadn't he captured any bandits — on the contrary, the bandits had taken him in. What a joke. When they got back to the hills, they'd surely laugh at him. He was just one big joke. The more he thought obout it, the worse You felt.

The best thing to do was capture some opium. Could opium be considered illegal? Yes. But what a dull pastime for an inspector of a special bureau. Anyhow, he couldn't resign. First he'd collect some opium; it wasn't a bad idea. You determined his policy. He'd confiscate opium for a while, then he'd see. At least here he knew his ground.

A week passed. Several stores of opium were brought in. Commissioner Li wanted bandits, but You couldn't push his men. His

武,一腰的傢伙,想开枪都不行;人家完全信任尤二哥,就那么交出枪来,人家想不到尤二哥会翻脸不认人;尤老二连想拿他们也不想了,他们有根,得佩服他们! 八十块办公费,赔出十六块去! 尤老二没办法,一百二的薪水也保不住,大概!

尤老二的午饭吃得不香,倒喝了两盅窝心酒,什么也不用说了,自己没本事! 对不起李司令,尤老二不是不顾脸的人,看吧,再有这么一当子,只好辞职,他心里研究着。多么难堪,辞职! 这年头哪里去找一百二的事? 再找李司令,万难;拿不了匪,倒叫匪给拿了,多么大的笑话! 人家上了山以后,管保还笑着俺尤老二,尤老二整个是个笑话! 越想越懊心。

只好先办烟土吧,烟土算反动不算呢? 算,也没劲哪! 反正不能辞职,先办办烟土也好,尤老二决定了政策,不再提反动,过些日子再说,老刘们办烟土是有把握的。

一个星期里,办下几件烟土来,李司令可是嘱咐办反动派! 他不能催伙计们,办公费已经

英汉对照
English-Chinese
中国文学宝库
Gems of Chinese Literature
现代文学系列
Modern Literature

expense money was already sixteen dollars overdrawn.

It was a Monday, and his men were all out looking for opium, (opium!) when a big swarthy fellow swaggered into You's office.

"Brother You," he called smilingly.

"You, Money Five? You've got your nerve."

"With Brother You in office, what have I to fear?" Money Five sat down. "Give me a smoke."

"What have you come for?" You reached for his money pouch. More railway fare.

"First to congratulate you, second to thank you. When the brothers got back to the hills, they all praised you. That's the truth."

Oh? They didn't laugh at me? You thought to himself.

"Brother," Money Five pulled out a roll of bills. "We can't let you lose anything. The brothers in the hills will never forget your kindness."

"Really —" You tried to make a show of courteous refusal.

"Not a word, brother. Take it. Now where is Brother Song's hardware?"

Am I a weapons keeper, or something? You didn't dare say it aloud. "Chu's got them," he replied.

"Good, I'll ask him for them."

"Just down from the hills?" You felt he ought to make conversation.

"Just down from the hills. I've come to advise you to chuck this job." Money Five was very sincere.

"You want me to resign?"

贴出十六块了。

是个星期一吧,伙计们都出去采烟土(烟土!),进来个傻大黑粗的傢伙,大摇大摆的。

"尤老二!"黑脸上笑着。

"谁?钱五!你好大胆子!"

"有尤老二哥在这儿,我怕谁。"钱五坐下了;"给根烟吃吃。"

"干吗来了?"尤老二摸了摸腰里——又是路费!

"来?一来贺喜,二来道谢!他们全到了山上,很念你的好处!真的!"

"呕?他们并没笑话我!"尤老二心里说。

"二哥!"钱五掏出一卷票子来;"不说什么了,不能叫你赔钱,弟兄们全到了山上,永远念你的好处。"

"这——"尤老二必须客气一下。

"别说什么,二哥,收下吧!宋大哥的家伙呢?"

"我是管看家伙的?"尤老二没敢说出来,"老褚手里呢。"

"好啦,二哥,我和老褚去要。"

"你从山上来?"尤老二觉得该闲扯了。

"从山上来,来劝你别往下干了。"钱五很诚恳。

"叫我辞职?"

英汉对照
English-Chinese
中国文学宝库
Gems of Chinese Literature
现代文学系列
Modern Literature

"That's right. Maybe you're one of us, maybe you're not. Anyhow, with you in office, we stay out of the way. You couldn't operate if we were here. You're good to us, and we're good to you. Leave this job. That's all I've got to say. I have over three hundred men up in the hills, but I've come down to say this to you personally. We're friends. When I tell you to quit, you'd better quit. A smart fellow catches on fast. I'm going, brother. Tell Chu I'll be waiting for him in the inn by the lakeshore."

"Tell me one thing, brother." You stood up. "If I quit, what will our friends think?"

"No one will laugh. Don't worry about that, brother. Well, goodbye."

Two or three days later, there was a new man in the post of inspector. You, fat and stately, often strolled down the street. At times, he glanced serenely at the Mountain of the Thousand Buddhas.

Translated by Sidney Shapiro

"就是!你算是我们的人也好,不算也好,论事说,有你没有我们,有我们没有你;论人说,你待弟兄们好,我们也待你好,你不用再干了。话说到这儿为止。我在山上有三百多人,可是我亲自来了,朋友吗!我叫你不干,你顶好就不干。明白人不用多费话。我走了,二哥。告诉老褚我在湖边小店里等他。"

"再告诉我一句,"尤老二立起来:"我不干了,朋友们怎想?"

"没人笑话你!怕笑,二哥?好了,再见!"

稽察长换了人,过了两三天吧。尤老二,胖胖的,常在街上溜着,有时候也看千佛山一眼。

英汉对照
English-Chinese
中国文学宝库
Gems of Chinese Literature
现代文学系列
Modern Literature

The Soul-Slaying Spear

Everything in life is a game; this thought often occurred to me in the past; only now do I understand the truth of it.

The headquarters of the escort agency where Dragon Sha used to work had long been converted into an inn.

The time had come for Asia to wake up from its dream. The sound of rifle fire overpowered the roaring of tigers in the jungles of the Malay Peninsula and India. Half awake, the peoples of Asia rubbed their sleepy eyes and offered prayers to their ancestors and gods; but before long, they lost all of their land, their freedom and their rights. Men with different-colored faces stood outside their doors, the barrels of their guns still warm. Of what use were their long spears, powerful bows and poisonous arrows, and thick shields covered in gorgeous snakeskin? Their ancestors and the divinities worshipped by their ancestors were totally impotent. China, with its dragon banners, was no longer the great mystery it had been in the past. Now China had railroads running through its graveyards, destroying all auspicious geomantic influences. The fringed maroon banner of the escort agency, the steel sword in a green sharkskin sheath, the horse hung with a string of bells, the accumulated wisdom and argot of the escort trade as well as the code of justice and pride of reputation — for Dragon Sha, all of

断魂枪

"生命是闹着玩,事事显出如此;
从前我这么想过,现在我懂得了。"

沙子龙的镖局已改成客栈。

东方的大梦没法子不醒了。炮声压下去马来与印度野林中的虎啸。半醒的人们,揉着眼,祷告着祖先与神灵;不大会儿,失去了国土、自由与权利。门外立着不同面色的人,枪口还热着。他们的长矛毒弩,花蛇斑彩的厚盾,都有什么用呢;连祖先与祖先所信的神明全不灵了啊!龙旗的中国也不再神秘,有了火车呀,穿坟过墓的破坏着风水。枣红色多穗的镖旗,绿鲨皮鞘的钢刀,响着串铃的口马,江湖上的智慧与黑话,义气与声名,连沙子龙,他的武艺、事业,都

英汉对照
English-Chinese
中国文学宝库
Gems of Chinese Literature
现代文学系列
Modern Literature

these things, including his mastery of the martial arts and his career as a swordman — had vanished like a dream. This was the age of the iron horse, of automatic rifles, of treaty ports and of terrorism. There were even rumors about that people were out to chop off the emperor's head!

At the point in history when our story takes place, acting as an armed escort was no longer a viable profession, though this was before either the Revolutionary Party or the educationalists had begun to promote the traditional martial arts as a national pastime.

In the past, Dragon Sha was known far and wide for his short and lean figure, his agility, his powerful physique and his piercing eyes which shone like stars on a frosty winter night. By now, however, he'd put on some weight. When the escort agency was converted into an inn, he moved into the northernmost rooms in the small rear courtyard. His long spear stood in one corner of his room, and he raised pigeons in the courtyard as well. In the evenings, he would close the gate leading into his courtyard and run through the routine which had made him famous: the "Five Tigers Soul-slaying Spear." His spear, and the series of exercises he performed with it, represented twenty years of experience in the Northeast, and had earned him the name "Magic Spear Sha." In those days, he had never suffered a single defeat. Now, however, his spear no longer could confer glory upon him or win him any victories; only when he passed his hand over the spear's cool, smooth, quivering staff could he lessen his despair somewhat. And only at night, when he practiced by himself in the privacy of his courtyard, did "Magic Spear Sha" come back to life. During the

梦似的变成昨夜的。今天是火车、快枪、通商与恐怖。听说,有人还要杀下皇帝的头呢!

这是走镖已没有饭吃,而国术还没被革命党与教育家提倡起来的时候。

谁不晓得沙子龙是短瘦、利落、硬捧,两眼明得像霜夜的大星?可是,现在他身上放了肉。镖局改了客栈,他自己在后小院占着三间北房,大枪立在墙角,院子有几支楼鸽。只是在夜间,他把小院的门关好,熟习熟习他的"五虎断魂枪"。这条枪与这套枪,二十年的工夫,在西北一带,给他创出来:"神枪沙子龙"五个字,没遇见过敌手。现在,这条枪与这套枪不会再替他增光显胜了;只是摸摸这凉、滑、硬而发颤的杆子,使他心中少难过一些而已。只有在夜间独自拿起枪来,才能相信自己还是"神枪沙"。在

英汉对照
English-Chinese
中国文学宝库
Gems of Chinese Literature
现代文学系列
Modern Literature

165

daytime, he rarely talked about the martial arts or the past; his world had been blown away by a storm.

Some of the young men he had trained as boys came to see him frequently. Most of them were unemployed. They had mastered some of the martial arts, but had no real opportunity to use them. Some of them gave performances at temple fairs. First flexing their legs, they would go through a series of exercises which would conclude with a few fancy somersaults; after such a display, they'd try to peddle some tonic pills. In this way they could earn themselves a few strings of cash. Those who couldn't afford to live in this manner hauled big baskets of fruit or beans into town in the early morning and hawked them in the streets. In those days, rice and pork were relatively inexpensive, and a man willing to do a little hard physical labor could easily earn enough to fill his belly. But this kind of life couldn't satisfy Dragon Sha's disciples. Not only did they have huge appetites; they also had to eat well — no hard buns or hot pepper pancakes for them. Moreover, they frequently took part in pilgrimages into the mountains, which included contests of "Five-Tiger Cudgels," wielding a sword at the head of the procession, and donning huge masks to participate in the lion dances. Although these pilgrimages never brought in much money — in comparison with working as an armed escort — they at least gave these young men an opportunity to get out in public and flex their muscles. These affairs were also a way of advertising one's skills. The participants had to dress up in their finest costumes: a typical outfit would include a pair of trousers made of European-style black crepe, a short jacket of fine white bleached cotton and a pair of

白天,他不大谈武艺与往事;他的世界已被狂风吹了走。

在他手下创练起来的少年们还时常来找他。他们大多数是没落子的,都有点武艺,可是没地方去用。有的在庙会上去卖艺:踢两趟腿,练套家伙,翻几个跟头,附带着卖点大力丸,混个三吊两吊的。有的实在闲不起了,去弄筐果子,或挑些毛豆角,赶早儿在街上论斤吆喝出去。那时候米贱肉贱肯卖膀子力气本来可以混个肚儿圆,他们可是不成:肚量既大,而且得吃口当事儿的;干饽饽辣饼子咽不下去。况且他们还时常去走会:五虎棍、开路、太狮少狮……虽然算不了什么——比起走镖来——可是到底有个机会活动活动,露露脸。是的,走会捧场是买脸的事,他们打扮得像个样儿,至少得有条青洋绉裤子,新漂白细市布的小褂,和一双鱼鳞洒

英汉对照
English-Chinese
中国文学宝库
Gems of Chinese Literature
现代文学系列
Modern Literature

167

fancy cotton shoes, though black satin fighting boots were generally considered more impressive. They were the disciples of "Magic Spear Sha" — though Dragon Sha himself would never have acknowledged this. Public performances often meant incurring some expenses, not to mention risking the possibility of getting into a brawl. When they ran out of money, these "disciples" often came to Dragon Sha for a loan. Dragon Sha was not one to beat around the bush in such matters, and would help them out as best he could; in any case, they never went away empty-handed. On the other hand, if they wanted to learn a new fighting trick or a fancy display piece, or asked their master to show them some countermoves, such as "snatching a sword empty-handed" or "spear vs. tiger-head hooks," Dragon Sha would usually brush them off with a quip, "What countermoves can I show you? I'd sooner shoo you!" And sometimes he would simply kick them out of his house. They had no idea why Master Sha acted this way, and often left rather reluctantly.

These disciples, however, sang Dragon Sha's praises wherever they went. On the one hand, they wanted people to know that they were the inheritors of an authentic martial arts tradition and had studied under a real master; and on the other, they all wanted to stir up Master Sha's pride: if someday a particularly stubborn adversary insisted on meeting Dragon Sha in person, they wanted to be sure he would show them his stuff. Thus they boasted that Master Sha could knock a bull off its feet with a single blow, and could easily send a man flying over the roof with a single kick. Though no one had ever seen him perform these miracles, the more they

鞋——顶好是青缎子抓脚虎靴子。他们是神枪沙子龙的徒弟——虽然沙子龙并不承认——得到处露脸,走会得赔上俩钱,说不定还得打场架。没钱,上沙老师那里去求。沙老师不含糊,多少不拘,不让他们空着手儿走。可是,为打架或献技去讨教一个招数,或是请给说个对子——什么空夺刀,或虎头钩进枪——沙老师有时说句笑话,马虎过去:"教什么?拿开水浇吧!"有时直接把他们逐出去。他们不大明白沙老师是怎么了,心中也有点不乐意。

可是,他们到处为沙老师吹腾,一来是愿意使人知道他们的武艺有真传授,受过高人的指教;二来是为激动沙老师:万一有人不服气而找上老师来,老师难道还不露一两手真的么?把以:沙老师一拳就砸倒了个牛!沙老师一脚把人踢到房上去,并没使多大的劲!他们谁也没

spoke about them, the more sincerely they believed they were true. They even went so far as to specify the time and place these miracles had taken place, and swore to the ends of the earth that they weren't exaggerating.

One day, Wang Sansheng — "Three Victories Wang" — one of Dragon Sha's more mature disciples, marked off a circle in the courtyard of the Temple of the Earth God and laid out his weapons. After taking a big pinch of snuff the color of tea leaves he began to swing his long segmented iron whip around his head to enlarge the circle. He put his whip down on the ground and without performing the customary bow to the assembled crowd, placed his hands on his hips and recited the following couplet: "I'm a man who's fought his way through this world; my fists have made me a hero throughout the length and breadth of the empire." He surveyed the crowd with a sweeping glance, and continued: "My good friends and neighbors, my name is Wang Sansheng. I'm no sideshow performer, but a true expert of the martial arts. When I worked as an escort in the Northeast, I met some of the best men in the business. I'm out of work now and have a bit of time to spare, so I thought I'd set up here and offer you gentlemen a chance to step into the ring with me. Anyone here who loves the martial arts is welcome; but remember, it's friendship first with me. If one of you would be so kind as to step up here, I'll be glad to entertain you. My master is Dragon Sha with a magic spear; that means my fighting is the real McCoy. Gentlemen, is there anyone here willing to join me?"

He surveyed the crowd once again, but he knew that no one

见过这种事,但是说着说着,他们相信这是真的了,有年月,有地方,千真万确,敢起誓!

　　王三胜——沙子龙的大伙计——在土地庙拉开了场子,摆好了家伙。抹了一鼻子茶叶末色的鼻烟,他抡了几下竹节钢鞭,把场子打大一些。放下鞭,没向四围作揖,叉着腰念了两句:"脚踢天下好汉,拳打五路英雄!"向四围扫了一眼:"乡亲们,王三胜不是卖艺的;玩艺儿会几套,西北路上走过镖,会过绿林上的朋友。现在闲着没事,拉个场子陪诸位玩玩。有爱练的尽管下来,王三胜以武会友,有赏脸的,我陪着。神枪沙子龙是我的师傅;玩艺地道! 诸位,有愿下来的没有?"他看着,准知道没人敢下来,他的

would have the nerve to step forward. His speech was impressive, but his iron whip was more so, weighing some nine kilograms.

Wang Sansheng was tall and had a tough muscular face. He opened his big black eyes wide and glanced through the crowd a third time. No one made a single sound. He removed his short jacket and tightened his wide pale blue fighting belt, which aided him in contracting his stomach. Spitting into the palms of his hands, he picked up his long-handled broadsword.

"Gentlemen, first I'll give you all a little sword demonstration. I'm not doing this for nothing, mind you, so when I'm finished, if you've got a few spare coins, toss 'em this way; but if you don't, then just shout a little something encouraging. Just remember, I'm not in it for the money. Alright then, here we go."

He held the sword against his body and opened his eyes wide, stretching all the muscles in his face. His chest muscles stuck out like two twisted birch roots. He stamped his foot and raised his sword before him, its long red tassels swinging back and forth in front of his shoulders. He brandished the sword in a series of fancy movements, squatted down, and spun around. The sword revolved like a tornado with a loud whirring. Finally, he bent down and set the sword spinning on the palm of his right hand. Not a single sound arose from the crowd; all that could be heard was the tinkling of the bells attached to the tassels of his sword. With an elegant gesture, he placed his sword on the ground in front of him and stamped his foot again. Straightening up until he was a head taller than anyone in the crowd, he stood there like a black pagoda, and then resumed his normal posture. "Ladies and gentlemen!" Hold-

话硬,可是那条钢鞭更硬,十八斤重。

王三胜,大个子,一脸横肉,努着对大眼珠,看着四围。大家不出声。他脱了小褂,紧了紧深月白的腰里硬,把肚子杀进去。给手心一口吐沫,抄起大刀来:

"诸位,王三胜先练趟瞧瞧。不白练,练完了,带着的扔几个;没钱,给喊个好,助助威。这儿没生意口。好,上眼!"

大刀靠了身,眼珠努出多高,脸上绷紧,胸脯子鼓出像两块老桦木根子。一跺脚,刀横起,大红缨子在肩前摆动,削砍劈拨,蹲越闪转,手起风生,忽忽直响。忽然刀在右手心上旋转,身弯下去,四围鸦雀无声,只有缨铃轻叫。刀顺过来,猛的一个跺泥,身子直挺,比众人高着一头,黑塔似的。收了势:"诸位!"一手持刀,一手叉

英汉对照
English-Chinese
中国文学宝库
Gems of Chinese Literature
现代文学系列
Modern Literature

ing the sword in one hand and placing his other hand on his waist, he surveyed the crowd once again. A few people tossed a few coins at his feet; he nodded in approval. "Ladies and gentlemen!" He waited a few more minutes, but the scattered bright and well-worn coins on the ground failed to grow in number, and people on the periphery of the circle began to leave. He took a deep breath. "No one appreciates me." Though he said this under his breath, everyone heard him clearly.

"Well done!" an old man with a scraggly beard shouted from the northwest corner of the circle.

"Eh?" Wang Sansheng uttered as if he hadn't heard the man.

"I said: You ... performed ... very ... well!" The man's tone of voice was slightly abrasive.

Putting his sword down on the ground, Wang Sansheng looked in the direction the voice was coming from. No one in the crowd had noticed this old man before, but now they all turned to look at him. He was short and wiry and had a coarse blue cotton long gown slung over his shoulder. His face was wizened and his eyes were set deeply in their sockets; his beard was composed of little more than a few sparse brownish hairs. The queue resting on his shoulder seemed to be made of straw. It was about as thick as a chopstick, but much less straight. Despite the old man's unformidable appearance, Wang Sansheng could tell he possessed real fighting skills. His forehead shone with a mysterious radiance, and his pupils were like two tiny wells shimmering with a black lustre. But Wang Sansheng had nothing to fear. His ability to identify a real fighter boosted his confidence in his own fighting: he

腰,看着四围。稀稀的扔下几个铜钱,他点点头。"诸位!"他等着,等着,地上依旧是那几个亮而削薄的铜钱,外层的人偷偷散去。他咽了口气:"没人懂!"他低声的说,可是大家全听见了。

"有工夫!"西北角上一个黄胡子老头儿答了话。

"啊?"王三胜好似没听明白。

"我说:你——有——工——夫!"老头子的语气很不得人心。

放下大刀,王三胜随着大家的头往西北看。谁也没看起这个老人:小干巴个儿,披着件粗蓝布大衫,脸上窝窝瘪瘪,眼陷进去很深,嘴上几根细黄胡,肩上扛着条小黄草辫子,有筷子那么细而绝对不像筷子那么直顺。王三胜可是看出这老家伙有工夫,脑门亮,眼睛亮、眼眶虽深,眼珠可黑得像两口小井,深深的闪着黑光。王三胜不怕:他看得出别人有工夫没有,叫更相信自

英汉对照
English-Chinese
中国文学宝库
Gems of Chinese Literature
现代文学系列
Modern Literature

175

was Dragon Sha's righthand man.

"How about joining me for a few rounds, Uncle?" Wang Sansheng addressed him with due deference.

Nodding his head, the old man entered the ring. At this moment, the crowd broke out laughing at the way he walked. His arms hardly moved at all; and each time he took a step with his left foot, he had to slide his right foot along the ground to catch up with it. In this fashion, he dragged himself forward, bending over and straightening up at each step. He looked as if he had suffered from paralysis at some time in the past. Making his way to the center of the circle, he threw his gown on the ground, oblivious to the ridicule being directed at him from all sides.

"So, you're a disciple of Dragon Sha with his magic spear, eh? Well then, you fight with a spear, but what about me?" The old man came right to the point; he seemed to be itching for a fight.

All those who had started to stray from the circle came back to watch. And no matter how loudly the man with the trained bear banged on his gong, no one paid any attention to him.

"How about me fighting with a spear and you using a set of triple-sticks?" Wang Sansheng wanted to give the old man a chance to prove himself. The triple-sticks — three heavy wooden rods connected in a line with two short chains — was not the sort of weapon an amateur could fight with.

The old man nodded and picked the sticks up from the ground.

Wang Sansheng glared at his opponent and started rattling his spear. He had a very unpleasant expression on his face.

The pupils of the old man's eyes darkened and receded into their

己的本事,他是沙子龙手下的大将。

"下来玩玩,大叔!?"王三胜说得很得体。

点点头,老头儿往里走。这一走,四外全笑了。他的胳臂不大动;左脚往前迈,右脚随着拉上来,一步步的往前拉扯,身子整着,像是患过瘫痪病。蹭到场中,把大衫扔在地上,一点没理会四围怎样笑他。

"神枪沙子龙的徒弟,你说?好,让你使枪吧;我呢?"老头子非常的干脆,很像久想动手。

人们全回来了,邻场耍狗熊的无论怎敲锣也不中用了。

"三截棍进枪吧?"王三胜要看老头子一手,三截棍不是随便就拿得起来的家伙。

老头子又点点头,拾起家伙来。

王三胜弩着眼,抖着枪,脸上十分难看。

老头子的黑眼珠更深更小了,像两个香火

英汉对照
English-Chinese
中国文学宝库
Gems of Chinese Literature
现代文学系列
Modern Literature

The Soul-Slaying Spear

sockets; they resembled the burning tips of two incense sticks, and followed the tip of Wang Sansheng's spear as he swung it in circles through the air. Wang Sansheng had a strange feeling that the old man was about to swallow the tip of his spear with those eyes of his. The spectators surged forward to the edge of the circle until there was hardly any breathing space between them. They were all aware that the old man possessed extraordinary powers. In order to divert the old man's eyes, Wang Sansheng executed an elaborate flourish with his spear.

The old man's scraggly beard fluttered once. He said, "After you." Wang Sansheng held his spear out in front of him and lunged forward, bending one knee. The sharp point of his spear was aimed directly at the old man's throat, and the red tassels surrounding the shaft swung around with the thrust. All at once the old man came alive; leaning slightly to one side to avoid the tip of the spear, he struck the spear with a downward stroke of one section of his triple-sticks while forcing Wang Sansheng's hands upwards with the other. There were two loud cracks and Wang Sansheng's spear fell to the ground. The crowd shouted their approval. Wang Sansheng blushed deep purple from his face down to his chest and picked up his spear. With a fancy flourish, he charged forward again, this time directing the tip of his spear towards the old man's belly. The old man's jet black eyes glowed in anger. Nimbly bending one leg, he parried the spearhead with one section of his triple-sticks and with another struck the spear's handle just as Wang was about to pull it away. With a bang, Wang Sansheng's spear fell to the ground once again.

断魂枪

头,随着面前的枪尖儿转,王三胜忽然觉得不舒服,那俩黑眼球似乎要把枪尖吸进去!四外已围得风雨不透,大家都觉出老头子确是有威。为躲那对眼睛,王三胜耍了个枪花。老头子的黄胡子一动:"请!"王三胜一扣枪,向前躬步,枪尖奔了老头子的喉头去,枪缨打了一个红旋。老人的身子忽然活展了,将身微偏,让过枪尖,前把一挂,后把撩王三胜的手。拍,拍,两响,王三胜的枪撒了手。场外叫了好。王三胜连脸带胸口全紫了,抄起枪来,一个花子,连枪带人滚了过来,枪尖奔了老人的中部。老头子的眼亮得发着黑光;腿轻轻一屈,下把掩裆,上把打着刚要抽回的枪杆;拍,枪又落在地上。

英汉对照
English-Chinese
中国文学宝库
Gems of Chinese Literature
现代文学系列
Modern Literature

More applause and cheers arose from the crowd. Wang Sansheng was now sweating all over. But this time he didn't pick up his spear; he simply remained standing there fixed to the spot, staring straight ahead. The old man threw down the sticks, picked up his gown and, dragging his right leg behind him, started walking at a somewhat faster pace than before. With his robe over his shoulder, he went up to Wang Sansheng and patted him on the arm. "You need a little more practice, boy."

"Where do you think you're going?" Wang Sansheng wiped the sweat from his brow. "Stay here a minute. I lost this one, but there's something I want to ask you. Do you dare take on Master Sha?"

"That's what I came here for in the first place." The old man twisted up his wizened face in a semblance of a smile. "Let's go. Get your things together. I'm taking you to dinner."

Wang Sansheng gathered up his weapons and left them with the magician Second Pockmarks. As they walked out of the temple, a large crowd was following them. Wang Sansheng shouted a few obscenities in their direction and they scattered.

"What is your family name?" Wang Sansheng asked.

"Sun's the name." The old man's speech was as coarse as the rest of him. "I love the martial arts, and I've always wanted to meet Dragon Sha."

"Dragon Sha's going to beat you into a pulp," Wang Sansheng thought to himself. He quickened his pace, but Mr Sun had no problem keeping up with him. Wang Sansheng knew that the old man's way of walking with consecutive leaps was characteristic of

场外又是一片彩声。王三胜流了汗,不再去拾枪,努着眼,木在那里。老头子扔下家伙,拾起大衫,还是拉拉着腿,可是走得很快了。大衫搭在臂上,他过来拍了王三胜一下:"还得练哪,伙计!"

"别走!"王三胜擦着汗:"你不离,姓王的服了!可有一样,你敢会会沙老师?"

"就是为会他才来的!"老头子的干巴脸上皱起点来,似乎是笑呢。"走;收了吧;晚饭我请!"

王三胜把兵器拢在一处,寄放在变戏法二麻子那里,陪着老头子往庙外走。后面跟着不少人,他把他们骂散。

"你老贵姓?"他问。

"姓孙哪,"老头子的话与人一样,都那么干巴。"爱练;久想会会沙子龙。"

沙子龙不把你打扁了!王三胜心里说。他脚底下加了劲,可是没把孙老头落下。他看出来,老头子的腿是老走查拳门中的连跳步;交起

英汉对照
English-Chinese
中国文学宝库
Gems of Chinese Literature
现代文学系列
Modern Literature

181

Zha Family Boxing — there was no doubt in his mind that he could kick up a storm in a fight. But no matter how agile his legs were, he was certainly no match for Dragon Sha. Convinced of this, Wang Sansheng felt a little better inside, and slowed his pace.

"Uncle Sun, where is your hometown?"

"Hejian County. Just a small town." Sun seemed to be warming up a little. "You can master the cudgel in a month. You can master the sword in a year. But it takes a lifetime to master the spear. To tell you the truth, you've got a really fine pair of hands there."

Beads of sweat broke out on Wang Sansheng's forehead, but he said nothing.

When they arrived at the inn, Wang Sansheng's heart was beating wildly. His worst fear was that Master Sha would not be at home; he was very eager to get his revenge. He knew Master Sha generally avoided becoming involved in conflicts of this sort, and that many of his fellow disciples had been spurned by Master Sha in similar situations. But Wang Sansheng believed Master Sha would agree this time; first, since he was Master Sha's eldest disciple, in a different class from the rest of those youngsters who hung around him; and second, because Dragon Sha's name had come up in front of the crowd at the temple fair; he could hardly afford to lose "face" in such a situation.

"Sansheng, what brings you here?" Dragon Sha was lying in bed reading the classical novel *Canonization of the Gods*.

Sansheng blushed a deep crimson. His lips trembled but no sound came out.

Dragon Sha sat up. "What's the matter, Sansheng?"

手来,必定很快。但是,无论他怎样快,沙子龙是没对手的。准知道孙老头要吃亏,他心中痛快了些,放慢了些脚步。

"孙大叔贵处?"

"河间的,小地方。"孙老者也和气了些,"月棍年刀一辈子枪,不容易见工夫!说真的,你那两手就不坏!"

王三胜头上的汗又回来了,没言语。

到了客栈,他心中直跳,唯恐沙老师不在家,他急于报仇。他知道老师不爱管这种事,师弟们已碰过不少回钉子,可是他相信这回必定行,他是大伙计,不比那些毛孩子;再说,人家在庙会上点名叫阵,沙老师还能丢这个脸么?

"三胜,"沙子龙正在床上看着本封神榜,"有事吗?"

三胜的脸又紫了,嘴唇动着,说不出话来。

沙子龙坐起来,"怎了,三胜?"

英汉对照
English-Chinese
中国文学宝库
Gems of Chinese Literature
现代文学系列
Modern Literature

"I got whipped."

Master Sha yawned but said nothing to him.

Wang Sansheng was very upset, but didn't want to show it; it was much more important to rouse Master Sha to action.

"There's an old man named Sun waiting outside to see you. My spear ... he knocked my spear out of my hands twice!" Wang Sansheng knew the effect the word "spear" would have on Dragon Sha. Before Dragon Sha could say a word, Sansheng rushed out the door.

When the visitor entered, Dragon Sha was waiting for him in the main room of his flat. They greeted each other politely in the traditional manner and sat down. Dragon Sha told Wang Sansheng to make tea. Sansheng hoped they would get right down to business and start fighting, but resigned himself for the moment to making tea. Mr Sun remained silent and sized up Dragon Sha with his deepset eyes.

Master Sha was extremely deferential. "If Sansheng offended you in any way, forget about it. He's just a youngster."

Mr Sun was disappointed in this response, but knew Dragon Sha was very astute. Unsure of how to react, Mr Sun knew that a man's astuteness was not necessarily an indication of his attainments in the martial arts. "I've come to learn spear fighting from you," he spurted out.

Dragon Sha said nothing. Wang Sansheng came in holding a teapot — he was so eager for them to come to grips that he had poured the water into the pot before it had boiled.

Raising his tea bowl, Dragon Sha said, "Sansheng, go round up

"栽了跟头!"

只打了个不甚长的哈欠,沙老师没别的表示。

王三胜心中不平,但是不敢发作;他得激动老师:"姓孙的一个老头儿,门外等着老师呢;把我的枪,枪,打掉了两次!"他知道"枪"字在老师心中有多大分量。没等吩咐,他慌忙跑出去。

客人进来,沙子龙在外间屋等着呢。彼此拱手坐下,他叫三胜去泡茶。三胜希望两个老人立刻交了手,可是不能不沏茶去。孙老者没话讲,用深藏着的眼睛打量沙子龙。沙很客气:"要是三胜得罪了你,不用理他,年纪还轻。"

孙老者有些失望,可也看出沙子龙的精明。他不知怎样好了,不能拿一个人的精明断定他的武艺。"我来领教领教枪法!"他不由的说出来。

沙子龙没接碴儿。王三胜提着茶壶走进来——急于看二人动手,他没管水开了没有,就沏在壶中。

"三胜,"沙子龙起个茶碗来,"去找小顺们

Little Shun and the rest of them and tell them to meet us at the Tianhui Restaurant. We're taking Mr Sun out to dinner."

"What?" Wang Sansheng's eyes nearly fell out of their sockets. He glanced at Dragon Sha. Though his heart was filled with inexpressable anger, he responded with a simple "Yes, sir!" and walked out, pouting his big lips.

Mr Sun said, "It's hard work teaching disciples."

"I've never had any disciples. Let's go now, this water isn't boiled. We'll go to a teahouse and drink tea till we get hungry." Dragon Sha picked up his waistpouch from the table, put his snuffbottle in one pocket and some money in the other, and hung it over his belt.

"I'm not hungry. Let's not go out yet." Mr Sun's two "nots" were insistent enough to knock his little queue off his shoulder.

"We'll chat for a while longer then."

"I've come especially to observe the way you fight with a spear."

"Five Tigers Soul-slaying Spear?" Dragon Sha said, pointing to his belly. "Look how much weight I've put on."

"Here's my idea." Mr Sun looked intensely at Dragon Sha. "We don't have to fight. Just teach me your 'Five Tigers Soul-slaying Spear' routine."

"Five Tigers Soul-slaying Spear?" Dragon Sha laughed. "I haven't done that for years. I couldn't do it now if I tried. I've got a better idea. Why don't you stay here with me for a few days. I'll show you around town, and when you're ready to go, I'll give you a little something to help you out on the way home."

去,天汇见,陪孙老者吃饭。"

"什么?"王三胜的眼球几乎掉出来。看了看沙老师的脸,他敢怒而不敢言的说了声"是啦!"走出去,撅着大嘴。

"教徒弟不易!"孙老者说。

"我没收过徒弟。走吧,这个水不开!茶馆去喝,喝饿了就吃。"沙子龙从桌子拿起青缎子搭连,一头装着鼻烟壶,一头装着点钱,挂在腰带上。

"不,我还不饿!"孙老者很坚决,两个"不"字把小辫从肩上抡到后边去。

"说会子话儿。"

"我来为领教领教枪法。"

"工夫早搁下了,"沙子龙指着身上,"已经放了肉!"

"这么办也行,"孙老者深深的看了沙老师一眼:"不比武,教给我那趟五虎断魂枪。"

"五虎断魂枪?"沙子龙笑了,"早忘净了!早忘净了!告诉你,在我这儿住几天,咱们逛逛各处,临走,多少送点盘川。"

英汉对照
English-Chinese
中国文学宝库
Gems of Chinese Literature
现代文学系列
Modern Literature

"I don't want to go anywhere and I don't need any money from you. All I want is to learn the martial arts." Mr Sun stood up. "I'll go through one of my routines for you so you can decide if I'm qualified or not." He stood up and literally leaped into the courtyard in a single bound, scaring the pigeons away. Spreading his legs in the proper starting posture, he performed an entire routine of Zha Family Boxing. His footwork was nimble, his hands full of grace; leaping and landing on one leg, his little queue remained suspended in the air and descended slowly like a kite on a windless day. Though his movements were rapid, all his postures were well balanced and a delight to watch. He circled the courtyard six times, covering every inch of space in it; all of his movements were fluent and finely coordinated. His body remained in one place while his spirit permeated every corner of the courtyard. He finished by bringing his hands together in front of his chest, shrinking back to his normal posture. It was as if a flock of swallows flying madly about the courtyard had all returned to their nests.

"Excellent! Excellent!" Dragon Sha nodded his approval from his front steps. Still holding his hands together in front of him, Mr Sun said, "Teach me your spear routine!"

Dragon Sha came down the steps and returned the salutation. "My dear Mr Sun, to tell you the truth, that spear and that spear routine are going to be buried with me when I die."

"Then you won't teach me?"

"No."

Mr Sun's mouth and beard quivered nervously for a few moments, but there was very little he could say. He went back

"我不逛,也用不着钱,我来学艺!"孙老者立起来,"我练趟给你看看,看够得上学艺不够!"一屈腰已到了院中,把楼鸽都吓飞起去。拉开架子,他打了趟查拳:腿快,手飘洒,一个飞脚起去,小辫儿飘在空中,像从天上落下来一个风筝;快之中,每个架子都摆得稳,准,利落;来回六趟,把院子满都打到,走得圆,接得紧,身子在一处,而精神贯串到四面八方。抱拳收势,身儿缩紧,好似满院的乱飞的燕子忽然归了巢。

"好! 好!"沙子龙在阶上点着头喊。

"教给我那趟枪!"孙老者抱了抱拳。

沙子龙下了台阶,也抱着拳:"孙老者,说真的吧;那条枪和那套枪都跟我入棺材,一齐入棺材!"

"不传?"

"不传!"

孙老者的胡子嘴动了半天,没说出什么来。

英汉对照
English-Chinese
中国文学宝库
Gems of Chinese Literature
现代文学系列
Modern Literature

inside, picked up his blue cotton gown and limped out. "Sorry to bother you then. Goodbye."

"Why don't you stay for dinner?"

Mr Sun said nothing.

After escorting his guest to the gate of the courtyard, Dragon Sha returned to his room and stood nodding in the direction of the corner where his spear stood.

He went alone to the Tianhui Restaurant, since he was afraid Wang Sansheng and the others were waiting for him there. But when he got there, he found out that they had not come at all.

Wang Sansheng, Little Shun and the others stopped giving performances at the Temple of the God of Earth, and no longer boasted about Dragon Sha's feats. On the contrary, they began spreading the word that Dragon Sha had thrown in the towel and was even too scared to fight with an old man. In fact, they now began telling people that Mr Sun could kill a bull with a single kick. It meant very little to anyone that Wang Sansheng had lost to him; but Dragon Sha hadn't even tried. In any case, Wang Sansheng had had a chance to test himself in the ring with the old man, while Dragon Sha was too much of a coward even to stick up for himself. Before long, everyone seemed to have forgotten about "Magic Spear Sha."

One quiet evening when no one was about, Dragon Sha bolted the outside gate and ran through the sixty-four thrusts of his entire routine. Leaning on his spear in the middle of the courtyard, he gazed up at the stars and thought back on the good old days, when he enjoyed a fine reputation in the country inns and all through the

到屋里抄起蓝布大衫,拉拉着腿:"打搅了,再会!"

"吃过饭走!"沙子龙说。

孙老者没言语。

沙子龙把客人送到小门,然后回到屋中,对着墙角立着的大枪点了点头。

他独自上了天汇,怕是王三胜们在那里等着,他们都没有去。

王三胜和小顺们都不敢再到土地庙去卖艺,大家谁也不再为沙子龙吹腾;反之,他们说沙子龙栽了跟头,不敢和个老头儿动手;那个老头子一脚能踢死个牛。不要说王三胜输给他,沙子龙也不是"个儿"。不过呢,王三胜到底和老头子见了个高低,而沙子龙连句硬话也没敢说。"神枪沙子龙"慢慢似乎被人们忘了。

夜静人稀,沙子龙关好了小门,一气把六十四枪刺下来;而后,拄着枪,望着天上的群星,想

wilderness. Sighing, he rubbed his hands over the cool, smooth handle of his spear and smiled. "No, I won't teach this to anyone. I won't teach this to anyone."

Translated by Don J. Cohn

起当年在野店荒林的威风。叹一口气,用手指慢慢摸着凉滑的枪身,又微微一笑,"不传!不传!"

The Fire Chariot[①]

It was New Year's Eve, according to the lunar calendar. Nobody paid any attention to the western calendar in those days.

As the train started moving, one could hear the wailing of the train whistle and the soft sighing of the passengers. Some passengers were counting hours to themselves: seven, eight, nine, ten; if the train arrived at the station by ten o'clock, they could be home by midnight. That wasn't too late, though the children would probably be asleep by then. The overhead racks were piled high with canned food, fresh and dried fruit and toys. Glancing at these gifts, the travellers could hear their children calling out to them: "Daddy!" But before long, they would return to their daydreams. Others, knowing they would not reach home until the following morning, sought out a familiar face among the other passengers, but none were to be found. By the time they got home, it would be next year already! Others.... How slowly the train was moving! Though they'd already arrived home a hundred times in their minds, their bodies were very much on the train. They smoked, drank tea, yawned, daydreamed about going home, hoped, made wishes and looked out the window at the black and endless night; when they turned away from the windows, their faces were entirely

---

① Literally, "The train."

火 车

除夕。阴历的,当然;国历的那个还未曾算过数儿。

火车开了,车悲鸣,客轻叹。有的算计着:七,八,九,十;十点到站,夜半可以到家;不算太晚,可是孩子们恐怕已经睡了;架上放着罐头,干鲜果品,玩具;看一眼,似乎听到唤着,"爸",呆呆的出神。有的知道天亮才能到家,看看车上的人,连一个长得像熟人的都没有;到家,已是明年了! 有的……车走的多慢! 心已到家一百多次了,身子还在车上;吸烟,喝水,打哈欠,盼望,盼望,扒着玻璃看看,漆黑,渺茫;回过头

英汉对照
English-Chinese
中国文学宝库
Gems of Chinese Literature
现代文学系列
Modern Literature

devoid of expression; they would lower their heads, on the verge of tears, and yawn.

There were very few people in the second class car. Big fat Mr Zhang and scrawny little Mr Qiao sat across from each other. When they first boarded the train, they had each laid out their blankets across an entire seat as a way of reserving them for their exclusive use. When the train left and they discovered that there were very few other passengers on board, the bitterness they felt about having to travel on New Year's Eve became intensified, while at the same time they regretted having occupied only a single seat each; this gave them something to commiserate with each other about. Both gentlemen were holding borrowed railroad passes, but the passes' owners had been unwilling to part with them even a day earlier. The two of them agreed on the following point: if people with railroad passes chose to make you wait until the last day of the year, then you just had to wait. The passes' owners seemed to enjoy watching their friends get nervous and impatient, even to the point of blowing up in anger! They sighed together: friends today — can you really call them friends? It's not like what it used to be. Nowadays, no one gives their passes away until New Year's Eve, and even then you would owe the passes' owners numerous favors. They nodded in agreement: it was entirely their friends' fault that they wouldn't make it home for New Year's Eve. At any other time of the year, borrowing a railroad pass was never a problem; but come new year's time, people got stubborn and started making things difficult. The two travellers were perhaps too embarrassed to say what was really on their minds: Goddamn them all!

来,大家板着脸;低下头,泪欲流,打个哈欠。

　　二等车上人不多。胖胖的张先生和细瘦的乔先生对面坐着二位由一上车就把绒毯铺好,为独据一条凳。及至车开了,而车上旅客并不多,二位感到除夕奔驰的凄凉,同时也微觉独占一凳的野心似乎太小了些,同病相怜:二人都拿着借用免票,而免票早一天也匀不出来。意见相合:有免票的人教你等到年底,你就得到年底;而有免票的人就是愿意看朋友干着急,等到冒火!同声慨叹:今日的朋友——哼,朋友!——远非昔日可比了,免票非到除夕不撒手,还得搭老大的人情呀!一齐点头:把误了过年的罪过统统归到朋友身上;平常日子借借免票,倒还顺利,单等到年底才咬牙,看人一手儿,一齐没好意思出声:真他妈的!

英汉对照
English-Chinese
中国文学宝库
Gems of Chinese Literature
现代文学系列
Modern Literature

Fat Mr Zhang removed his fox fur riding jacket and attempted to sit cross-legged on his seat; but he was so fat it was nearly impossible for him to remain upright that way. It was also terribly hot in the train car and his broad forehead was covered with beads of sweat. "Steward! Bring me a hot towel!" He turned to skinny Mr Qiao and said, "Why do they always overheat these trains? It must be much cooler travelling by airplane."

Mr Qiao had taken off his overcoat, and although he was wearing a fur-lined robe with a satin padded vest on top of it, he wasn't feeling hot at all. "There're a lot of airplane passes floating around, actually," he said, smiling wryly.

"Better not take any risks!" Mr Zhang made another concerted effort to cross his stocky legs, but was again unsuccessful. "Steward! Bring me a towel!"

The steward came into the car supporting a tall stack of hot towels on the palm of his hand. He was about forty years old, extremely tall and thin, and gave one the impression that he could very comfortably disconnect his head from his shoulders and replace it whenever he pleased. Normally disposed to providing the finest service, he was nursing a particular grievance today. The moment he entered the car, he addressed Little Cui, "You know what happened, don't you? I worked two days in a row on the 27th and 28th, so I should have a day off on the 30th. Alright then, I was already to take off when Mr Liu comes in and tells me, 'Old Five, I'm afraid you've got to work on the 30th.' Ai! You know what I mean? More than sixty people working on this train and he still can't do without me? I don't care about celebrating New Year.

胖张先生脱下狐皮马褂,想盘腿坐一会儿;太胖,坐不牢;车上也太热,胖脑门上挂了汗,"茶房,打把手巾!"又对瘦乔先生:"车里,老弄这么热干吗?坐飞机大概可以凉爽一点。"

乔先生早已脱去大衣,穿着西皮筒皮袍,套着青缎子坎肩,并不觉得热:"飞机也有免票,不难找;可是。"瘦瘦的一笑。

"总以不冒险的为是!"张先生试着劲儿往上盘两只胖腿。还不易成功。"茶房手巾!"

茶房——四十多岁,个子很细很长,似乎可以随时把脑袋摘下来,再安上去,一点也不费事——扬着满手的热毛巾,很想热心服务,可是委屈太大了,一进门便和小崔聊起来:"看见了没有,廿七,廿八,连跟了两次车,算计好了大年三十歇班,好,事到临期,刘先生上来了:老五,三十还得跑一趟呀!唉,看见了没有?路上一共六十多伙计,单短我这么一个!过年不过,没什

英汉对照
English-Chinese
中国文学宝库
Gems of Chinese Literature
现代文学系列
Modern Literature

That's not the point. It's having to work today that pisses me off." He glanced down the aisle at fat Mr Zhang and shifted the hot towels from one hand to the other. He removed one from the pile and offered it to Little Cui. "Have a towel. Here's what I should have said to Mr Liu: 'I don't care about celebrating New Year. But I ought to get off on the 30th. After working a solid year on this train, why should I have such bad luck? There're more than sixty people working on this train. What's the big difference if I...?'" His resentment flowed, bubbling forth falteringly like water from an inverted bottle. It was nearly impossible for him to contain himself.

When Little Cui handed the towel back to him, Old Five continued, "What a pain in the ass! Who needs all this? I tell you, screw this whole crazy business! You kill yourself the whole goddamned year, and then...."

A touch of animation which one might interpret as a smile transfused Little Cui's sickly complexion. He nodded his head, and was about to bend it even further as a way of expressing his sympathy for Old Five, but stopped there in order not to compromise his principles in such a casual manner. All the people who worked on the train — from the chief conductor to Old Five and even the couplers at every station — were Little Cui's friends. His sickly face was a veritable second class ticket; if he ever got into trouble with the Ministry of Railroads, there were very few people who would deny this ticket's validity. Similarly, no one who knew he always carried a few hundred ounces of opium with him at all times dared to deny him the right to do this. Little Cui offended no one; if a

么;单说这股子别扭劲!"长个子往胖张先生那里探了探,毛巾换了手,揭起一条来,让小崔:"擦一把,我就可对刘先生说了:过年不过没什么,大年卅'该'我歇班;跑了一年的车了,恰好赶上这么个巧当儿!六十多伙计,单缺我……"长个子像倒流瓶儿似的,上下咕噜着气泡,憋得很难过。把小崔的毛巾接过来,才又说出话来:"妈的不混用了,不干了,告诉你,事情妈的来得邪!一年到头,好容易……"

小崔的绿脸上泛出一点活气儿来,几乎可以当作笑意;头微微的点着,又要往横下里摇着;很想同情于老五,而决不肯这么轻易的失去自己的圆滑。自车长至老五,连各站上的挂钩的,都是小崔的朋友,他的瘦绿脸便是二等车票,就是闹到铁道部去大概也没人能否认这张特别车票的价值,正如同谁也晓得他身上老带着那么一二百两烟土而不能不承认他应当带

英汉对照
English-Chinese
中国文学宝库
Gems of Chinese Literature
现代文学系列
Modern Literature

201

friend of his got into trouble, he could ill afford to show too much sympathy, lest his other friends become jealous. And since he never offended anyone, he was never afraid of anyone either. Little Cui's train ticket — his sickly face — was stamped all over with wisdom and intelligence.

"Shit, you work a whole goddamned year without a break!" By venting some of his own bitterness, Little Cui provided Old Five with an opportunity to relieve himself of some of the anger stored up in his heart. Evidently, he was aware of what Aristotle wrote about the effect of tragedy. "I'm in the same trap. It's the 30th, and here I am riding the same old train. But that's not all. Tomorrow, the first day of the New Year, I've got to go see that bitch Pinky. Everyone else's going after the God of Wealth, but I've got to go see that slut. Shit!" He parted his sickly lips, revealing several blackened teeth. Then he closed his mouth, cleared his throat and landed a huge gob of phlegm on the floor.

As expected, Old Five instantly ceased worrying about his own problems, and was moved by Little Cui's plight. When he extended his neck in Little Cui's direction, Old Five looked a lot like a camel — with a kind and tender face. The face towels had cooled, so he went to the next car and poured some hot water over them. When he returned and passed by Little Cui, he didn't say anything, though he winked once to indicate that his resentment hadn't died away altogether. The train shook, and he nearly lost his balance. Righting himself, he went up to Mr Gou. "Have a hot towel. Couldn't get away till the 30th, eh?" His real purpose in asking Mr Gou this question was to revive his own grumbling.

着。小崔不能得罪人,对朋友们的委屈他都晓得,可就是不能给任何人太大的脸,而引起别人吃醋。他谁也不得罪,所以谁也不怕;小崔这张车票——或是绿脸——印着全部人生的智慧。

"×,谁不是一年到头穷忙!"小崔想道出些自家的苦处,给老五一点机会抒散抒散心中的怨恨,像亚里士多德所说的悲剧的效果那样:"我还不是这样?大年卅还得跑这么一趟!这还不提,明天,大年初一,妈的还得看小红去!人家初一出门朝着财神爷走,咱去找那个臭货,×!"绿嘴唇咧开,露出几个乌牙;绿嘴唇并上,鼓起,拍,一口唾液,吐在地上。

老五果然忘了些自家的委屈,同病相怜,向小崔伸了伸长脖子,近似善表情的骆驼。手巾已凉,回去从新用热水浇过;回来,经过小崔的面前不再说什么,只微一闭眼,尚有余怨。车摇了一下,他身子微偏,把自己投到荀先生身旁。"擦一把!大年卅才动身。"问荀先生,以便重新

英汉对照
English-Chinese
中国文学宝库
Gems of Chinese Literature
现代文学系列
Modern Literature

Though Old Five knew Mr Gou quite well, he knew Little Cui better, so with Mr Gou it was necessary to approach his favorite subject by a slightly circuitous route.

Mr Gou was very well dressed. He apparently felt no need to take off his black woolen overcoat with its otter collar, nor his brand new black satin skullcap. Splendidly attired, he sat there quite formally; he could easily pass for the chairman of a large corporation preparing to address an audience from the rostrum. In order to take the towel proffered by Old Five, he had to stretch his arms forward, thus shortening somewhat the very long sleeves of his overcoat. Then, with the towel in his hands, instead of simply bending his arms, he made a wide semi-circular motion, and when his hands finally reached his face, he began to scrub in the most gentlemanly manner. His sparkling face set off his square head and large ears to good advantage. He nodded slightly to Old Five, but didn't explain why he was travelling on New Year's Eve.

"Do you know what we have to go through to make a living?" Old Five couldn't bear wasting an opportunity to vent his spleen in front of Mr Gou, but he wanted to avoid repeating the same old rigmarole to him. Thus by carefully measuring his words, he injected just the right dose of respect and intimacy into the conversation. "I ought to have a day off on the 30th, but here I am still working. There's no way out." Taking the towel back from Mr Gou, Old Five added, "How about another one?"

Mr Gou shook his head, both as a way of refusing a second towel as well as to show a little sympathy for Old Five. But he said nothing. Everyone on the line knew Mr Gou was related to Mr Song,

引起自己的牢骚,对苟先生虽熟,而熟的程度不似对小崔那么高,所以须小小的绕过弯儿。

苟先生很体面,水獭领的青呢大衣还未曾脱去,崭新的青缎子小帽也还在头上,衣冠齐楚,端坐如仪,像坐在台上,等着向大家致词的什么大会主席似的。接过毛巾,手伸出老远,为是把大衣的袖子缩短一些;然后,胳臂不往回诠,而画了个大半圆圈,手找到了脸,擦得很细腻的气派。把脸擦亮,更显出方头大耳朵的十分体面。只对老五点了点头,没有解释为什么在除夕旅行的必要。

"您看我们这个苦营生!"老五不愿意把苟先生放过去,可也不便再重述刚才那一套,更要把话说得有尺寸,正好于敬意之中带着些亲热:"卅晚上该歇,还不能歇!没办法!"接过来手巾:"您再来一把?"

苟先生摇了摇头,既拒绝了第二把手巾,又似乎是为老五伤心,还不肯说什么。路上谁不晓得苟先生是宋段长的亲戚,白坐二等车是当

head of this section of the railroad, which gave him every right to ride in the second class car for free. It was therefore quite beneath his dignity to enter into a casual conversation with a steward.

Old Five felt that Mr Gou's shaking his head was rather brusque, but when a relative of Mr Song, the section chief, deigned to shake his head, one ought to be grateful. A moment later, the train shook violently, and he walked down the aisle as if he were on a swingboat. With a flourish, he unfurled a towel that had been twisted up like a cruller, holding it by its corners in a manner both dainty and professional. "Wipe your face, sir?" Mr Zhang placed the hottest part of the towel over the palm of his hand, slapped himself in the face with it, and began rubbing as if he were polishing a mirror. "And you, sir?" Old Five offered a towel to Mr Qiao. Mr Qiao was not particularly keen on rubbing his face, and only left on his towel whatever finely ground fertile filth he could produce from inside his nostrils and under his fingernails.

"They'll be inspecting tickets shortly." Old Five thought it was wrong to start complaining to strangers, so he began with a short detour. "After we check your tickets, you two gentlemen can take a nice rest; if you need any pillows, just let me know. There're only a few passengers on the train, so you should be able to get some sleep. It's New Year's Eve, so it looks like you two gentlemen are going to have to celebrate on board this year. When you work on the railroad ... you don't even have a choice." He didn't want to say everything at once; better he should observe their reactions first. He offered Mr Zhang another towel. Mr Zhang was reluctant to exert so much effort a second time, but he had not yet wiped his

然的,而且要拿出点身分,不能和茶房一答一和的谈天。

　　老五觉得苟先生只摇了摇头有点发秃,可是宋段长的亲戚既已只摇了头也就得设法认为满意。车又摇动得很厉害,他走着浪木似的走到车中间,把毛巾由麻花形抖成长方,轻巧而郑重的提着两角:"您擦吧?"张先生的胖手心按触到毛巾最热的部份,往脸上一捂,而后用力的擦,像擦着一面镜子。"您……"老五让乔先生。乔先生不大热心擦脸,只稍稍的把鼻孔中与指甲里的细腻,肥美的,可以存着也可以不存着的黑物让给了毛巾。

　　"待会儿就查票,"老五不便于开口就对生客人发牢骚,所以稍微往远处支了一笔:"查过票去,二位该歇着了;要枕头自管言语一声。车上没什么人,还可以睡一会儿。大年卅,您二位也在车上过了!我们跟车……无法!"不便说得太多了,看看二位的神气再讲。又递给张先生一把。张先生不愿再卖那么大力量,可是刚推

英汉对照
English-Chinese
中国文学宝库
Gems of Chinese Literature
现代文学系列
Modern Literature

hair after his haircut earlier that morning. For this, a few passes of the towel would suffice, though his scalp required a little vigorous rubbing as well. After going through all the motions, he breathed a sigh of relief. At this point, Mr Qiao couldn't possibly accept a second towel, since it looked like Mr Zhang had used up all the energy available for rubbing. Instead, he started picking his teeth with his freshly-cleaned fingernails.

"Why do you have to make it so hot in this car?" Mr Zhang said when he tossed the towel back to Old Five.

"I wouldn't open that window if I were you unless you want to freeze. Believe me, no one gives a damn about anything that happens on this train." In a single leap, Old Five arrived at his favorite subject. "What do you think, shouldn't a guy who works the whole year have a day off on New Year's Eve? Ah, forget it, what's the use of talking about it?"

One good reason was because the train had stopped at a small station.

A number of people got off from the third class cars. They were all carrying sacks over their shoulders or baskets in their hands. As they headed out of the station, some hesitated for a moment, perhaps wondering whether they had left anything on the train. Those who remained on board stared out of the windows, envious of those who were nearly home, and anxious for the train to move a little faster. No one in the second class car got off, but seven or eight men in military uniforms boarded, their leather shoes pounding noisily through the carriage and their polished leather belts shining in the light. They carried on four bundles of extra-large fireworks

过的短发上还没有擦过,需要擦几把,而头皮上是须用力气的;很勉强的擦完,吐了口气,乔先生没要第二把,怕力气都教张先生卖了,乃轻轻的用刚被毛巾擦过的指甲刷着牙。

"车上干吗弄这么热!"张先生把毛巾扔给老五。

"您还是别开窗户;一开,准着凉!车上的事,没人管,我告诉你!"老五急转直下的来到本题,"您就说,一年到头跑车的好容易大年卅歇一天,好,得了,什么也甭说了……"

老五的什么也甭说了也一半因为车到了一小站。

三等车上去几个人,都背着包,提着篮,匆匆的往站外走,又忽然犹豫了一下,唯恐落在车上一点什么东西。不下车的扒着玻璃窗外看,有点羡慕人家已到了家,而急盼着车再快开了。二等车上没有下去的,反倒上来七八个军人,皮鞋乱响,皮带油亮,搭上来四包特别加人的花

英汉对照
English-Chinese
中国文学宝库
Gems of Chinese Literature
现代文学系列
Modern Literature

209

wrapped in red paper stamped with gold characters. These fireworks were so large there was hardly any place to put them. The soldiers marched up and down the aisles, shouting and cursing at each other. The more heated their arguments, the more difficult it became for them to reach any conclusions, until the assistant battalion commander ordered, "Lay 'em flat on the floor!" "Put 'em on the floor!" echoed the platoon lieutenant.

In perfect unison, the soldiers bent down, straightened up, patted the dust off their uniforms, stood at attention and saluted.

The assistant battalion commander returned the salute. "Alright then, dismissed!" The platoon lieutenant echoed, "Dismissed!" Accompanied by the sound of loud footsteps, all the grey caps, grey puttees and leather belts moved in the direction of the train door. "On the double!" The whistle sounded; the engine huffed and puffed. Electric lights, human shadows and the sound of turning wheels all blended into one as the train moved out of the station.

Old Five wandered up and down the aisle — whether this could be considered work it was hard to tell — and glanced at the assistant battalion commander, the platoon lieutenant and the fireworks piled on the floor. Feeling too timid to say anything to them, he sat down with Little Cui and started in on his favorite topic, this time with an even more detailed report about what it meant not to be able to take the day off. Little Cui responded by saying that both Pinky and Big Trumpet, another friend of his, were both stinking bitches.

Old Five was becoming slightly anxious about the fireworks, so

炮,血红的纸包,印着金字。花炮太大,放在哪里也不合适,皮鞋乱响,前后左右挪动,语气粗壮,主意越多越没有决定。"就平放在地上!"营副发了言。"放在地上!"排长随着。一齐弯腰,立直,拍拍,立正敬礼。营副还礼:"好啦,回去!"排长还礼:"回去!"皮鞋乱响,灰帽,灰裹腿,皮带,一齐往外活动。"快下!"噜——笛声:闷——车头放响。灯光,人影,轮声,浮动。车又开了。

老五似乎有事,又似乎没事,由这头走到那头,看了那营副及排长,又看了看地上的爆竹,没敢言语,坐下和小崔聊起来,他还是抱怨那一套,把不能歇班的经过又述说了一回,比上次更详细满意。小崔由小红说到大喇叭,都是臭×。

老五心中微微有点不放心那些爆竹,又溜

英汉对照
English-Chinese
中国文学宝库
Gems of Chinese Literature
现代文学系列
Modern Literature

211

he ambled back to where the two officers were sitting. The assistant battalion commander was lying down and appeared thoroughly exhausted. He had placed his gun on the little table next to his seat. The platoon lieutenant felt it would have been improper for him to lie down so soon, but in the meantime had removed his cap and was actively engaged in scratching his scalp. Old Five didn't want to disturb the battalion commander, so he smiled at the platoon lieutenant from a distance and said, "How about letting me put these firecrackers on the overhead rack for you?"

"Why?" The lieutenant took a deep breath and scratched his scalp with such force that his mouth was pulled out of shape.

"Someone might knock them over," Old Five said, retracting his neck.

"Who's going to knock them over? Why would anyone want to do that?" The lieutenant opened his singlefold eyelids, but the effect was lost on Old Five.

"Well, it doesn't matter then." Old Five smiled, but it was as if a boulder were pressing down on his head, giving his face a very squashed look. "It doesn't matter. Where are you getting off?"

"You looking for trouble?" The lieutenant felt a great vacuum inside himself, and thought it appropriate to vent a bit of spleen.

Old Five knew there was no use in picking a fight, so he withdrew tactfully to where Mr Zhang was sitting. "We're going to begin checking tickets now, sir."

Fatty Zhang and Scrawny Qiao were right in the midst of the liveliest conversation. It turned out that both gentlemen knew a man named Ziqing, and that Ziqing was actually a distant relative

回来,营副已经卧倒,似乎极疲乏,手枪放在小几上。排长还不敢卧倒,只摘了灰帽,拼命抓头皮。老五没敢惊动营副,老远就向排长发笑:"那什么,我把这些炮放在上面好不好?"

"干吗?"排长正把头皮抓到歪着嘴吸气的程度。

"怕教它给碰了,"老五缩着脖子说。

"谁敢碰!干吗碰?"排长的单眼皮的眼瞪得极大而并不威严。

"没关系,"老五像头上压了块极大石头,笑得脸都扁了,"没关系!您这是上哪儿?"

"找揍!"排长心中极空洞,而觉得应略发脾气。

老五知道没有找揍的必要,轻轻的退到张先生这边:"这就查票了,您哪。"

张先生此时已和乔先生一胖一瘦的说得挺投缘。张先生认识子清,乔先生也认识子清,说

英汉对照
English-Chinese
中国文学宝库
Gems of Chinese Literature
现代文学系列
Modern Literature

213

of Mr Qiao. From Ziqing their conversation shifted to Ganchen; both Mr Zhang and Mr Qiao knew Ganchen too. He could play twenty rounds of mahjong at a single sitting; even if he lost every penny he had, Ganchen always discarded his tiles in the most gracious manner, a broad smile perpetually spread across his lips. Ganchen was a man of the world, and extremely clever. Was it last year, or the year before, that Ganchen had found himself a lovely and gifted concubine? Ganchen was quite a guy, and a good friend as well.

The ticket inspectors began their rounds: The first two, wearing caps decorated with golden braids, came in frowning. In the second class car, however, one would smile while the other frowned. In the first class car, naturally, they both smiled. The third ticket collector, a tall husky Tianjin type, was sporting a pistol in a leather holster and a beltful of bullets. The fourth was a tall Shandong type, and in addition to pistol and bullets had a large knife in his kit. The fifth, Old Five, just stood there not knowing what to do with his long slender neck, so he simply tilted his head slightly to the right. They entered the car together and passed by where Little Cui was sitting.

By now, Little Cui's sickly complexion and stained teeth were familiar sights to them all. As usual, when they saw him this time and Little Cui smiled, it only made them all feel uncomfortable. The head ticket inspector with the golden braid on his cap stared off into the distance as if there were something on his mind and clicked his little silver ticket punch against his leg, while the second in command, wearing the same sort of cap, actually nodded to

起来子清还是乔先生的远亲呢。由子清引出干臣,张先生乔先生又都晓得干臣:坐下就能打廿圈,输掉了脑袋,人家干臣不能使劲摔一张牌,老那么笑不唧儿的,外场人,绝顶聪明。嗯,是去年,还是前年,干臣还娶了个人儿,漂亮,利落。干臣是把手,朋友!

查票:头一位,金箍帽的脸都板起;二等车,一板一开;头等车,都笑。第三位,天津大汉,手枪,皮带,子弹俱全;第四位,山东大汉,手枪,子弹外加大刀。第五位,老五,细长脖挺也不好,缩也不好,勉强向右边歪着。从小崔那边进来的。

小崔的绿脸乌牙已早在大家的记忆中,现在又见着了,小崔笑,大家反倒稍觉不得劲。头号金箍帽,眼视远处,似略有感触,把手中银亮的小剪子在腿上轻碰,第二金箍帽和小崔点点

英汉对照
English-Chinese
中国文学宝库
Gems of Chinese Literature
现代文学系列
Modern Literature

Little Cui. The Tianjin type smiled for an instant but immediately resumed his frown; he could turn his smile on and off like a light. The man from Shandong fidgeted with the peak of his cap, and though he had many things to say to Little Cui, decided to wait until later; there was a rather elusive look in his eyes. Old Five was feeling somewhat embarrassed for Little Cui, and apologized to him on behalf of all the ticket men. "Don't get up, there're hardly any passengers today. When we're done we'll come back for a chat." Little Cui felt left out, and a dark cloud passed over his sickly face as he sat down.

Old Five went up to Mr Gou and addressed him, "Mr Gou!" But the head ticket inspector thought this was rather presumptuous and immediately interrupted him by shaking Mr Gou's hand. "How's our section cheif Mr Song these days? How is it you're travelling today?" Mr Gou smiled and, looking more dignified than ever, quickly withdrew his shaking hand and clasped his two hands together in front of his chest in the traditional gesture of greeting. He mumbled something incomprehensible, but it was instantly understood by all present that he was just trying his best to be polite. The two men from Tianjin and Shandong stood there not knowing what to say or do, while feeling somewhat inferior to their colleagues. Nonetheless, they maintained their dignity by straightening their backs as stiff as boards.

At the apposite moment, Old Five walked briskly up to Mr Zhang and Mr Qiao and announced that it was time to inspect their tickets. When he saw that they were both carrying free passes, his respect for them rose to great heights. Old Five returned Mr

头。天津大汉一笑,赶紧板脸,似电灯的忽然一明一灭。山东大汉的手摸了摸帽沿,有许多话要对小崔说,暂且等回儿,眼神很曲折。老五似乎很替小崔难堪,所以须代大家向他道歉:"坐,坐,没多少客人,回来说话!"小崔略感孤寂,绿脸上黑了一下,坐下。

老五赶到面前去:"苟先生!"头号金箍帽觉得老五太张道好事,手早交给苟先生:"段长好吧?怎么今天才动身?"苟先生笑,更体面了许多,手退回来,拱起,有声无字说了些什么,客气的意思很可以使大家想象到。二位大汉愣着,怪僵,搭不上话,微觉身分不够,但维持住尊严,腰挺得如板。

老五看准了当儿,轻步上前,报告张乔二位先生,查票。接过来,知是免票,乃特别加紧的恭敬。张先生的票退回;乔先生的稍迟,因为票

Zhang's pass to him first and lingered for a few moments over Mr Qiao's since the latter's pass had been issued to a woman, and Mr Qiao, without a doubt, was a man. The number two ticket inspector poked his head in for a glance but withdrew immediately, nodding his head in forgiveness: on New Year's Eve, a woman could easily turn into a man. Holding Mr Qiao's pass in his two hands, Old Five returned it to him in the most apologetic manner.

The assistant battalion commander was snoring. Sensing the imminent arrival of the ticket inspectors, the platoon lieutenant quickly put his feet up on the seat in order to appear asleep and discourage them from disturbing him. As all eyes turned towards the fireworks on the floor, the man from Shandong nodded in admiration — they were so long and fat. The Tianjin type turned to the second in command and said, "These must be for Brigadier-General Cao!" And since nobody raised any objections, they continued on their way. As they were going out the door, the chief ticket inspector issued a brief order to Old Five: "Tell them to put those fireworks up on the rack." In an effort to lessen the difficulty of such a task, the second in command added, "You can do it for them." Old Five nodded several times, and his whole body nodded as well. He said nothing to them, but he had it all worked out in his mind: "Since you don't have the nerve to tell them yourselves, all I have to do is nod. Nodding my head and whether I put the firework on the rack are entirely different questions." The Tianjin type was the most conservative of them all: "Don't forget they're for Brigadier-General Cao." Hearing this, Old Five came to the enlightened conclusion that there was no way the fireworks could be

上注明是女性,而乔先生是男子汉,实无可疑。二金箍帽的头稍凑近一处,极快的离开,暗中谅解:除夕原可女变为男。老五双手将票递回,甚多歉意。

营副已打呼。排长见查票的来到急把脚放在椅上,表示就寝,不可惊动。大家都视线下移,看地上的巨炮,山东大汉点头佩服,爆竹既长且大。天津大汉对二号金箍帽:"准是给曹旅长送去的!"听者无异议,一齐过去。到了车门,头号金箍帽下令给老五:"教他们把炮放到上面去!"二号金箍帽补充上,亦可以略减老五的困难:"你给他们搬上去!"老五连连点头,身子极灵动,口中不说,心里算好:"你们既不敢去说,我只好点头而已;点头与作不作向来相距很远。"天津大汉最为慎重:"虽是给曹旅长送去的,"老五心中透亮,知爆竹必不可动。

英汉对照
English-Chinese
中国文学宝库
Gems of Chinese Literature
现代文学系列
Modern Literature

moved.

When Old Five returned to where Little Cui was sitting, he could tell from the shadow on his face that he needed a glass of water, and went to fetch it for him without saying a word. Little Cui couldn't afford the time to thank him at this moment, and took a tiny piece of something out of his pocket — not even Old Five could see what it was. He placed the tip of his right thumb on his left palm and curled up the fingers of his left hand so that it resembled the sort of shoe worn by a woman with bound feet; at the same time he grinned, but his face was sickly pale and he was sweating; he looked like an onion which had sprouted after being stored in a warm place. He placed the little shoe over his mouth, tossed back his head and closed his eyes. Bringing the glass to his lips, he drew in his hollow cheeks as if he were gargling, and took a deep breath which produced a sound in his throat. When he opened his eyes, a broad smile appeared on his sickly face.

Old Five cocked his head and nodded in approval. "It's so important to eat well."

"Yes, eating well's very important," Little Cui replied, his spirits restored.

Mr Gou could no longer stand the heat with his overcoat on. As he began to remove it, he glanced around him and stopped. On the one hand, he wanted to put his coat in the safest possible position; on the other, he was concerned about maintaining his dignity. The coat hooks were placed too low. If he hung it there, the coat's lower half would rest on the seat, resulting in a few unattractive creases. Laying it flat on an empty seat would place it at a disadvanta-

老五回到小崔那里,由绿脸上的锈暗,他看出小崔需要一杯开水。没有探问,他就把开水拿来。小崔已顾不得表示谢意,掏出来——连老五也没看清———点:么,右手大姆指按在左手的手心上,左手弯如一弓鞋;咧嘴,脸绿得要透白,有汗气,如受热放芽之洋葱。弓鞋扣在嘴上,微有起落,闭目,唇就水杯,瘦腮稍作漱势;纳气,喉内作响;睁闭眼,绿脸上分明有笑纹。

"吃饭要紧!"老五歪着头赞叹。

"吃饭要紧!"小崔神足,所以话也直爽。

荀先生没法再不脱去大衣,脱下,眼珠欲转而定,欲定而转,一面是想把大衣放在最妥当的地方,一面是表示自己的态度雍重。衣钩太低,挂上去,衣的下半截必窝在椅上,或至出一二小折。平放在空椅上,又嫌离自己稍远,减少水獭

英汉对照
English-Chinese
中国文学宝库
Gems of Chinese Literature
现代文学系列
Modern Literature

geous distance from himself, and estrange him from the otter-fur collar. Nor was it proper for him to hold it on his lap for very long, just as it was unacceptable to have one's concubine sitting on one's lap in public. Unable to make up his mind, he looked up at the overhead luggage rack where his eighteen pieces of luggage were arranged in a row: four bundles, five large baskets, two small baskets, two suitcases, one handbag, two bottles, a parcel wrapped in newspaper and another wrapped in glossy paper. He counted them. They occupied some six meters of space on the rack. To his great satisfaction, they were laid out without the slightest crowding. He was still clinging to his overcoat, and since he couldn't figure out what to do with it, he sat up even straighter.

"New Year's Eve, not home yet. New Year's Eve, not home yet." The rhythmic clicking of the wheels urged the train forward, but it moved as slowly as ever. The starry sky rose and fell; clusters of mountains, trees, villages and cemeteries receded into the darkness. After breaking out of one spell of blackness, the train would rush into the next. Smoke and sparks belched forth from the engine, while clouds of white steam and spray gushed out from the wheels and remained suspended in space after the train had gone; rushing ahead, rushing ahead, not missing a single breath, the train flew through the night. One moment of darkness, richly textured, faded away; another moment of darkness, perfectly empty, faded into the distance. Here there were snow banks, there a small range of hills; the snow was glistening white, the hills were dark and murky; all these things quickly disappeared. However, the train moved slowly, relentlessly slowly. "New Year's Eve, not

领与自己的亲密关系,亦不能久放在怀中,正如在公众场所不便置妾于膝上。不能决定。眼珠向上转去,架上放自己的行李十八件三四卷,五篮,二小筐,二皮箱,一手提箱,二瓶,一报纸包,一书皮纸包。一、二、三、四……占地方长约二丈余,没有压挤之虞,尚满意。大衣仍在怀中,几乎无法解决,更须端坐。

　　快去过年,还不到家!快去过年,还不到家!轮声这样催动。可是跑得很慢。星天起伏,山树村坟集团的往后急退,冲开一点黑暗,奔入另一片黑暗;上面灰烟火星急躁的冒出,后退;下面水点白气流落,落在后边;跑,跑,不喘气,飞驰。一片黑,黑得复杂,过去了;一片黑,黑得空洞,过去了。一片积雪,一列小山,明一下,暗一下,过去了。但是,还慢,还慢,快去过

home yet." The carriages were brightly lit and comfortably heated, but the passengers were anxious and impatient. Who could go to sleep at a time like this? "New Year's Eve, not home yet." Out with the old, in with the new; sacrifice to the Gods; bow down to the ancestors; paste New Year couplets up on door panels; set off firecrackers; make dumplings; eat mixed sweets. Fine wines and sumptuous cuisine were all there in their minds, in their mouths, by their ears, before their noses; but their laughter quickly faded into melancholy. Here they were on the train, but the only sounds they could hear were "New Year's Eve, not home yet." Outside, one dark shadow followed upon another; the starry sky rose and fell; out among the snow drifts, no human voices could be heard, nor a single horse-drawn cart; there was simply nothing to be seen. This unending, unfathomable darkness embraced the well-lit and comfortably heated train cars, dragging them along as if it would never let go. "New Year's Eve, not home yet."

Mr Zhang took two bottles of strong liquor down from the rack and rinsed out two tea bowls. "We're old friends now. Let's drink to it. We can celebrate again when we get home, but there's no reason we shouldn't enjoy ourselves here on the train. Enjoy today, forget tomorrow. Bottoms up, bottoms up! This is vintage wine from Yingkou — twenty years old. You can't buy this anywhere. I got it from a Manchurian bigwig who had a few bottles to spare. Drink up, this is fine stuff!"

Mr Qiao was hard put to refuse, but at the same time didn't feel like drinking right away. He stared at the little bowl in front of him, not knowing whether to take it or not. He sat for a moment

年,还不到家!车上,灯明,气暖,人焦燥;没有睡意,快去过年,还不到家!辞岁,祭神,拜祖,春联,爆竹,饺子,杂拌儿。美酒佳肴,在心里,在口中,在耳旁,在鼻端,刚要笑,转成愁,身在车上,快去过年,还不到家!车外,黑影,黑影,星天起伏,积雪高低,没有人声,没有车马,全无所见,一片退不完,走不尽的黑影,抱着扯着一列灯明气暖的车,似永不散手,快去过年,还不到家……

张先生由架上取下两瓶白酒来,一边涮茶碗,一边说:

"弟兄一见如故!咱们喝喝。到家过年。在车上也得过年,及时行乐!尝尝!真正廿年营口原封,买不到,我和一位'满洲国'的大官匀来的。来,杀口。"

乔先生不好意思拒绝,也不好意思就这么接着。眼看着碗,手没处放,心里想主意。他由

英汉对照
English-Chinese
中国文学宝库
Gems of Chinese Literature
现代文学系列
Modern Literature

225

trying to figure out what to do. From the overhead rack, he took down a large package wrapped in paper and opened it gently. Inside were a large number of small paper packages, each of which he felt with his fingers, the same way clerks in Chinese medicine shops check the contents of medicine bags against the doctor's prescription. He identified three bags accurately: dried lichees, dates, and five-spice-flavored dried beancurd. He only smiled in the direction of the wine after opening these packages. "Just like old friends. Let's not stand on ceremony!"

Mr Zhang cracked open a lichee with his fat fingers. The shell split with a festive "pop," a proper reminder of New Year's firecrackers. He watched while Mr Qiao took a drink and when he'd finished swallowing asked him, "How do you like it?"

"Excellent! Excellent!" Mr Qiao rolled back his tongue to prevent the heady fragrance from escaping from his mouth. "This is wine money can't buy!"

After exchanging several polite toasts, their faces turned bright red. They chatted about their families, their jobs, their friends, the difficulty of making a living, railroad passes.... When they clinked their bowls together, their hearts touched as well; their eyes were moist with tears, and their hearts burned so passionately that they couldn't help but open up to each other: Mr Qiao took out a package of candied kumquats. Mr Zhang thought he ought to open up a few packages of his own, but since he had already opened *two* bottles of wine, why not capitalize on that and prove to Mr Qiao that he wasn't a stingy person? "We're going to empty both of these bottles, one for you and one for me; down to the last

架上取下个大纸包来,轻轻的打开,里面还有许多小纸包,逐一的用手指摸过,如药铺伙计抓完了药对着药方摸摸药包那样。摸准了三包:干荔支,金丝枣,五香腐干,都打开,对着酒碗才敢发笑:"一见如故!彼此不客气了!"

张先生的胖手捏破了一个荔支,拍,响得有意思,恰似过年时节应有的响声。看着乔先生喝了一口酒,还看着,等酒已走下去才问:"怎样?"

"太好了!"乔先生团着点舌头,似不肯多放走口中的酒香,"太好了!有钱也买不到!"

对喝。相让。慢慢的脸全红起来。随便的说,谈到家里,谈到职业,谈到朋友,谈到挣钱的不易,谈到免票……碗碰了碗,心碰了心,眼中都微湿,心中增多了热气与热烈,不能不慷慨:乔先生又打开一包蜜钱金桔。张先生本也想取下些纸包来,可是看了看酒,"两"瓶,乃就题发挥,消极的表示自家并不吝啬:"全得喝上!一人一瓶,一滴也不能剩!这个年过得还真不差

英汉对照
English-Chinese
中国文学宝库
Gems of Chinese Literature
现代文学系列
Modern Literature

drop! We're going to celebrate New Year's Eve! Anyway, it's not wine that makes you drunk. When good friends get together, it doesn't matter if we drink our fill. Drink up! Drink up!"

"But I'm not much of a drinker."

"What are you talking about? This is vintage stuff, twenty years old. You'll be perfectly all right. It's destiny that brings good people together for the first time on New Year's Eve."

Mr Qiao was moved by his candor. "Alright, then, I'll drink with you, to hell with the consequences!"

Little Cui seemed to have something on his mind, but Old Five felt the urge to go to the dining car for a nip or two and leave Little Cui behind to take a nap. "What do you say, shall we head for the dining car?" Old Five stood up and surveyed the interior of the car.

Little Cui made no response. Old Five noticed that Mr Gou was lying down across his seat, his feet resting on the armrest. He also noticed that Mr Gou's new light brown cotton and wool blend socks still had fresh creases in them. Mr Zhang and Mr Qiao, the two free pass holders, were drinking merrily. The battalion commander and the lieutenant were soundly asleep. The fireworks were resting quietly on the floor of the car, their red wrappers glistening like fresh blood. Old Five sneaked off to the dining car.

Little Cui curled up on his seat and closed his eyes, a half-smoked cigarette dangling from his lips.

Mr Zhang had nearly finished his bottle. He loosened his clothing, and sweat dripped down from his temples to his cheeks. His eyes were bloodshot and his tongue was numb, but he never

呢！酒不醉人；哥儿俩投缘，喝多少也不碍事！干上！"

"我的量可——"

"没的话！廿年的原封，决不能出毛病，大年卅交的朋友，前缘！"

乔先生颇受感动："好，我舍命陪君子！"

小崔也不怎么有点心事似的，谈着谈着老五觉得有到饭车上找点酒风的必要，而让小崔安静的忽个盹儿。"怎么着？饭车上去？"老五立起来，向车里瞭望。

小崔没拾碴儿。老五见苟先生已躺下，一双脚在椅子上扶手上仰着，新半毛半线的棕黄色袜子还带着中间那道折儿。张乔二位免票喝得正高兴。营副排长都已睡熟，爆竹静悄而热烈的在地上放着，纸色血红。老五偷偷的奔了饭车去。

小崔团了一团，窝在椅子上，闭上眼，嘴上叼着半截香烟。

张先生的一瓶已剩下不多，解开了钮扣，汗从鬓角流到腮上，眼珠发红，舌头也木，话极多。

stopped babbling. Because he'd lost partial control of his tongue, some of the things he said were somewhat on the coarse side, though he was still thinking straight. He was about to use abusive language with Mr Qiao, but he managed to curb his tongue, transforming his denunciations into bursts of strong emotion. But he didn't become impolite on account of having too much to drink. Mr Qiao had only drunk half a bottle, but his face was a ghostly pale. He fished out a pack of cigarettes and threw one to Mr Zhang. They both lit up. With smoke streaming from his mouth, Mr Zhang lay down on his back, his legs dangling over the edge of his seat. He had no cares in the world. He would have started singing "I've fallen into a drunken stupor...." but his throat was hot and dry, in no condition for singing. He snorted through his nose like an angry bull. Mr Qiao lay down as well, cigarette in hand, with his eyes fixed diagonally across the aisle upon the lieutenant's feet. His heart was beating rapidly, he burped, and his pallid face felt itchy.

"New Year's Eve, not home yet." The sound of the train wheels clicked rapidly in Mr Zhang's ears. The faster they went, the more rapidly his heart beat, and soon all he could hear was a loud buzzing. His head started to spin like a rope swinging in the breeze. Everything around him — including his mind and his body — turned bright red, and a series of red circles appeared before his eyes. But a minute later, the buzzing stopped, the spinning diminished to a gentle sensation inside his body, and he opened his eyes cautiously. He recovered somewhat and, as if nothing at all had happened, groped for a match with his pudgy fingers. He relit

因舌头不利落,所以有些话从横着来,但是心中还微微有点力量,在要对乔先生骂街之际,还能卷住舌头,把乱骂变为豪爽,并非闹酒不客气。乔先生只吞了半瓶,脸可已经青白,白得可怕。掏出烟卷,扔给了张先生一支。都点着了烟。张先生烟在口中,仰卧椅上,腿的下半截悬空,满不在乎。想唱"孤王酒醉"嗓子干辣无音,用鼻子吐气,如怒牛。乔先生也歪下去,手指夹烟卷,眼直视斜对过的排长的脚,心跳,喉中作嗝,脸白而微痒。

快去过年,还不到家!轮声在张先生耳中响得特别快,轮声快,心跳得快,忽然嗡——,头在空中绕弯,如绳子盘空,到处红亮,心与物一色,成若干红圈。忽然,嗡声收敛,心盘旋落身内,微敢睁眼,胆子稍壮,假装没事,胖手取火

英汉对照
English-Chinese
中国文学宝库
Gems of Chinese Literature
现代文学系列
Modern Literature

his half-smoked cigarette and tossed the match away. Instantly, a large thick puff of amoke rose up from the table; the bowls, bottles and table top began to glow with a faint green light which shuddered as it rose gradually and began to spread. Mr Qiao woke up startled to discover that his cigarette was on fire. He tossed it onto the floor and groped in the direction of the table, knocking over the bottles and bowls and spilling the liquor, while the little paper packages started to burn in a rainbow of colors. A ring of flames revolved around Mr Zhang's face like a torch dance. Mr Qiao thought about getting up and running away, but the flames from the burning packages on the table spread to all the paper parcels on the luggage rack, which seemed to stretch out their arms to embrace them. Mr Qiao was on fire head to toe; his eyebrows were singed off; his hair smoldered with a crackle; and when the flames reached his lips, still dripping with liquor, they too started to burn. Mr Qiao looked like the statue of the celestial judge who spits forth flames from his mouth.

Suddenly there was a loud series of explosions. The platoon lieutenant had just awoken from his nap when a "double charger" blew up by the side of his nose, spattering blood and sparks all over him; he stood up in a panic; there were more explosions all around him, as if he had walked into the center of a minefield. Before the battalion commander could stand up, his entire body was covered in flames, and his right eye had been blown to bits.

Mr Gou awoke with a start. He glanced up at the luggage rack, and noticed that some of his paper packages were burning. The flames bore down upon him like a fiery dragon with its pointed

柴,点着已灭了的香烟。火柴顺手抛出。忽然,桌上烟气极强,碗,瓶,几上,都发绿光,飘渺,活动,渐高,四散。乔先生惊醒,手中烟卷已成火焰。抛出烟卷,双手急扑几上,瓶倒,碗倾,纸包吐火苗各色。张先生脸上已满是火,火苗旋转,如舞火球。乔先生想跑,几上火随纸灰上腾,架上纸包仿佛探手取火,火苗联成一片。他自己已成火人,火至眉,眉焦;火至发,发响;火至唇,唇上酒燃起,如吐火判官。

忽然,拍,拍,拍……连珠炮响。排长刚睁眼,鼻上一"双响",血与火星并溅;起来,狂奔,脚下,身上,万响俱发如践地雷。营副不及立起,火及全身,右眼被击碎。

苟先生惊醒,先看架上行李,一部分纸包已烧起,火自上而下,由远而近,若横行火龙,混身

scales made of flames. He made up his mind to break a window and jump out, and removed one of his shoes to accomplish this. The window shattered; the wind rushed in, feeding the flames. His otter-fur collar, his four bundles and five baskets, and all his clothing were perfect fuel for the flames. The train sped on through the night, the wind whistling and the fireworks exploding one after another. Mr Gou panicked.

Little Cui was so inured to train travel that nothing could wake him up. The fire began at his feet, searing his entire body, fussing all the opium he was carrying on his person into a single sticky mass. He sat up quickly, and was nearly blinded by the smoke, explosions, flames and light. The burning opium gave off a wonderfully intoxicating odor, but his legs were so badly burned that he could not budge. Gradually the opium oozed its way upwards along the length of his body, forming a huge bubble which enveloped him like a cocoon.

Little Cui couldn't move. Mr Zhang was too drunk to move; Mr Qiao was panicking; Mr Gou was panicking; the lieutenant was panicking; and the battalion commander was kneeling on his seat, screaming in pain. The train car itself was now on fire, and the smell of sulphur permeated the air. The paper and cloth stopped burning as the fireworks fizzled out. There were fewer explosions, and the smoke thickened; while the flames burned on, the smoke spread to every corner of the car; those who attempted to escape fell down; those who were kneeling down ceased screaming; the smoke thickened; the flames attacked the wooden seats; the train sped on; the wind rushed in through the windows; red tongues of

火舌。急起飞智,打算破窗而逃,拾鞋打玻璃,玻璃碎,风入,火狂;水獭领,四卷五篮,身上都成燃料。车疾走,呼,呼,呼,风;拍,拍,拍,爆竹;苟先生狂奔。

小崔惯于旅行,闻声尚不肯睁眼,火已自足部起,身上极烫,烟土烧成膏,急坐起,烟,炮,火,光,不见别物。身上烟膏发奇香,至烫腿已不能动,渐及上部,成最大烟泡,形如茧。

小崔不能动,张先生醉得不知道动,乔先生狂奔,苟先生狂奔,排长狂奔,营副跪椅上长号。火及全车,硫磺气重,纸与布已渐随爆竹声残灭,声敛,烟浓;火炙,烟塞,奔者倒,跪者声竭,烟更浓,火入木器,车疾走,风呼呼,烟中吐红

英汉对照
English-Chinese
中国文学宝库
Gems of Chinese Literature
现代文学系列
Modern Literature

flame darted out from the clouds of smoke, seeking an escape route. The flames burned brighter, white smoke and flames streamed out of the windows, illuminating the entire train in a gorgeous blazing spectacle. More flames trailed behind the train like a tail composed of a hundred torches.

The train came to a small station but did not stop. When the staff exchanger exchanged staffs with the engineer, he said to himself, "Fire!" When the signal man gave the green light he said to himself, "Fire!" When the switchman threw the switch, and when the railroad policeman stood at attention on the platform, they both said to themselves, "Fire!" The stationmaster was half drunk. By the time he made it to the platform, the train had already left the station. When he looked down the tracks, he thought he saw flames, but he told himself he was seeing things. The staff exchanger replaced the staff in its proper place; the signal man snuffed out his lamp; the switchman readjusted the switch; and the policeman shouldered his rifle and returned to the waiting room. They all remembered they had seen a fire on the train, but none of them felt it worthwhile mentioning. A few minutes later, all that remained of this particular fire turned to ashes in their minds, and they sat around chatting about how they were going to celebrate the New Year. They then set off firecrackers, drank wine and played mahjong — here, at least, all the world was at peace.

After leaving the station, the train increased speed. The wind fed the flames and sparks flashed in every direction. The night was as dense as black lacquer; the train burned like a giant lamp, spitting up and swallowing countless tongues of fire. All that remained

焰,四处寻出路。火更明,烟白火舌吐窗外,全车透亮,空明多姿,火舌长曳,如悬百十火把。

车入了一小站,不停。持签的换签,心里说"火!"持灯的放行,心里说"火!"搬闸的搬闸,路警立正,都心里说"火!"站长半醉,尚未到站台,车已过去,及到站台,微见火影,疑是眼花。持签的交签,持灯的灭灯,搬闸的复闸,路警提枪入休息室,心里都存着些火光,全不想说什么。过了一会儿,心中那点火光渐熄,群议如何守岁,乃放炮,吃酒,打牌,天下极太平。

车出站,加速度。风火交响,星火四落,夜黑如漆,车走如长灯,火舌吞吐。二等车但存屋

英汉对照
English-Chinese
中国文学宝库
Gems of Chinese Literature
现代文学系列
Modern Literature

237

now of the second class carriage was its shape, a charred skeleton engulfed in flames. Hungry flames licked at the air, but disappointed in finding no flammable objects, inched their way down the aisles in both directions and entered the third class cars. Smoke took up the vanguard — smoke scented with the putrid odor of raw meat and the sickening sweetness of charred flesh. First smoke, then flames, then the frenzied cries of "Fire! Fire! Fire!" as the third class passengers panicked. In the chaos which followed, some broke windows, but just stood before them too terrified to jump; some tried to make their way to the doors but collided with others who had the same intentions; some remained in their seats, rendered mute by their fear; some gathered up their bamboo baskets.... It was a scene of helplessness, chaos and terror. The flames burned before their very eyes, setting their torsos and heads on fire. People screamed, covered their heads with their hands, patted their clothing, rushed for the exits, leaped off the train....

The blaze had discovered a new territory to colonize; with such an abundance of people and things, it went mad with joy. One flame shot out in a short leap while another flew off into the distance; one flame disguised itself in a cloud of smoke while another slipped out of the window; one flame wandered aimlessly about while another shunted back and forth through the car, leaving a trail of fire behind it. Assuming countless guises and forms, the flames came together in a fiery dance. Some merged to form balls of fire and flaming comets; others became burning walls of red and green flames; flashing on and off, they crept forward at the whim of the wind; suddenly they would break through a barrier of smoke

形,火光里实存炭架。火舌左右扑空,似乎很失望,乃前乃后,入三等车。火舌的前面,烟为导军,腥臭焦甜。烟到,火到,"火! 火! 火!"人声忽狂,胆要裂。人多,志昏,有的破窗而迟疑不肯跳下,有的奔逃,相挤俱仆,有的呆坐,欲哭无声,有的拾起筐篮……乱,怕,无济于事,火已到面前,到身上,到头顶,哭喊,抱头,拍衣,狂奔,跳车……

火找到新殖民地,物多人多,若狂喜,一舌吐出一舌远掷,一舌半隐烟中,一舌突挺窗外,一舌徘徊,一舌左右联烧,姿体万端,百舌齐舞;渐成一团,为火球,为流星,或滚或飞;又成一片,为红为绿,忽暗忽明,随风爬得,突裂烟成

英汉对照
English-Chinese
中国文学宝库
Gems of Chinese Literature
现代文学系列
Modern Literature

and surge ahead like a giant wave of flame. With audible crackling, human flesh roasted and hair burned, the sounds growing more complex as boxes and baskets fell off the racks and passengers moaned and wailed; further fiery blasts were spurred on by the whistling wind. The entire train was on fire now; dense smoke and leaping flames turned it into a mass cremation of tragic proportions.

The train came to another station where it was scheduled to stop. The staff exchanger, signalman, ticket collector, policemen, porters, stationmaster, assistant stationmaster, clerks, secretaries, and factotums all stared at the train, but there wasn't a single fire extinguisher in the station. On the second class car and the two third class cars in front and behind, there were no sounds and no movement. All that remained were several slowly-rising columns of white smoke and a few steadily burning flames. It was a scene of perfect quietude.

The reports said that a total of fifty-two corpses were recovered on the train. Another eleven bodies were found along the line; these were the remains of passengers who had jumped from the train.

After the Lantern Festival, two weeks after New Year's Day, the investigation team arrived on the scene. There were dinner invitations from many quarters and a busy banquet schedule ensued. After three days of feasting and drinking, there was hardly any time left for a proper investigation. The members of the team had some personal business to attend to, and since this naturally came first, the investigation was postponed for another three days.

焰,急流若惊浪;吱吱作响,炙人肉,烧毛发;响声渐杂,物落人嚎,呼呼借风成火阵;全车烧起,烟浓火烈,为最惨的火葬!

又到站,应停。持签的,打灯的,收票的,站岗的,脚行,正站长,副站长,办事员,书记,闲员,都干睁眼,站上没有救火设备。二等车左右三等车各一辆,无人声,无动静,只有清烟缓动,明焰静燃,至为闲适。

据说事后检尸,得五十二具;沿路拾取,跳车而亡者又十一人。

元宵节后,调查员到。各方面请客,应酬很忙。三日酒肉,顾不及调查。调查专员又有些私事,理应先办,复延迟三日。宴残事了,乃着手调查。

英汉对照
English-Chinese
中国文学宝库
Gems of Chinese Literature
现代文学系列
Modern Literature

The Fire Chariot

The chief conductor knew nothing about what happened, the chief ticket inspector knew nothing about what happened, the second ticket inspector knew nothing about what happened, and the man from Tianjin knew nothing about what happened. Also, the Shandong man knew nothing and Old Five knew nothing, so the cause of the fire was never discovered. The total number of tickets sold at all the stations along the line tallied with the number of tickets inspected on the train. Precisely sixty-three tickets were missing; it was assumed that all the tickets went up in smoke along with the train, since this was the exact number of corpses recovered. No stations reported selling any second class tickets. Since the second class car had been empty, it was eliminated as a possible source of the fire.

Old Five was questioned. Though he knew nothing about what happened, he was in the dining car when the fire started. His job was second class steward. Why had he left his post without proper authorization? Though the cause of the fire remained undetermined, this was a serious breach of railroad regulations and Old Five was dismissed from his job as a punishment.

The investigation team returned to their offices. Their detailed final report was written in an elegant literary style.

"I was supposed to get off on New Year's Eve. Then they insist I have to work that night. So who gives a damn if I keep that job or not." Old Five extended his long neck towards his wife. "Let 'em fire me. That's fine with me. If they don't want me, I can still take care of myself. Don't worry about it. You think getting kicked off the railroad means we're going to starve to death?"

车长无所知,头号金箍帽无所知,二号金箍帽无所知,天津大汉无所知,山东大汉无所知,老五无所知,起火原因不明。各站报告售出票数与所收票数,正相合,恰少六十三张,似与车俱焚,等于所拾尸数。各站俱未售出二等票,二等车必为空车,绝对不能起火。

审问老五,虽无所知,但火起时老五在饭车上,既系二等车的看车夫,为何擅离职守,到饭车上去?起火原因虽不明,但擅离职守,罪有当得,开除示惩!

调查专员回衙复命,报告详细,文笔甚佳。

"大年卅歇班,硬还叫我跟车,妈的干不干没多大关系!"老五伸着长脖对五嫂说,"开除,正好,此处不留爷,自有留爷处! 你甭着急,离了火车还不能吃饭是怎着?"

英汉对照
English-Chinese
中国文学宝库
Gems of Chinese Literature
现代文学系列
Modern Literature

"I'm not worried about that," Old Five's wife said, trying to console her husband, "but it still bugs me the way those fresh turnips you were bringing me got burned in the fire."

Translated by Don J. Cohn

"我倒不着急。"五嫂想安慰安慰老五,"我倒真心疼你带来那些青菲,也叫火给烧了!"

英汉对照
English-Chinese
中国文学宝库
Gems of Chinese Literature
现代文学系列
Modern Literature

Crescent Moon

1

Yes, I've seen the crescent moon again — a chill sickle of pale gold. How many times have I seen crescent moons just like this one, how many times.... It stirred many different emotions, brought back many different scenes. As I sat and stared at it, I recalled each time I had seen it hanging in the blue firmament. It awakened my memories like an evening breeze blowing open the petals of a flower that is craving for sleep.

2

The first time, the chill crescent moon really brought a chill. My first recollection of it is a bitter one. I remember its feeble pale gold beams shining through my tears. I was only seven then — a little girl in a red padded jacket. I wore a blue cloth hat Mama had made for me. There were small flowers printed on it. I remember. I stood leaning against the doorway of our small room, gazing at the crescent moon. The room was filled with the smell of medicine and smoke, with Mama's tears, with Papa's illness. I stood alone on the steps looking at the moon. No one bothered about me, no one cooked my supper. I knew there was tragedy in that room, for

月牙儿

一

是的,我又看见月牙儿了,带着点寒气的一钩儿浅金。多少次了,我看见跟现在这个月牙儿一样的月牙儿;多少次了。它带着种种不同的感情,种种不同的景物,当我坐定了看它,它一次一次的在我记忆中的碧云上斜挂着。它唤醒了我的记忆,像一阵晚风吹破一朵欲睡的花。

二

那第一次,带着寒气的月牙儿确是带着寒气。它第一次在我的云中是酸苦,它那一点点微弱的浅金光儿照着我的泪。那时候我也不过是七岁吧,一个穿着短红棉袄的小姑娘。戴着妈妈给我缝的一顶小帽儿,蓝布的,上面印着小小的花,我记得。我倚着那间小屋的门垛,看着月牙儿。屋里是药味,烟味,妈妈的眼泪,爸爸的病;我独自在台阶上看着月牙,没人招呼我,没人顾得给我作晚饭。我晓得屋里的惨凄,因

英汉对照
English-Chinese
中国文学宝库
Gems of Chinese Literature
现代文学系列
Modern Literature

everyone said Papa's illness was.... But I felt much more sorry for myself. I was cold, hungry, neglected.

I stood there until the moon had set. I had nothing; I couldn't restrain my tears. But the sound of Mama's weeping drowned out my own. Papa was silent; a white cloth covered his face. I wanted to raise the cloth and look at him, but I didn't dare. There was so little space in our room, and Papa occupied it all.

Mama put on white mourning clothes. A white robe without stitched hems was placed over my red jacket. I remember because I kept breaking off the loose white threads along the edges. There was a lot of noise and grief-stricken crying, everyone was very busy; but actually there wasn't much to be done. It hardly seemed worth so much fuss. Papa was placed in a coffin made of four thin boards; the coffin was full of cracks. Then five or six men carried him out. Mama and I followed behind, weeping. I remember Papa; I remember his wooden box. That box meant the end of him. I knew unless I could break it open I'd never see him again. But they buried it deep in the ground in a cemetery outside the city wall. Although I knew exactly where it was, I was afraid it would be hard to find that box again. The earth seemed to swallow it like a drop of rain.

3

Mama and I were both wearing white gowns again the next time I saw the crescent moon. It was a cold day, and Mama was taking me to visit Papa's grave. She had bought some gold and silver

为大家说爸爸的病……可是我更感觉自己的悲惨,我冷,饿,没人理我。一直的我立到月牙儿落下去。什么也没有了,我不能不哭。可是我的哭声被妈妈的压下去;爸,不出声了,面上蒙了块白布。我要掀开白布,再看看爸,可是我不敢。屋里只有那么点点地方,都被爸占了去。妈妈穿上白衣,我的红袄上也罩了个没缝襟边的白袍,我记得,因为不断地撕扯襟边上的白丝儿。大家都很忙,嚷嚷的声儿很高,哭得很恸,可是事情并不多,也似乎值不得嚷:爸爸就装入那么一个四块薄板的棺材里,到处都是缝子。然后,五六个人把他抬了走。妈和我在后边哭。我记得爸,记得爸的木匣。那个木匣结束了爸的一切:每逢我想起爸爸来,我就想到非打开那个木匣不能见着他。但是,那木匣是深深的埋在地里,我明知在城外哪个地方埋着它,可又像落在地上的一个雨点,似乎永难找到。

三

妈和我还穿着白袍,我又看见了月牙儿。那是个冷天,妈妈带我出城去看爸的坟。妈拿

"ingots" made of paper to burn and send to Papa in the next world. Mama was especially good to me that day. When I was tired, she carried me piggy-back; at the city gate she bought me some roasted chestnuts. Everything was cold, only the chestnuts were hot. Instead of eating them, I used them to warm my hands.

I don't remember how far we walked, but it was very, very far. It hadn't seemed nearly so far the day we buried Papa, perhaps because a lot of people had gone with us. This time there was only Mama and me. She didn't speak. I didn't feel like saying anything either. It was very quiet out there. On that yellow dirt road there wasn't a breath of sound.

It was winter, and the days were short. I remember the grave — a small mound of earth. There were some brown hills in the distance, with the sunlight slanting on them. Mama seemed to have no time for me. She set me down on the side and embraced the head of the grave and wept. I sat holding the hot chestnuts. After crying a while, Mama burned the paper ingots. The ashes swirled before us in little spirals, then lazily settled back on the ground. There wasn't much wind, but it was very cold.

Mama began to cry again. I thought of Papa too, but I didn't cry for him. It was Mama's pitiful weeping that brought tears to my eyes. I pulled her by the hand and said, "Don't cry, Mama, don't cry." But she sobbed all the harder and hugged me to her bosom.

The sun was nearly set and there wasn't another person in sight. Only Mama and me. That seemed to scare Mama a little. With tears in her eyes she led me away. After we had walked a while, she turned and looked back. I did too. I couldn't tell Papa's grave

着很薄的一摞儿纸。妈那天对我特别的好,我走不动便背我一程,到城门上还给我买了一些炒栗子。什么都是凉的,只有这些栗子是热的;我舍不得吃,用它们热我的手。走了多远,我记不清了,总该是很远很远吧。在爸出殡的那天,我似乎没觉得这么远,或者是因为那天人多;这次只是我们娘儿俩,妈不说话,我也懒得出声,什么都是静寂的;那些黄土路静寂得没有头儿。天是短的,我记得那个坟:小小的一堆儿土,远处有一些高土岗儿,太阳在黄土岗儿上头斜着。妈妈似乎顾不得我了,把我放在一旁,抱着坟头儿去哭。我坐在坟头的旁边,弄着手里那几个栗子。妈哭了一阵,把那点纸焚化了,一些纸灰在我眼前卷成一两个旋儿,而后懒懒的落在地上;风很小,可是很够冷的。妈妈又哭起来。我也想爸,可是我不想哭他;我倒是为妈妈哭得可怜而也落了泪。过去拉住妈妈的手:"妈不哭!不哭!"妈妈哭得更恸了。她把我搂在怀里。眼看太阳就落下去,四外没有一个人,只有我们娘儿俩。妈似乎也有点怕了,含着泪,扯起我就走,走出老远,她回头看了看,我也转过身去:爸

英汉对照
English-Chinese
中国文学宝库
Gems of Chinese Literature
现代文学系列
Modern Literature

from the others any more. There were nothing but graves on the hillside. Hundreds of small mounds, right to the foot of the hill. Mama sighed.

We walked and walked, sometimes fast, sometimes slow. We still hadn't reached the city gate when I saw the crescent moon again. All around us was darkness and silence. Only the crescent moon gave off a cold glow. I was worn out. Mama carried me. How we got back to the city I don't know. I only remember hazily that there was a crescent moon in the sky.

4

By the time I was eight, I had learned how to take things to the pawnshop. I knew that if I didn't come back with some money, Mama and I would have nothing to eat that night — Mama would never send me except as a last resort. Whenever she handed me a small package it meant there wasn't even thin gruel in the bottom of our pot. Our pot was often cleaner than a neat young widow.

One day I was sent to the pawnshop with a mirror. This seemed to be the only thing we could spare, though Mama used it every day. It was spring, and our padded clothes had just been placed in hock. I knew how to be careful. Carrying the mirror, I walked carefully but quickly to the pawnshop. It was already open.

I was afraid of that pawnshop's big red door, afraid of its high counter. Whenever I saw that door, my heart beat fast. But I'd go in just the same, even if I had to crawl over the high door-sill. Taking a grip on myself, I would hand up my package and say

的坟已经辨不清了;土岗的这边都是坟头,一小堆一小堆,一直摆到土岗底下。妈妈叹了口气。我们紧走慢走,还没有走到城门,我看见了月牙儿。四外漆黑,没有声音,只有月牙儿放出一道儿冷光。我乏了,妈妈抱起我来。怎样进的城,我就不知道了,只记得迷迷糊糊的天上有个月牙儿。

四

刚八岁,我已经学会了去当东西。我知道,若是当不来钱,我们娘儿俩就不要吃晚饭;因为妈妈但凡有点主意,也不肯叫我去。我准知道她每逢交给我个小包,锅里必是连一点粥底儿也看不见了。我们的锅有时干净得像个体面的寡妇。这一天,我拿的是一面镜子。只有这件东西似乎是不必要的,虽然妈妈天天得用它。这是个春天,我们的棉衣都刚脱下来就入了当铺。我拿着这面镜子,我知道怎样小心,小心而且要走得快,当铺是老早就上门的。我怕当铺的那个大红门,那个大高长柜台。一看见那个门,我就心跳。可是我必须进去,似乎是爬进去,那个高门坎儿是那么高。我得用尽了力量,

英汉对照
English-Chinese
中国文学宝库
Gems of Chinese Literature
现代文学系列
Modern Literature

loudly, "I want to pawn this." After getting my money and the pawn ticket, I would hold them carefully and hurry home. I knew Mama would be worried.

But this time they didn't want the mirror. They said I should add another item to it. I knew what that meant. Putting the mirror in my shirt, I ran home as fast as my legs could carry me. Mama cried; she couln't find anything else to pawn. I had always thought there were a lot of things in our little room. But now, helping Mama look for a piece of clothing to raise some money on, I saw that we didn't have much at all.

Mama decided not to send me to the pawnshop again, but when I asked her, "Mama, what are we going to eat?" she cried and gave me her silver hairpin. It was the last bit of silver she had left. She had taken it out of her hair several times before, but she had never been able to part with it. Grandma had given it to her when she got married. Now Mama gave it to me — her last bit of silver — to pawn together with the mirror.

I ran with all my might to the pawnshop, but the big door was already shut tight. Clutching the silver hairpin, I sat down on the steps and cried softly, not daring to make too much noise. I looked up at the sky. Ah, there was the crescent moon shining through my tears again.

I wept for a long time. Then Mama came out of the shadows and took me by the hand. Oh, what a nice warm hand. I forgot all my troubles, even my hunger. As long as Mama's warm hand was holding mine, everything was all right.

"Ma," I sobbed, "let's go home and sleep. I'll come again

递上我的东西,还得喊:"当当!"得了钱和当票,我知道怎样小心的拿着,快快回家,晓得妈妈不放心。可是这一次,当铺不要这面镜子,告诉我再添一号来。我懂得什么叫"一号"。把镜子搂在胸前,我拼命的往家跑。妈妈哭了;她找不到第二件东西。我在那间小屋住惯了,总以为东西不少;及至帮着妈妈一找可当的事物,我的小心里才明白过来,我们的东西很少,很少。妈妈不叫我去了。可是,"妈妈咱们吃什么呢?"妈妈哭着递给我她头上的银簪——只有这一件东西是银的。我知道,她拔下过来几回,都没肯交给我去当。这是妈妈出门子时,姥姥家给的一件首饰。现在,她把这末一件银器给了我,叫我把镜子放下。我尽了我的力量赶回当铺,那可怕的大门已经严严的关好了。我坐在那门墩上,握着那根银簪。不敢高声的哭,我看着天,啊,又是月牙儿照着我的眼泪!哭了好久,妈妈在黑影中来了,她拉住了我的手,呕,多么热的手。我忘了一切的苦处,连饿也忘了,只要有妈妈这只热手拉着我就好。我抽抽搭搭的说:"妈! 咱

early tomorrow morning."

Mama didn't say anything. After we had walked a while I said, "Ma, you see that crescent moon? It hung crooked just like that the day Pa died. Why is it always so slant?"

Mama remained silent. But her hand trembled a little.

5

All day long, Mama washed clothes for people. I wanted to help her, but there wasn't any way I could do it. I would wait for her; I wouldn't go to sleep until she finished. Sometimes, even after the crescent moon had already risen, she would still be scrubbing away. Those smelly socks, hard as cowhide, were brought in by salesmen and clerks from the shops. By the time Mama finished washing the "cowhide" she never had any appetite.

I would sit beside her, looking at the moon, watching the bats flit through its rays, like big triangular water-chestnuts flashing across beams of silver then quickly dropping into the darkness again.

The more I pitied Mama, the more I loved the crescent moon. Gazing at it always eased my heart. I loved it in the summer most of all. It was always so cool, so icy. I loved the faint shadows it cast upon the ground, though they never lasted very long. Soft and grey, they soon vanished, leaving the earth especially dark and the stars especially bright and the flowers especially fragrant. Our neighbours had many flower bushes. Blossoms from a tall locust tree used to drift into our courtyard and cover the ground like a

们回家睡觉吧。明儿早上再来!"妈一声没出。又走了一会儿:"妈!你看这个月牙;爸死的那天,它就是这么斜斜着。为什么她老这么斜斜着呢?"妈还是一声没出,她的手有点颤。

五

妈妈整天的给人家洗衣裳。我老想帮助妈妈,可是插不上手。我只好等着妈妈,非到她完了事,我不去睡。有时月牙儿已经上来,她还哼哧哼哧的洗。那些臭袜子,硬牛皮似的,都是买卖地的伙计们送来的。妈妈洗完这些牛皮就吃不下饭去。我坐在她旁边,看着月牙,蝙蝠专会在那条光儿底下穿过来穿过去,像银线上穿着个大菱角,极快的又掉到暗处去。我越可怜妈妈,便越爱这个月牙,因为看着它,使我心中痛快一点。它在夏天更可爱,它老有那么点凉气,像一条冰似的。我爱它给地上的那点小影子,一会儿就没了;迷迷糊糊的不甚清楚,及至影子没了,地上就特别的黑,星也特别的亮,花也特别的香——我们的邻居有许多花木,那棵高高的洋槐总把花儿落到我们这边来,像一层雪似的。

英汉对照
English-Chinese
中国文学宝库
Gems of Chinese Literature
现代文学系列
Modern Literature

layer of snow.

6

Mama's hands became hard and scaly. They felt wonderful when she rubbed my back. But I hated to trouble her, because her hands were all swollen from the water. She was thin too; often she couldn't eat a thing after washing those stinking socks. I knew she was trying to think of a way out. I knew. She used to push the pile of dirty clothes to one side and become lost in thought. Sometimes she would talk to herself. What was she planning? I couldn't guess.

7

Mama told me to be good and call him "Pa" — she had found me another father. Mama didn't look at me when she told me this. There were tears in her eyes, and she said, "I can't let you starve!"

Oh, so it was to keep me from starving that she found me another Pa? I didn't understand much, and I was a little afraid. But I was kind of hopeful too — maybe we really wouldn't go hungry any more.

What a coincidence! As we were leaving our tiny flat, a crescent moon again hung in the sky. It was brighter and more frightening than I had ever seen it before. I was going to leave the small room I had grown so accustomed to. Ma sat in a red bridal sedan-chair. Ahead of her marched a few tootling musicians who played

六

妈妈的手起了层鳞,叫她给搓搓背顶解痒痒了。可是我不敢常劳动她,她的手是洗粗了的。她瘦,被臭袜子熏的常不吃饭。我知道要想主意了,我知道。她常把衣裳推到一边,愣着。她和自己说话。她想什么主意呢?我可是猜不着。

七

妈妈嘱咐我不叫我别扭,要乖乖的叫"爸":她又给我找到一个爸。这是另一个爸,我知道,因为坟里已经埋好一个爸了。妈嘱咐我的时候,眼睛看着别处。她含着泪说:"不能叫你饿死!"呕,是因为不饿死我,妈才另给我找了个爸!我不明白多少事,我有点怕,又有点希望——果然不再挨饿的话。多么凑巧呢,离开我们那间小屋的时候,天上又挂着月牙。这次的月牙比哪一回都清楚,都可怕;我是要离开这住惯了的小屋了。妈坐了一乘红轿,前面还有几个鼓手,吹打的一点也不好听。轿在前边走,我

very badly. The man and I followed behind. He held me by the hand. The crescent moon gave off faint rays that seemed to tremble in the cool breeze.

The streets were deserted except for stray dogs that barked at the musicians. The sedan-chair moved very quickly. Where was it going? Was it taking Mama outside the city, to the cemetery? The man pulled me along so fast I could hardly catch my breath. I couldn't even cry. His sweating palm was cold, like a fish. I wanted to call "Ma!" but I didn't dare. The crescent moon looked like a large half-closed eye. In a little while, the sedan-chair entered a small lane.

8

During the next three or four years I somehow never saw the crescent moon.

My new Pa was very good to me. He had two rooms. He and Ma lived in the inner room; I slept on a pallet in the outside one. At first I still wanted to sleep with Mama, but after a few days I began to love "my" little room. It had clean whitewashed walls, a table and a chair. They all seemed to belong to me. My bedding was thicker and warmer, too.

Mama gradually put on some weight.

Colour came back to her cheeks, and the scales left her hands. I hadn't been to the pawnshop in a long time. My new father let me go to school. Sometimes he even played with me. I don't know why I couldn't bring myself to call him "Pa" — I liked him a lot. He

和一个男人在后边跟着,他拉着我的手。那可怕的月牙放着一点光,仿佛在凉风里颤动。街上没有什么人,只有些野狗追着鼓手们咬;轿子走得很快。上哪去呢?是不是把妈抬到城外去,抬到坟地去?那个男人扯着我走,我喘不过气来,要哭都哭不出来。那男人的手心出了汗,凉得像个鱼似的,我要喊"妈",可是不敢。一会儿,月牙像个要闭上的一道大眼缝,轿子进了个小巷。

八

我在三四年里似乎没再看见月牙。新爸对我们很好,他有两间屋子,他和妈住在里间,我在外间睡铺板。我起初还想跟妈妈同睡,可是几天之后,我反倒爱"我的"小屋了。屋里有白白的墙,还有条长桌,一把椅子。这似乎都是我的。我的被子也比从前的厚实暖和了。妈妈也渐渐胖了点,脸上有了红色,手上的那层鳞也慢慢掉净。我好久没去当当了。新爸叫我去上学。有时候他还跟我玩一会儿。我不知道为什么不爱叫他"爸",虽然我知道他很可爱。他似

seemed to understand. He used to just grin at me. His eyes looked very nice then. Mama would privately urge me to call him "Pa." I didn't really want to be stubborn. I knew it was because of him that Mama and I had food to eat and clothes to wear. I understood all that.

Yes, for three or four years I don't recall seeing the crescent moon; maybe I saw it and don't remember.

But I can never forget the crescent moon I saw when Pa died, or the one that rode before Ma's bridal sedanchair. That pale chill light will always remain in my heart, shiny and cool as a piece of jade. Sometimes when I think of it, it seems as if I can almost reach out my hand and touch it.

9

I loved going to school. I had the feeling that the schoolyard was full of flowers, though, actually, this wasn't so. Yet whenever I think of school I think of flowers. Just as whenever I think of Papa's grave I think of a crescent moon outside the city — hanging crooked in the wind blowing across the fields.

Mama loved flowers too. She couldn't afford them, but if anyone ever sent her one, she pinned it in her hair. Once I had the chance to pick a couple for her. With a fresh flower in her hair, she looked very young from the back. She was happy, and so was I.

Going to school also made me very glad. Perhaps this is the reason whenever I think of school I think of flowers.

乎也知道这个,他常常对我那么一笑;笑的时候他有很好看的眼睛。可是妈妈偷偷告诉我叫爸,我也不愿十分的别扭。我心中明白,妈和我现在是有吃喝的,都因为有这个爸,我明白。是的,在这三四年里我想不起曾经看见过月牙儿;也许是看见过而不大记得了。爸死时那个月牙,妈轿子前面那个月牙,我永远忘不了。那一点点光,那一点寒气,老在我心中,比什么都亮,都清凉,像块玉似的,有时候想起来仿佛能用手摸到似的。

九

我很爱上学。我老觉得学校里有不少的花,其实并没有;只是一想起学校就想到花罢了,正像一想起爸的坟就想起城外的月牙儿——在野外的小风里歪着。妈妈是很爱花的,虽然买不起,可是有人送给她一朵,她就顶喜欢的戴在头上。我有机会便给她折一两朵来;戴上朵鲜花,妈的后影还很年轻似的。妈喜欢,我也喜欢。在学校里我也很喜欢。也许因为这个,我想起学校便想起花来?

英汉对照
English-Chinese
中国文学宝库
Gems of Chinese Literature
现代文学系列
Modern Literature

10

The year I was to graduate from primary school, Mama sent me to the pawnshop again. I don't know why my new father suddenly left us. Mama didn't seem to know where he went either. She told me to continue going to school; she thought he'd probably come back soon.

Many days passed and there was still no sign of him. He didn't even write. I was afraid Mama would have to start washing dirty socks again, and I felt very badly about it.

But Mama had other plans. She still dressed prettily and wore flowers in her hair. How strange! She didn't cry; in fact she was always smiling. Why? I didn't understand. For several days whenever I came home from school, I'd find her standing in the doorway. Not long after, men began to hail me on the street:

"Hey, tell your Ma I'll be calling on her soon!"

"Young and tender, are you selling today?"

My face burning like fire, I hung my head till it couldn't go any lower. I knew now, but there wasn't anything I could do about it. I couldn't question Mama, no, I couldn't do that. She was so good to me, always urging, "Read your books, study hard."

But she was illiterate herself. Why was she so anxious for me to study? I grew suspicious. But then I would think — she's doing this because she has no way out. When I felt suspicious, I wanted to curse her. At other times, I would want to hug her and beg her not to do that kind of thing any more.

十

当我要在小学毕业那年,妈又叫我去当当了。我不知道为什么新爸忽然走了。他上了哪儿,妈似乎也不晓得。妈妈还叫我上学,她想爸不久就会回来。他许多日子没回来,连封信也没有。我想妈又该洗臭袜子了,这使我极难受。可是妈妈并没这么打算。她还打扮着,还爱戴花;奇怪! 她不落泪,反倒好笑;为什么呢? 我不明白! 好几次,我下学来,看她在门口儿立着。又隔了不久,我在路上走,有人"嗨"我了:"嗨! 给你妈捎个信儿去!""嗨! 你卖不卖呀? 小嫩的!"我的脸红得冒出火来,把头低得无可再低。我明白,只是没办法。我不能问妈妈,不能。妈对我很好,而且有时候极庄重的说我:"念书! 念书!"妈是不识字的,为什么这样催我念书呢? 我疑心;又常由疑心而想到妈是为我才作那样的事。妈是没有更好的办法。疑心的时候我恨不能骂妈妈一顿。再一想,我要抱住

英汉对照
English-Chinese
中国文学宝库
Gems of Chinese Literature
现代文学系列
Modern Literature

I hated myself for not being able to help Mama. I was worried. Even when I graduated from primary school, what use would I be? I heard from the girls in my class that several of the students who graduated last year became concubines; a few, they said, were working "in dark doorways." I didn't quite understand these things, but from the way my classmates spoke, I guessed it was something bad. The girls in my class seemed to know everything; they loved to whisper about things which they knew perfectly well were not nice. It made them blush, yet, at the same time, look quite self-satisfied.

My suspicion of Mama increased. Was she waiting for me to graduate, so that she could make me...? When I thought like this, I didn't dare to go home. I was afraid to face Mama. I used to save the pennies she gave me to buy afternoon snacks, and go to physical training class on an empty stomach. I was often faint. How I envied the other kids, munching their pastries. But I had to save money. With a little money I could run away if Mama insisted that I....

At my richest, I never managed to save more than ten or fifteem cents. Even during the day, I used to gaze up at the sky, looking for my crescent moon. If the misery in my heart could be compared to anything physical, it should be that crescent moon — hanging helpless and unsupported in the grey-blue sky, its feeble rays soon swallowed up by the darkness.

11

What made me feel worst of all was that I was slowly learning to

她,央告她不要再作那个事。我恨自己不能帮助妈妈。所以我也想到:我在小学毕业后又有什么用呢?我和同学们打听过了,有的告诉我,去年毕业的有好几个作姨太太的。有的告诉我,谁当了暗门子。我不大懂这些事,可是由她们的说法,我猜到这不是好事。她们似乎什么都知道,也爱偷偷的谈论她们明知是不正当的事——这些事叫她们的脸红红的而显出得意。我更疑心妈妈了,是不是等我毕业好去作……这么一想,有时候我不敢回家,我怕见妈妈。妈妈有时候给我点心钱,我不肯花,饿着肚子去上体操,常常要晕过去。看着别人吃点心,多么香甜呢!可是我得省着钱,万一妈妈叫我去……我可以跑,假如我手中有钱。我最阔的时候,手中有一毛多钱!在这些时候,即使在白天,我也有时望一望天上,找我的月牙儿呢。我心中的苦处假若可以用个形状比喻起来,必是个月牙儿形的。它无倚无靠的在灰蓝的天上挂着,光儿微弱,不大会儿便被黑暗包住。

叫我最难过的是我慢慢的学会了恨妈妈。

hate Mama. But whenever I hated her, I couldn't help remembering how she carried me piggy-back to visit Papa's grave — and then I couldn't hate her any more. Yet I had to. My heart ... my heart was like that crescent moon — only able to shine a little while, surrounded by a darkness that was black and limitless.

Men constantly came to Mama's room now; she no longer tried to hide it from me. They looked at me like dogs — drooling, their tongues hanging out. In their eyes I was an even tastier morsel than Mama. I could see it.

In a short time, I suddenly came to understand a lot. I knew I had to protect myself. I could feel that my body had something precious; I was aware of my own fragrance. I felt ashamed; I was torn by one emotion after another. There was a force within me that I could use to protect myself — or destroy myself. At times I was firm and strong. At times I was weak, defenceless, confused.

I wanted to love Mama. There were so many things I wanted to ask her. I needed her comforting. But it was just at that time that I had to shun her, hate her — or lose my own existence.

Lying sleepless on my bed and considering the matter calmly, I could see that Mama deserved to be pitied. She had to feed the two of us. But then I would think — how could I eat the food she earned that way?

That was how my mood kept changing. Like a winter wind — halting a moment, then blowing fiercer than ever. I would quietly watch my fury rising within me, and be powerless to stop it.

12

Before I could think of a solution, things became worse. Mama

可是每当我恨她的时候,我不知不觉的便想起她背着我上坟的光景。想到了这个,我不能恨她了。我又非恨她不可。我的心像——还是像那个月牙儿,只能亮那么一会儿,而黑暗是无限的。妈妈的屋里常有男人来了,她不再躲避着我。他们的眼像狗似的看着我,舌头吐着,垂着涎。我在他们的眼中是更解馋的,我看出来。在很短的期间,我忽然明白了许多的事。我知道得保护我自己,我觉出我身上好像有什么可贵的地方,我闻得出我已有一种什么味道,使我自己害羞,多感。我身上有了些力量,可以保护自己,也可以毁了自己。我有时很硬气,有时候很软。我不知怎样好。我愿爱妈妈,这时候我有好些必要问妈妈的事,需要妈妈的安慰;可是正在这个时候,我得躲着她,我得恨她;要不然我自己便不存在了。当我睡不着的时节,我很冷静的思索,妈妈是可原谅的。她得顾我们俩的嘴。可是这个又使我要拒绝再吃她给我的饭菜。我的心就这么忽冷忽热,像冬天的风,休息一会儿,刮得更要猛;我静候着我的怒气冲来,没法儿止住。

十二

事情不容我想好方法就变得更坏了。妈妈

英汉对照
English-Chinese
中国文学宝库
Gems of Chinese Literature
现代文学系列
Modern Literature

asked me, "What about it?" If I really loved her, she said, I ought to help her. Otherwise, she couldn't continue taking care of me. These didn't seem like words that Mama could speak, yet she said them. To make it even clearer, she added:

"I'm getting old. In another year or two, men won't want me even if I offer myself for nothing."

It was true. Lately you could see the wrinkles on Mama's face no matter how much powder she used. She no longer had the energy to entertain a lot of men; she was thinking of giving herself to only one. There was a man who ran a steamed bread shop who wanted her. She could go to him right away. But I was a big girl now. I couldn't trail after her bridal sedan-chair like I did when I was a child. I would have to look after myself. If I would agree to "help" Mama, she wouldn't have to go to him. I could earn money for us both.

I was quite willing to earn money, but when I thought of the way she wanted me to do it, it made me shiver. I knew next to nothing; how could I peddle myself like some middle-aged woman? Mama's heart was hard, and the need for money was harder still. She didn't force me to take this road or that. She left the choice to me. Either help her, or we two would go our separate ways. Mama didn't cry. Her eyes had long since gone dry.

What was I to do?

13

I spoke to the principal of my school. She was a stout woman of

问我,"怎样?"假若我真爱她呢,妈妈说,我应该帮助她。不然呢,她不能再管我了。这不像妈妈能说得出的话,但是她确是这么说了。她说得很清楚:"我已经快老了,再过二年,想白叫人要也没人要了!"这是对的,妈妈近来擦许多的粉,脸上还露出摺子来。她要再走一步,去专伺候一个男人。她的精神来不及伺候许多男人了。为她自己想,这时候能有人要她——是个馒头铺掌柜的愿要她——她该马上就走。可是我已经是个大姑娘了,不像小时候那样容易跟在妈妈轿后走过去了。我得打主意安置自己。假若我愿意"帮助"妈妈呢,她可以不再走这一步,而由我代替她挣钱。代她挣钱,我真愿意;可是那个挣钱方法叫我哆嗦。我知道什么呢,叫我像个半老的妇人那样去挣钱?!妈妈的心是狠的,可是钱更狠。妈妈不逼着我走哪条路,她叫我自己挑选——帮助她,或是我们娘儿俩各走各的。妈妈的眼没有泪,早就干了。我怎么办呢?

十三

我对校长说了。校长是个四十多岁的妇

about forty, not very bright, but a warm-hearted generous person. I was really at my wit's end, otherwise how could I have said anything about Mama...? Actually, I didn't know the principal very well, and every word I spoke seared my throat like a ball of fire. I stammered and took a long time to get out what I had to say.

The principal said she was willing to help me. She couldn't give me any money, but she could give me two meals a day and a place to live — I could move in with an old woman servant who lived at the school. She said I could help the scribe with his writing — but not right away, because I still needed more practice with my handwriting.

Two meals a day and a place to live — that settled the biggest problem. I didn't have to be a burden to Mama any more.

Mama didn't ride in a bride's sedan-chair when she left this time. She simply took a rickshaw and went off into the night. She let me keep my bedding.

Mama tried not to cry as she was leaving, but the tears in her heart gushed out after all. She knew I couldn't come to see her — her own daughter. As for me, I had forgotten even how to weep properly — I sobbed open-mouthed, the tears smothering my face. I was her daughter, her friend, her solace. But I couldn't help her. Not unless I agreed to something I just couldn't do.

After she had gone, I sat and thought. We two, mother and daughter, were like a couple of stray dogs. For the sake of our mouths, we had to accept all kinds of suffering, as if no other parts of our bodies mattered. Only our mouths. We had to sell all the rest of us to feed our mouths.

人,胖胖的,不很精明,可是心热。我是真没了主意,要不然我怎会开口述说妈妈的……我并没和校长亲近过。当我对她说的时候,每个字都像烧红了的煤球烫着我的喉,我哑了,半天才能吐出一个字。校长愿意帮助我。她不能给我钱,只能供给我两顿饭和住处——就住在学校和个老女仆作伴儿。她叫我帮助书记员写写字,可是不必马上就这么办,因为我的字还需要练习。两顿饭,一个住处,解决了天大的问题。我可以不连累妈妈了。妈妈这回连轿也没坐,只坐了辆洋车,摸着黑走了。我的铺盖,她给了我。临走的时候,妈妈挣扎着不哭,可是心底下的泪到底翻上来了。她知道我不能再找她去,她的亲女儿。我呢,我连哭都忘了怎么哭了,我只裂着嘴抽达,泪蒙住了我的脸。我是她的女儿,朋友,安慰。但是我帮助不了她,除非我得作那种我决不肯作的事。在事后一想,我们娘儿俩就像两个没人管的狗,为我们的嘴我们得受着一切的苦处,好像我们身上没有别的,只有一张嘴。为这张嘴,我们得把其余一切的东西

英汉对照
English-Chinese
中国文学宝库
Gems of Chinese Literature
现代文学系列
Modern Literature

I didn't hate Mama. I understood. It wasn't her fault; it wasn't wrong of her to have a mouth. The fault lay with food. By what right were we deprived of food? Recollections of past troubles flooded back on me. But the crescent moon that was most familiar with my tears didn't appear this time. It was pitch dark, without even the glow of fireflies. Mama had disappeared into the darkness like a ghost, silent, shadowless. If she were to die tomorrow, she probably couldn't be buried beside Papa. I wouldn't even be able to find her grave. She was my only Mama, my only friend. And now I was left alone in the world.

14

I could never see Mama again. Love died in my heart, like a spring flower nipped by frost. I practised hard with my writing so that I could help the scribe copy minor documents for the principal. I had to become useful — I was eating other people's food. I couldn't be like the other girls in my class, who did nothing but watch others all day long — observing what other people ate, what they wore, what they said. I concentrated on myself. My shadow was my only friend. "I" was always in my mind, because no one loved me. I loved myself, pitied, encouraged, scolded myself. I knew myself, as if I were another person.

My body changed in a way that frightened and pleased me, yet left me puzzled. When I touched them with my hand it was like brushing against delicate, tender flowers.

I was concerned only with the present. There was no future; I

都卖了。我不恨妈妈了,我明白了。不是妈妈的毛病,也不是不该长那张嘴,是粮食的毛病,凭什么没有我们的吃食呢? 这个别离,把过去一切的苦楚都压过去了。那最明白我的眼泪怎流的月牙这回没出来,这回只有黑暗,连点荧火的光也没有。妈妈就在暗中像个活鬼似的走了,连个影子也没有。即使她马上死了,恐怕也不会和爸埋在一处了,我连她将来的坟在哪里都不知道。我只有这么个妈妈,朋友。我的世界里剩下我自己。

十四

妈妈永不能相见了,爱死在我心里,像被霜打了的春花。我用心的练字,为是能帮助校长抄写些不要紧的东西。我必须有用,我是吃着别人的饭。我不像那些女同学,她们一天到晚注意别人,别人吃了什么,穿了什么,说了什么;我老注意我自己,我的影子是我的朋友。"我"老在我的心上,因为没人爱我。我爱我自己,可怜我自己,鼓励我自己,责备我自己;我知道我自己,仿佛我是另一个人似的。我身上有一点变化都使我害怕,使我欢喜,使我莫明其妙。我在我自己手中拿着,像捧着一朵娇嫩的花。我只能顾目前,没有将来,也不敢深想。嚼着人家

didn't dare to think too far ahead. Because I was eating other people's food, I had to know when it was noon and when it was evening. Otherwise I wouldn't have thought of time at all. Without hope there isn't any time. I seemed nailed down to a place that had no days or months. When I thought of my life with Mama, I knew I had existed for fifteen or sixteen years. My schoolmates were always looking forward to vacations, festivals, the New Year holiday. What had these things to do with me?

But my body was continuing to mature. I could feel it. It confused me. I couldn't trust myself. I knew I was growing prettier. Beauty raised my social stature. That was a consolation — until I remembered that I never had any social stature to begin with; then the consolation turned sour. Still, in the end, I was proud of my good looks. Poor but pretty! Suddenly, a frightening thought came to me — Mama wasn't bad looking either.

15

I hadn't seen the crescent moon for a long time. Even though I wanted to see it, I didn't dare to look. I had already graduated and was still living at the school. In the evenings I was alone with two old servants — a man and a woman. They didn't quite know how to treat me. I was no longer a student, yet I wasn't a teacher; nor was I a servant, though in some ways I resembled one.

At night I walked alone in the courtyard. Often I was driven into my room by the crescent moon. I hadn't the courage to face it. But in my room I would picture it, especially when there was a slight

的饭,我知道那是晌午或晚上了,要不然我简直想不起时间来;没有希望,没有时间。我好像钉在个没有日月的地方。想起妈妈,我晓得我曾经活了十几年。对将来,我不像同学们那样盼望放假,过节,过年;假期,节,年,跟我有什么关系呢?可是我的身体是往大了长呢,我觉得出。觉出我又长大了一些,我更渺茫,我不放心我自己。我越往大了长,我越觉得自己好看,这是一点安慰;美使我抬高了自己的身分,可是我根本没身分,安慰是先甜后苦的,苦到末了又使我自傲。穷,可是好看呢!这又使我怕:妈妈也是不难看的。

十五

我又老没看月牙了,不敢去看,虽然想看。我已毕了业,还在学校里住着。晚上,学校里只有两个老仆人,一男一女。他们不知怎样对待我好,我既不是学生,也不是先生,又不是仆人,可有点像仆人。晚上,我一个人在院中走,常被月牙给赶进屋来,我没有胆子去看它。可是在屋里,我会想象它是什么样,特别是在有点小风

英汉对照
English-Chinese
中国文学宝库
Gems of Chinese Literature
现代文学系列
Modern Literature

breeze. The breeze seemed able to blow those pale beams directly to my heart, making me recall the past, intensifying my forebodings of tragedy. My heart was like a bat in the moonlight — a dark thing in spite of the light; black — even though it could fly, still black. I had no hope. But I didn't cry. I only frowned.

16

I earned a little money, knitting for some of the girl students. The principal let me. But I couldn't make much because they knew how to knit too. The girls only came to me when they were too busy to do it themselves. Still, my heart felt lighter. I even thought — if Mama could come back, I could support her.

When I counted my money, I knew this was just an idle dream. But it made me feel better anyhow. I wished I could find her. If she would see me, she'd surely come away with me. We could get along, I thought. But I didn't altogether believe this myself. I was always thinking of Mama. Often, I saw her in my dreams.

One day I went with the students on an outing in the country. On the way back, because it was getting late, we took a shortcut through a small lane. There I saw Mama! Outside this steamed bread shop was a big basket with a large wooden object in it painted white to look like a steamed bread. Mama sat by the wall, pulling and pushing a lever that blew up the fire in the oven. While we were still quite a distance away I saw Mama and that white wooden steamed bread. I recognized her from the back. I wanted to rush over and embrace her. But I didn't dare. I was

的时候。微风仿佛会给那点微光吹到我的心上来,使我想起过去,更加重了眼前的悲哀。我的心就好像在月光下的蝙蝠,虽然是在光的下面,可是自己是黑的;黑的东西,即使会飞,也还是黑的,我没有希望。我可是不哭,我只常皱着眉。

十六

我有了点进款:给学生织些东西,她们给我点工钱。校长允许我这么办。可是进不了许多,因为她们也会织。不过她们急于要用,自己赶不来,或是给家中人打双手套或袜子,才来照顾我。虽然是这样,我的心似乎活了一点,我甚至想:假若妈妈不走那一步,我是可以养活她的。一数我那点钱,我就知道这是梦想,可是这么想使我舒服一点。我很想看看妈妈。假若她看见我,她必能跟我来,我们能有方法活着,我想——不十分相信。我想妈妈,她常到我的梦中来。有一天,我跟着学生们去到城外旅行,回来的时候已经是下午四点多了。为是快点回来,我们抄了个小道。我看见了妈妈!在个小胡同里,有一家卖馒头的,门口放着个元宝筐,筐上插着个顶大的白木头馒头。顺着墙坐着妈妈,身儿一仰一弯地拉风箱呢。从老远我就看见了那个大木馒头与妈妈,我认识她的后影。我要过去抱住她。可是我不敢,我怕学生们笑

英汉对照
English-Chinese
中国文学宝库
Gems of Chinese Literature
现代文学系列
Modern Literature

afraid the students would laugh at me. They wouldn't let me have such a Mama.

We came closer and closer. I lowered my head and looked at her through my tears. She didn't see me. The whole group of us brushed by her. Intent on pulling the bellows' lever, evidently she didn't see a thing.

When we were far beyond her, I turned around and looked back. She was still plying that lever. I couldn't see her features clearly; I had only the impression of a few stray locks hanging down over her forehead. I made a mental note of the name of the lane.

17

It was as if a little bug was gnawing at my heart. I had to see Mama or I'd have no peace.

Just at this time, a new principal was appointed to the school. The stout lady who was leaving told me I'd better start making other plans. As long as she remained she could give me food and lodgings, but she couldn't guarantee that the new principal would do the same.

I counted my money. Altogether I had two dollars and seventy some odd cents. This would keep me from starving for the next few days. But where was I to go?

There was no point in sitting around worrying. I had to think of something.

Go see Mama — that was my first idea. But could she let me

话我,她们不许我有这样的妈妈。越走越近了,我的头低下去,从泪中看了她一眼,她没看见我。我们一群人擦着她的身子走过去,她好像是什么也没看见,专心的拉她的风箱。走出老远,我回头看了看,她还在那儿拉呢。我看不清她的脸,只看到她的头发在额上披散着点。我记住这个小胡同的名儿。

十七

像有个小虫在心中咬我似的,我想去看妈妈,非看见她我心中不能安静。正在这个时候,学校换了校长。胖校长告诉我得打主意,她在这儿一天便有我一天的饭食与住处,可是她不能保险新校长也这么办。我数了数我的钱,一共是两块七毛零几个铜子。这几个钱不会叫我在最近的几天中挨饿,可是我上哪儿呢?我不敢坐在那儿呆呆地发愁,我得想主意。找妈妈去是第一个念头。可是她能收留我吗?假若她

stay with her? If she couldn't, it might provoke a quarrel between her and the steamed bread seller; at least it would make her feel very badly. I had to think of things from her viewpoint. She was my Mama, and yet she wasn't. We were separated by a wall of poverty.

After mulling it over, I decided not to go to her. I had to bear my own burdens. But how? I didn't know. The world seemed very small — there was no place for me and my little roll of bedding. Even a dog was better off. He could lie down anywhere and sleep. I wouldn't be permitted to sleep on the street. Yes, I was a person, but a person was less than a dog.

What if I should refuse to leave? Would the new principal drive me out? I couldn't wait for that. It was spring. I saw the flowers and the green leaves, but I felt no breath of warmth. The red of the flowers and the green of the leaves were only colours to me; they had no special significance. Spring, in my heart, was something cold and dead. I didn't want to cry, but the tears flowed from my eyes.

18

I went job-hunting. I wouldn't go to Mama. I wouldn't depend on anyone. I would earn my own food.

Hopefully, I searched for two whole days. But I brought back a harvest of only dust and tears. There was no work for me to do. It was then that I truly understood Mama, really forgave her. At least she had washed smelly socks. I wasn't even able to do that. Mama

不能收留我,而我找了她去,即使不能引起她与那个卖馒头的吵闹,她也必定很难过。我得为她想,她是我的妈妈,又不是我的妈妈,我们母女之间隔着一层用穷作成的障碍。想来想去,我不肯找她去了。我应当自己担着自己的苦处。可是怎么担着自己的苦处呢? 我想不起。我觉得世界很小,没有安置我与我的小铺盖卷的地方。我还不如一条狗,狗有个地方便可以躺下睡;街上不准我躺着。是的,我是人,人可以不如狗,假若我扯着脸不走,焉知新校长不往外撵我呢? 我不能等着人家往外推。这是个春天。我只看见花儿开了,叶儿绿了,而觉不到一点暖气。红的花只是红的花,绿的叶只是绿的叶,我看见些不同的颜色,只是一点颜色;这些颜色没有任何意义,春在我的心中是个凉的死的东西。我不肯哭,可是泪自己往下流。

十八

我出去找事了。不找妈妈,不依赖任何人,我要自己挣饭吃。走了整整两天,抱着希望出去,带着尘土与眼泪回来。没有事情给我作。我这才真明白了妈妈,真原谅了妈妈。妈妈还洗过臭袜子,我连这个都作不上。妈妈所走的

took the only road that was left. The learning and morality the school had given me were just jokes, playthings for people with full stomachs and time to spare. The students wouldn't permit me to have a Mama like mine; they sneered at women who sold themselves. That was all right for them; they got their meals regularly.

I practically made up my mind — I would do anything. If only some one would feed me. Mama was admirable. I wouldn't kill myself — although I had thought of it. No, I wanted to live. I was young, pretty. I wanted to live. Any shame would be none of my doing.

19

Thinking like that, it was as if I had already found a job. I dared to walk in the courtyard in the moonlight. A spring crescent moon hung in the sky. I saw it and it was beautiful. The sky was dark blue, without a speck of cloud. Bright and warm, the crescent moon bathed the willow branches with its soft beams. A breeze, laden with the fragrance of flowers, blew the shadow of the willow branches back and forth from the bright corner of the courtyard wall to the darkened section. The light was not strong; the shadows were not deep. The breeze blew tenderly. Everything was warm, drowsy, yet gently in motion. Below the moon and above the willows a pair of stars like the smiling eyes of a fairy maiden winked mischievously at that slanting crescent moon and those trailing branches. A tree by the wall was a galaxy of white blossoms. In the moonlight, half the tree was snowy white, half was

路是唯一的。学校里教给我的本事与道德都是笑话,都是吃饱了没事的玩艺。同学们不准我有那样的妈妈,她们笑话暗门子;是的,她们得这样看,她们有饭吃。我差不多要决定了:只要有人给我饭吃,什么我也肯干;妈妈是可佩服的。我才不去死,虽然想到过;不,我要活着。我年轻,我好看,我要活着。羞耻不是我造出来的。

十九

这么一想,我好像已经找到了事似的。我敢在院中走了,一个春天的月牙在天上挂着。我看出它的美来。天是暗蓝的,没有一点云。那个月牙清亮而温柔,把一些软光儿轻轻送到柳枝上,院中有点小风,带着南边的花香,把柳条的影子吹到墙角有光的地方来,又吹到无光的地方去;光不强,影儿不重,风微微地吹,都是温柔,什么都有点睡意,可又要轻软的活动着。月牙下边,柳梢上面,有一对星儿好像微笑的仙女的眼,逗着那歪歪的月牙和那轻摆的柳枝。墙那边有棵什么树,开满了白花,月的微光把这团雪照成一半儿白亮,一半儿略带点灰影,显出

英汉对照
English-Chinese
中国文学宝库
Gems of Chinese Literature
现代文学系列
Modern Literature

dappled with soft grey shadows. A picture of incredible purity.

That crescent moon is the beginning of my hope, I said to myself.

20

I went to see the stout lady principal again, but she wasn't home. A young man let me in. He was very handsome, and very friendly. Usually, I'm afraid of men, but this young man didn't frighten me a bit. I couldn't very well refuse to answer his questions — he had such a winning smile. I told him why I wanted to see the principal. He was very concerned. He promised to help me.

That same night, he came and gave me two dollars. When I tried to refuse, he said the money was from his aunt — the stout principal. She had already found me a place to live, he added. I could move in the next day. I was a little suspicious at first, but his smiles went right to my heart. I felt it was wrong to doubt a person who was so considerate, so charming.

21

His smiling lips were on my cheek, and I could see the crescent moon, smiling too, upon his hair. The intoxicated spring breeze had blown open the spring clouds to reveal the crescent moon and a pair of spring stars. Trailing willow branches stirred along the river bank, frogs throbbed their love songs, the fragrance of young rushes filled the spring night. I could hear water flowing, bringing

难以想到的纯净。这个月牙是希望的开始,我心里说。

二十

我又找了胖校长去,她没在家。一个少年的男子把我让进去。他很体面,也很和气。我平素很怕男人,但是这个少年不叫我怕他。他叫我说什么,我便不好意思不说;他那么一笑,我心里就软了。我把找校长的意思对他说了,他很热心,答应帮助我。当天晚上,他给我送了两块钱来,我不肯收,他说这是他婶母——胖校长——给我的。他并且说他的婶母已经给我找好了地方住,第二天就可以搬过去。我要怀疑,可是不敢。他的笑脸像笑到我的心里去。我觉得我要疑心便对不起人,他是那么温和可爱。

二十一

他的笑唇在我的脸上,从他的头发上我看着那也在微笑的月牙。春风像醉了,吹破了春云,露出月牙与一两对儿春星。河岸上的柳枝轻摆,春蛙唱着恋歌,嫩蒲的香味散在春晚的暖气里。我听着水流,像给嫩蒲一些生力,我想象

nourishment to the tender rushes so that they might quickly grow tall and strong. Young shoots were growing on the moist warm earth; every living thing was absorbing spring's vitality and giving off a lovely perfume.

I forgot myself; I had no self. I seemed to dissolve into that gentle spring breeze, those faint moon beams. Suddenly, a cloud covered the moon. I had lost the crescent moon, and myself as well. I was the same as Mama!

22

I was regretful, yet eased. I wanted to cry, but was very happy I didn't know how I felt. I wanted to go away and never see him again. But he was always on my mind, and I was lonesome without him.

I lived alone in a small room. He came to me every night — always handsome, always tender. He provided me with food, he bought me clothing. When I put on a new gown, I could see that I was beautiful. I hated the clothes, but I couldn't bear to part with them.

I didn't dare to think; I was too indolent to think. I drifted about in a daze, rouge on my cheeks. I didn't feel like dressing up, yet I had to. There was no other way to kill time. While putting my finery on, I adored my image in the mirror; then, when I finished, I hated myself.

Tears came easily to my eyes now, though I managed not to weep. My eyes — always moist and glistening — looked lovely.

着蒲梗轻快的往高里长。小蒲公英在潮暖的地上似乎正往叶尖花瓣上灌着白浆。什么都在溶化着春的力量,把春收在那微妙的地方,然后放出一些香味,像花蕊顶破了花瓣。我忘了自己,像四外的花草似的,承受着春的透入;我没了自己,像化在了那点春风与月的微光中。月儿忽然被云掩住,我想起来自己,我觉得他的热力压迫我。我失去那个月牙儿,也失去了自己,我和妈妈一样了!

二十二

我后悔,我自慰,我要哭,我喜欢,我不知道怎样好。我要跑开,永不再见他;我又想他,我寂寞。两间小屋,只有我一个人,他每天晚上来。他永远俊美,老那么温和。他供给我吃喝,还给我作了几件新衣。穿上新衣,我自己看出我的美。可是我也恨这些衣服,又舍不得脱去。我不敢思想,也懒得思想,我迷迷糊糊的,腮上老有那么两块红。我懒得打扮,又不能不打扮,太闲在了,总得找点事作。打扮的时候,我怜爱自己;打扮完了,我恨自己。我的泪很容易下来,可是我设法不哭,眼终日老那么湿润润的,

英汉对照
English-Chinese
中国文学宝库
Gems of Chinese Literature
现代文学系列
Modern Literature

Sometimes I would kiss him madly, then push him away, even curse him. He never stopped smiling.

23

I knew there was no hope from the start. Any wisp of cloud could cover a crescent moon. My future was dark.

Sure enough, not long after, as spring was changing to summer, my spring dream ended.

One day, just about noon, a young woman came to see me. She was very pretty, in a vapid, doll-like way. The moment she entered the room she began to weep. There was no need for her to say anything; I knew already.

She hadn't come to raise a row, nor did I want to quarrel with her. She was a simple, honest sort. Crying, she took my hand, "He deceived us both!" she said.

I had thought she was also a "sweetheart." But no, she was his wife. She didn't berate me. She just kept repeating, "Please let him go!"

I didn't know what to do. I felt very sorry for the young woman. Finally, I consented and, at once, she was all smiles. She appeared to be completely guileless, and quite naive. All she knew was that she wanted her husband.

24

I walked the streets for hours. It had been easy enough to agree to what that young woman had asked, but what was I to do now? I

可爱。我有时候疯了似的吻他,然后把他推开,甚至于破口骂他;他老笑。

二十三

我早知道,我没希望;一点云便能把月牙遮住,我的将来是黑暗。果然,没有多久,春便变成了夏,我的春梦作到了头儿。有一天,也就是刚晌午吧,来了一个少妇。她很美,可是美得不玲珑,像个磁人儿似的。她进到屋中就哭了。不用问,我已明白了。看她那个样儿,她不想跟我吵闹,我更没预备着跟她冲突。她是个老实人。她哭,可是拉住我的手:"他骗了咱们俩!"她说。我以为她也只是个"爱人"。不,她是他的妻。她不跟我闹,只口口声声的说:"你放了他吧!"我不知怎么才好,我可怜这个少妇。我答应了她。她笑了。看她这个样儿,我以为她是缺个心眼,她似乎什么也不懂,只知道要她的丈夫。

二十四

我在街上走了半天。很容易答应那个少妇呀,可是我怎么办呢?他给我的那些东西,我不

didn't want the things he had given me. Since we were parting, I ought to make the break complete. But they were all I had to my name. Where was I to go? Would I be able to eat that day? His gifts at least were worth a little money. Very well, I'd keep them. I had no choice.

Quietly, I moved away. Though I had no regrets, there was an emptiness in my heart. I was like a lone and drifting cloud.

I rented a small room. Then I went to bed and slept right around the clock.

25

I was good at economizing. Since childhood I had known how precious money was. I still had a couple of dollars, but I decided to go out and look for a job immediately. Though I had no great hopes, it seemed like the safest course.

But job-hunting hadn't become any easier just because I was a year or two older than last time. I kept trying, not that I thought it would do any good, but because I felt it was the proper thing to do.

Why was it so hard for a woman to earn a living? Mama was right. She took the only road open to a woman. Though I knew it was waiting for me, not far off, I didn't want to take that road yet.

The more I struggled, the more frightened I became. My hope was like the light of a new moon; in a little while it would be gone.

Two weeks later, just as I was about to give up, I stood in a line

愿意要;既然要离开他,便一刀两断。可是,放下那点东西,我还有什么呢?我上哪儿呢?我怎么能当天就有饭吃呢?好吧,我得要那些东西,无法。我偷偷的搬了走。我不后悔,只觉得空虚,像一片云那样的无倚无靠。搬到一间小屋里,我睡了一天。

二十五

我知道怎样俭省,自幼就晓得钱是好的。凑合着手里还有那点钱,我想马上去找个事。这样,我虽然不希望什么,或者也不会有危险了。事情可是并不因我长了一两岁而容易找到。我很坚决,这并无济于事,只觉得应当如此罢了。妇女挣钱怎这么不容易呢!妈妈是对的,妇人只有一条路走,就是妈妈所走的路。我不肯马上就往那么走,可是知道它在不很远的地方等着找呢。我越挣扎,心中越害怕。我的希望是初月的光,一会儿就要消失。一两个星期过去了,希望越来越小。最后,我去和一排年

of girls in a cheap restaurant. The restaurant was very small; the boss, who was looking us over, was very big. We were a rather attractive bunch — all primary school graduates, but we waited for that great broken-down tub of a boss to pick one of us as if he were an emperor.

He chose me. Though I wasn't the least grateful, at the moment I couldn't help feeling good. The girls all seemed to envy me. As they left, some had tears in their eyes. A few cursed under their breath — "How can women be worth so little!"

26

I became the small restaurant's Second Hostess. I didn't know anything about waiting on tables and I was rather scared. The First Hostess told me not to worry — she didn't either. She said the waiter took care of that. All the hostess had to do was serve tea, hand out damp face cloths and present the bill at the end of the meal.

Strange. First Hostess wore her sleeves rolled up to her elbow, but the white linings were quite spotless. Tied to her wrist was a fancy handkerchief embroidered with the words "Little Sister, I love you." She was always powdering her face, and the lipstick on her big mouth made it look like bloody ladle. When lighting a cigarette for a customer, she would press her knee against his leg. She also poured the drinks: sometimes she took a sip herself. To some customers she was very attentive; others she would completely ignore. She had a way of batting her eyes and pretending she

轻的姑娘们在小饭馆受选阅。很小的一个饭馆,很大的一个老板;我们这群都不难看,都是高小毕业的女子们,等皇赏似的,等着那个破塔似的老板挑选。他选了我。我不感谢他,可是当时确有点痛快。那群女孩子们似乎很羡慕我,有的竟自含着泪走去,有的骂声"妈的!"女子够多么不值钱呢!

二十六

我成了小饭馆的第二号女招待。摆菜,端菜,算账,报菜名,我都不在行。我有点怕。可是"第一号"告诉我不用着急,她也都不会。她说,小顺管一切的事;我们当招待的只要给客人倒茶,递手巾把,和拿账条;别的不用管。奇怪!"第一号"的袖口卷起来很高,袖口的白里子上连一个污点也没有。腕上放着一块白丝手绢,绣着"妹妹我爱你"。她一天到晚往脸上拍粉,嘴唇抹得血瓢似的。给客人点烟的时候,她的膝往人家腿上倚;还给客人斟酒,有时候她自己也喝了一口。对于客人,有的她伺候得非常的周到;有的她连理也不理,她会把眼皮一耷拉,

didn't see them. It was up to me to look after the ones she neglected.

I was afraid of men. I had learned from that little experience of mine — love or no love, men were monsters. The customers at our restaurant were particularly repulsive. They put on a great show of grabbing for the bill. They played noisy drinking games and ate like pigs. They picked fault over the smallest trifles, and cursed and raged.

While serving them tea or handing out face cloths, I kept my head down and blushed. They talked to me and tried to make me laugh. But I wanted nothing to do with them. At nine o'clock when my first day's work was over, I was worn out. I went to my little room and lay down; without even taking my clothes off, I slept until the next day. When I awoke, I felt better. I was self-supporting, earning my own keep. I reported for work very early.

27

When First Hostess showed up, after nine, I had already been on the job two hours. Contemptuously, but not altogether unkindly, she explained, "You don't have to come so early. Who eats here at eight o'clock in the morning? And another thing, droopy puss, don't always be pulling such a long face. You're supposed to be a hostess, not a pallbearer. Keep your head down like that all the time and nobody'll order any extra drinks. What do you think you're here for? You're dressed all wrong, too. Your gown should have a high collar — and where's your chiffon handkerchief? You

假装没看见。她不招待的,我只好去。我怕男人。我那点经验叫我明白了些,什么爱不爱的,反正男人可怕。特别是在饭馆吃饭的男人们,他们假装义气,打架似的让座让账;他们拼命的猜拳,喝酒;他们野兽似的吞吃,他们不必要而故意的挑剔毛病,骂人。我低头递茶递手巾,我的脸发烧。客人们故意的和我说东说西,招我笑;我没心情说笑。晚上九点多钟完了事,我非常的疲乏了。到了我的小屋,连衣裳没脱,我一直地睡到天亮。醒来,我心中高兴了一些,我现在是自食其力,用我的劳力自己挣饭吃。我很早的就去上工。

二十七

"第一号"九点多才来,我已经去了两点多钟。她看不起我,可也并非完全恶意的教训我:"不用那么早来,谁八点来吃饭? 告诉你,丧气鬼,把脸别耷拉得那么长;你是女跑堂的,没让你在这儿送殡玩。低着头,没人多给酒钱;你干什么来了? 不为挣子儿吗? 你的领子太矮,咱这行全得弄高领子,绸子手绢,人家认这个!"我

英汉对照
English-Chinese
中国文学宝库
Gems of Chinese Literature
现代文学系列
Modern Literature

don't even look like a hostess!"

I knew she meant well. If I didn't smile at the customers, I'd lose out and so would she, for we all split the tips equally. I didn't look down on her; in one sense, I even admired her — she knew how to earn money. Playing up to men — that was the only way a woman could get along.

But I didn't want to imitate her, though I could see clearly enough that the day might be coming when I would have to be even more free and easy than she to earn my food. But that would be only when all other means failed. The "last resort" was always lying in wait for us women. I was just trying to make it wait a little longer.

Angrily, I gritted my teeth and struggled on. But a woman's fate is never in her own hands. Three days later the boss warned me — he'd give me two more days; if I wanted to keep the job, I'd have to act like First Hostess. Half in jest, First Hostess also dropped me a hint:

"One of the customers has been asking about you. Why don't you quit holding back and playing so dumb? We all know the score. Hostesses have married bank managers — there've been cases. We're not so cheap. If we're not too prissy, we can ride around in a goddam limousine with the best of 'em!"

That burned me up. "When did you ever ride in a limousine?" I queried.

Her big red mouth opened so wide with surprise, I thought her jaw was going to drop off. Then she snapped, "None of your nasty lip. You're no lily-arsed lady. You wouldn't be here if you were!"

知道她是好意,我也知道设若我不肯笑,她也得挂落,少分酒钱;小账是大家平分的。我也并非看不起她,从一方面看,我实在佩服她,她是为挣钱。妇女挣钱就得这么着,没第二条路。但是,我不肯学她。我仿佛看得很清楚:有朝一日,我得比她还开通,才能挣上饭吃。可是那得到了山穷水尽的时候;"万不得已"老在那儿等我们女子,我只能叫它多等几天。这叫我咬牙切齿,叫我心中冒火,可是妇女的命运不在自己手里。又干了三天,那个大掌柜的下了警告:再试我两天,我要是愿意往长了干呢,得照"第一号"那么办。"第一号"一半嘲弄,一半劝告的说:"已经有人打听你,干吗藏着乖的卖傻的呢?咱们谁不知道谁是怎着?女招待嫁银行经理的,有的是;你当是咱们低搭呢?闯开脸儿干呀,咱们也它妈的坐几天汽车!"这个,逼上我的气来,我问她:"你什么时候坐汽车?"她把红嘴唇撇得要掉下去:"不用你耍嘴皮子,干什么说什么;天生下来的香屁股,还不会干这个呢!"我

I quit. I took my pay — a dollar and five cents — and went home.

28

The final shadow had taken another big step towards me. To avoid it, I first had to come closer to it. I didn't care about losing the job, but I was really afraid of that shadow. I knew how to sell myself. Ever since that affair, I understood quite a bit about relations between men and women. A girl had only to relax her hold on herself a little, and the men would sense it and come running. What they wanted was flesh; when they had satisfied their lust, they would feed you and clothe you for a time. Afterwards, they might curse and beat you, and cut off your income.

That's the way it is when a girl sells herself. At times she's very content. I've known that feeling myself. It's all sweet love talk for a while; later you become depressed and ache all over. When you sell yourself to one man, at least you get words of love and bliss. But when you're on sale to the general public, you don't even get that. Then you hear lots of words Mama never used.

The degree of fear was different too. Though I just couldn't accept the advice of First Hostess, I wasn't quite as afraid of a private affair with one man. Not that I was thinking of selling myself. I had no need of a man — I was less than twenty. I only thought that it might be fun to go around with one. How was I to know that as soon as I went out a few times with a new friend he would demand what I feared the most!

干不了,拿了一块另五分钱,我回了家。

二十八

最后的黑影又向我迈了一步。为躲它,就更走近了它。我不后悔丢了那个事,可我也真怕那个黑影。把自己卖给一个人,我会。自从那回事儿,我很明白了些男女之间的关系。女子把自己放松一些,男人闻着味儿就来了。他所要的是肉,他所给的也是肉。他咬了你,压着你,他发散了兽力,你便暂时有吃有穿;然后他也许打你骂你,或者停止了你的供给。女人就这么卖了自己,有时候还很得意,我曾经觉到得意。在得意的时候说的净是一些天上的话;过了会儿,你觉得身上的疼痛与丧气。不过,卖给一个男人,还可以说些天上的话;卖给大家,连这些也没法说了,妈妈就没说过这样的话。怕的程度不同,我没法接受"第一号"的劝告;"一个"男人到底使我少怕一点。可是,我并不想卖我自己。我并不需要男人,我还不到二十岁。我当初以为跟男人在一块儿必定有趣,谁知道到了一块他就要求那个我所害怕的事。是的,

英汉对照
English-Chinese
中国文学宝库
Gems of Chinese Literature
现代文学系列
Modern Literature

It was true I had once abandoned myself to the spring breeze, and let a young man have his will. But later I knew he had taken advantage of my innocence, hypnotized me with his honeyed words. When I awoke, I realized it was all an empty dream, with nothing to show for it but a few meals and some new clothes. I didn't want to earn my food that way again. Food was a proper practical object that should be earned in a proper practical way. But if that proved impossible, a woman had to admit she was a woman, and sell her flesh.

More than a month passed. I still was unable to find a new job.

29

I ran into some of my old classmates. A few had gone on to middle school; some were just living at home. I wasn't much interested in them. Talking with them, I could see that I was cleverer than they. In school, they used to be the smart ones. Now the tables were reversed. They seemed to be living in a world of dreams. All very smartly turned out, they were like merchandise in a store. Their eyes shone when they met a young man and their hearts seemed to melt in a poetic reverie.

Those girls made me laugh, but I had to forgive them. Food was no problem to them; it's easy to think of love when your belly is full. Men and women weave nets to ensnare one another. The ones with the most money have the biggest nets. After bagging a few prospects, they leisurely take their pick. I had no money. I couldn't even find a quiet corner to weave my net. But I had to

那时候我像把自己交给了春风,任凭人家摆布;过后一想,他是利用我的无知,畅快他自己。他的甜言蜜语使我走入梦里;醒过来,不过是一个梦,一些空虚;我得到的是两顿饭,几件衣服。我不想再这样挣饭吃,饭是实在的,实在的去挣好了。可是,实在挣不上饭吃,女子得承认自己是女子,得卖肉! 一个多月,我找不到事作。

二十九

我遇见几个同学,有的升入了中学,有的在家里作姑娘。我不愿理她们,可是一说起话儿来,我觉得我比她们精明。原先,在学校的时候,我比她们傻;现在,"她们"显着呆傻了。她们似乎还都作梦呢。她们都打扮得很好,像铺子里的货物。她们的眼溜着年轻的男人,心里好像作着爱情的诗。我笑她们。是的,我必定得原谅她们,她们有饭吃,吃饱了当然只好想爱情,男女彼此织成了网,互相捕捉;有钱的,网大一些,捉住几个,然后从容的选择一个。我没有钱,我连个结网的屋角都找不到。我得直接的

catch someone, or be caught myself. I was clearer on such matters than my ex-classmates, more practical.

30

One day I ran into the doll-faced young wife again. She greeted me as if I were one of her dearest friends, but there was some confusion in her manner.

"You're a good person," she stammered, very earnest. "I was sorry later I asked you to let him go. I would have been better off if he stayed with you. Now he's found himself another. He's gone away with her and I haven't seen him since!"

Questioning her, I discovered that she and he had married for love. Apparently she still loved him, but he had run off again. I was sorry for the little wife. She was still dreaming; she still believed that love was sacred.

I asked her what she was going to do now. She said she had to find him, that they were mated for life. But suppose you can't find him? I asked. She bit her lips. She had parents and in-laws; she was under their control. She envied me my freedom.

So someone actually envied me. I wanted to laugh. My freedom — what a joke! She had food, I had freedom. She had no freedom, I had nothing to eat. We both were women, both were frustrated.

31

After meeting the little doll-face, I gave up the idea of selling

捉人,或是被捉,我比她们明白一些,实际一些。

三十

有一天,我碰见那个小媳妇,像磁人似的那个。她拉住了我,倒好像我是她的亲人似的。她有点颠三倒四的样儿。"你是好人!你是好人!我后悔了,"她很诚恳的说,"我后悔了!我叫你放了他,哼,还不如在你手里呢!他又弄了别人,更好了,一去不回头了!"由探问中,我知道她和他也是由恋爱而结的婚,她似乎还很爱他。他又跑了。我可怜这个小妇人,她也是还作着梦,还相信恋爱神圣。我问她现在的情形,她说她得找到他,她得从一而终。要是找不到他呢?我问。她咬上了嘴唇,她有公婆,娘家还有父母,她没有自由,她甚至于羡慕我,我没有人管着。还有人羡慕我,我真要笑了!我有自由,笑话!她有饭吃,我有自由;她没自由,我没饭吃,我俩都是女人。

三十一

自从遇上那个小磁人,我不想把自己专卖

myself to one man. I decided to play around; in other words, I was going to use "romance" to earn my meals. I couldn't be bothered about moral responsibility any more when I was hungry.

Romance would cure hunger, just as a full stomach was necessary before you could concentrate on romance. It was a perfect circle, no matter where you started from.

There wasn't much difference between me and my classmates and the little doll-face. They had a few more illusions; I was a bit more straightforward. There is no truth more vital than the empty stomach.

I sold my meagre possessions and bought myself a complete new outfit. I didn't look bad at all. Then I entered upon the market.

32

I had imagined I could play at romance, but I was wrong. I didn't know as much about the world as I had thought. Men weren't trapped quite that easily. I was after the more cultured types, men I could satisfy with a kiss or two. Ha-ha, they didn't go for that line, not one bit. They wanted to take advantage the very first time we met. What's more, they only invited me to see a movie, or go out for a walk, or have some ice-cream. I still went home hungry.

The so-called cultured men never failed to ask what school I graduated from, what business my family was in. It was plain enough — they didn't want you unless you had something to offer. If you couldn't bring them any real gain, the best they were willing

给一个男人了,我决定玩玩了;换句话说,我要浪漫的挣饭吃了。我不再为谁负着什么道德责任,我饿。浪漫足以治饿,正如同吃饱了才浪漫,这是个圆圈,从哪儿走都可以。那些女同学与小磁人都跟我差不多,她们比我多着一点梦想,我比她们更直爽,肚子饿是最大的真理。是的,我开始卖了,把我所有的一点东西都折卖了,作了一身新行头,我的确不难看。我上了市。

三十二

我想我要玩玩,浪漫。啊,我错了。我还是不大明白世故。男人并不像我想的那么容易勾引。我要勾引文明一些的人,要至多只赔上一两个吻。哈哈,人家不上那个当,人家要初次见面就摸我的乳。还有呢,人家只请我看电影,或逛逛大街,吃杯冰激凌;我还是饿着肚子回家。所谓文明人,懂得问我在哪儿毕业,家里作什么事。那个态度使我看明白,他若是要你,你得给他相当的好处;你若是没有好处可供献呢,人家

英汉对照
English-Chinese
中国文学宝库
Gems of Chinese Literature
现代文学系列
Modern Literature

to give was ten cents worth of ice-cream in exchange for a kiss.

It was strictly a cash on delivery proposition. The doll-faces didn't understand this, but I did. Mama and I both understood. I thought of Mama a lot.

33

They say some girls can earn a living playing at romance. But I just didn't have the capital; I had to drop the idea. For me it had to be straight business. My landlord ordered me to get out. He was a respectable man, he said. I didn't even give him a second glance. I moved back to the small flat where Mama and my first new Papa used to live. This landlord didn't say anything about being respectable. He was much nicer and more honest.

Business was very good. The cultured types came too. As soon as they found out I was for sale, they were willing to buy. With this kind of arrangement they got their money's worth, with no reflection on their social status.

When I first started I was very scared. I wasn't yet twenty. But after a couple of days I wasn't afraid any more. I could turn them limp as sacks of wet sand. They were pleased and satisfied; they advertised me to their friends.

By the end of several months, I knew a lot. I learned to size a man up the first time we met. The rich customer would always inquire about my background, and make it plain that he could afford me. Very jealous, he would always want me all to himself. Even in brothels he wanted to monopolize — because he had money.

只用一角钱的冰激凌换你一个吻。要卖,得痛痛快快的,拿钱来,我陪你睡。我明白了这个。小磁人们不明白这个。我和妈妈明白,我很想妈了。

三十三

据说有些女人是可以浪漫的挣饭吃,我缺乏资本;也就不必再这样想了。我有了买卖。可是我的房东不许我再住下去,他是讲体面的人。我连瞧他也没瞧,就搬了家,又搬回我妈妈和新爸爸曾经住过的那两间房。这里的人不讲体面,可也更真诚可爱。搬了家以后,我的买卖很不错。连文明人也来了。文明人知道了我是卖,他们是买,就肯来了;这样他们不吃亏,也不丢身分。初干的时候,我很害怕,因为我还不到二十岁。及至作过了几天,我也就不怕了,身体上哪部分多运动都可以发达的。况且我不留情呢,我身上的各处都不闲着,手,嘴……都帮忙。他们爱这个。多咱他们像了一摊泥,他们才觉得上了算,他们满意,还替我作义务的宣传。干过了几个月,我明白的事情更多了,差不多每一见面我就能断定他是怎样的人。有的很有钱,这样的人一开口总是问我的身价,表示他买得起我。他也很嫉妒,总想包了我;逛暗娼他也想

To that type of man I wasn't very courteous. If he raged I didn't care. I could quiet him down by threatening to go to his wife. Those years at school weren't spent in vain. I didn't scare easily. Education has its advantages. I was convinced of that.

Some men would show up with only a dollar in their hands, terrified of being cheated. To this sort, I would explain the terms of our transaction in careful detail. They would then meekly go home and get some more money. It was really a scream.

The worst of the lot were the small-time punks. Not only didn't they want to spend any money, but they were always trying to make something on the deal — stealing half a pack of cigarettes, or a small jar of cold cream. It was bad policy to offend these boys — they had connections. Get tough with them, and they put the cops on you.

I didn't offend them. I played them along until I got to know an official on the police force, then I finished them off one by one. It's a dog-eat-dog world; the worse you are the better you make out.

Most pitiful of all were the young student types, with only a dollar and a handful of small change clinking in their pockets, nervous perspiration standing out on their noses. I pitied them, but I took their money just the same. What else could I do?

Then there were the elderly men — all quite respectable, some of them grandfathers. I didn't really know how to treat them. But I knew they had money; they wanted to buy a little happiness before they died. So I gave them what they were after.

These experiences taught me to recognize the true nature of

独占,因为他有钱。对这样的人,我不大招待。他闹脾气,我不怕,我告诉他,我可以找上他的门去,报告给他的太太。在小学里念了几年书,到底是没白念,他唬不住我。教育是有用的,我相信了。有的人呢,来的时候,手里就攥着一块钱,唯恐上了当。对这种人,我跟他细讲条件,干什么多少钱,干什么多少钱,他就乖乖的回家去拿钱,很有意思。最可恨的是那些油子,不但不肯花钱,反倒要占点便宜走,什么半盒烟卷呀,什么一小瓶雪花膏呀,他们随手拿去。这种人还是得罪不得的,他们在地面上很熟,得罪了他们,他们会叫巡警跟我捣乱。我不得罪他们,我喂着他们;及至我认识了警官,才一个个的收拾他们。世界就是狼吞虎咽的世界,谁坏谁就有便宜。顶可怜的是那像中学学生样儿的,袋里装着一块钱,和几十铜子,叮当的直响,鼻子上出着汗。我可怜他们,可是也照常卖给他们。我有什么办法呢!还有老头子呢,都是些规矩人,或者家中已然儿孙成群。对他们,我不知道怎样好;但是我知道他们有钱,想在死前买些快乐,我只好供给他们所需要的。这些经验叫我

英汉对照
English-Chinese
中国文学宝库
Gems of Chinese Literature
现代文学系列
Modern Literature

money and man. Money is the more powerful of the two. If man is an animal, then money is his gall.

34

I discovered I had caught a disease. It made me so miserable I wanted to die. I rested, I strolled about the streets. I longed for Mama. She could give me some comfort. I thought of myself as someone who hadn't long to live.

I went to the little lane where I had last seen her plying the bellows' lever. But the steamed bread shop had closed down. No one knew where they had moved to. But I persisted. I simply had to find her. For days I roved the streets like a ghost. It was no use. I wondered whether she was dead, or whether the shop had moved to somewhere outside the city, maybe hundreds of miles away.

In this gloomy frame of mind, I broke down and cried. I put on my best clothes, made up my face, and lay down on my bed and waited for death. I was sure I wouldn't last long.

But I didn't die. There was a knock at the door. Someone had come looking for me. All right, show him in. With all my strength, I gave him a full charge of my infection. I didn't think I was wrong. The fault wasn't mine to begin with.

I began to feel a little better. I smoked, I drank, I behaved like an old hand of thirty or forty. There were dark circles under my eyes, my hands were feverish. I didn't care. Money was everything. The idea was to eat your fill first; then you could talk about

认识了"钱"与"人"。钱比人更厉害一些,人是兽,钱是兽的胆子。

三十四

我发现了我身上有了病。这叫我非常的苦痛,我觉得已经不必活下去了。我休息了,我到街上走去;无目的,乱走。我想去看看妈,她必能给我一些安慰,我想象着自己已是快死的人了。我绕到那个小巷,希望见着妈妈;我想起她在门外拉风箱的样子。馒头铺已经关了门。打听,没人知道搬到哪里去。这使我更坚决了,我非找到妈妈不可。在街上丧胆游魂的走了几天,没有一点用。我疑心她是死了,或是和馒头铺的掌柜的搬到别处去,也许在千里以外。这么一想,我哭起来,我穿好了衣裳,擦上了脂粉,在床上躺着,等死。我相信我会不久就死去的。可是我没死。门外又敲门了,找我的。好吧,我伺候他,我把病尽力的传给他。我不觉得这对不起人,这根本不是我的过错。我又痛快了些,我吸烟,我喝酒,我好像已是三四十岁的人了。我的眼圈发青,手心很热,我不再管,有钱才能

英汉对照
English-Chinese
中国文学宝库
Gems of Chinese Literature
现代文学系列
Modern Literature

other things.

And I ate not badly at all. Why not have the best! I had to have good food and nice clothing. That was the only way I could do a little justice to myself.

35

One morning as I sat draped in a long gown — it must have been about ten o'clock — I heard some footsteps out in the courtyard. I had just got out of bed. Sometimes I didn't get dressed until noon. I had become very lazy lately. I could sit around like this for an hour, sometimes two, thinking of nothing, not wanting to think of anything either.

The footsteps approached my door, softly, slowly. I saw a pair of eyes peering in through the door's small glass panel. After a moment, they vanished. I sat listless, too lazy to move. A few minutes later, the eyes came back again. This time I recognized them. I got up and quietly opened the door. "Ma!"

36

What happened next I can't exactly say. Nor do I remember how long we cried together. Mama had aged terribly. Her husband had gone back to his native village, sneaking away without a word. He didn't leave her a cent. She sold the shop's few implements, gave the store back to the landlord and moved into a cheap room.

She had already been searching for me over half a month. Finally, she thought of coming to her old flat, just on the off chance

活着,先吃饱再说别的吧。我吃得并不错,谁肯吃坏的呢!我必须给自己一点好吃食,一些好衣裳,这样才稍微对得起自己一点。

三十五

一天早晨,大概有十点来钟吧,我正披着件长袍在屋中坐着,我听见院中有点脚步声。我十点来钟起来,有时候到十二点才想穿好衣裳,我近来非常的懒,能披着件衣服呆坐一两个钟头。我想不起什么,也不愿想什么,就那么独自呆坐。那点脚步声向我的门外来了,很轻很慢。不久,我看见一对眼睛,从门上那块小玻璃看呢。看了一会儿,躲开了;我懒得动,还在那儿坐着。待了一会儿,那对眼睛又来了。我再也坐不住,我轻轻的开了门。"妈!"

三十六

我们母女怎么进了屋,我说不上来。哭了多久,也不大记得。妈妈已老得不像样儿了。她的掌柜的回了老家,没告诉她,偷偷的走了,没给她留下一个钱。她把那点东西变卖了,辞了房,搬到一个大杂院里去。她已找了我半个多月。最后,她想到上这儿来,并没希望找到

that she might run into me. Sure enough, there I was. She hadn't dared to speak to me. If I hadn't called her, perhaps she would have gone away again.

When we stopped crying at last, I began to laugh hysterically. What a farce! Mother finds daughter, but daughter is a whore. In order to bring me up, Mama had been forced to become one. Now it was my turn to look after her, so I would have to remain one.

This oldest profession is hereditary — a woman's speciality!

37

Though I knew that words of comfort were just empty talk, I was hoping to hear them from Mama's mouth. Mama was always good at fooling people, and I used to take her cajolery as consolation.

But now she had forgotten how to do even that. She was scared stiff by hunger, and I didn't blame her.

She began checking through my things, questioning me about income and expenses, apparently not the least troubled by the nature of my work. I told her I was sick, hoping she would urge me to rest a few days. Nothing of the sort. She said she'd buy me some medicine.

"Are we always going to remain in this business?" I asked her. She didn't answer.

Yet, in a way, she really loved me and wanted to protect me. She fed me, looked after my health. She was always stealing glances at me, the way a mother watches a sleeping child.

The only thing she wouldn't do for me was tell me to quit my

我,只是碰碰看,可是竟自找到了我。她不敢认我了,要不是我叫她,她也许就又走了。哭完了,我发狂似的笑起来:她找到了女儿,女儿已是个暗娼!她养着我的时候,她得那样;现在轮到我养着她了,我得那样!女子的职业是世袭的,是专门的!

三十七

我希望妈妈给我点安慰。我知道安慰不过是点空话,可是我还希望来自妈妈的口中。世上的妈妈都最会骗人,我们把妈妈的诓骗叫作安慰。我的妈妈连这个都忘了。她是饿怕了,我不怪她。她开始检点我的东西,问我的进项与花费,似乎一点也不以这种生意为奇怪。我告诉她,我有了病,希望她劝我休息几天。没有;她只说出去给我买药。"我们老干这个吗?"我问她。她没言语。可是从另一方面看,她确是想保护我,心疼我。她给我作饭,问我身上怎样,还常常的偷看我,像妈妈看睡着了的小孩那样。只是有一层她不肯说,就是叫我不用再干

profession.

I knew well enough — though I wasn't too pleased about it — that aside from this, there was nothing else I could do. Mama and I had to have food and clothing — that decided everything. Mother or daughter, respectable or not, the need for money was merciless.

38

Mama wanted to look after me, but she had to stand by and watch me be ruined. Though I wanted to be good to her, sometimes she was very annoying. She tried to run the whole show — especially where money was concerned. Her eyes had lost their youthful shine, but the sight of money could make them gleam again. She acted like a servant when there were customers around, yet if any man should pay less than the agreed price, she'd curse him and call him every name under the sun.

It made things awkward for me. Of course, I was in business for money, but that didn't mean we had to curse people. I knew how to be rude to a customer, but I had my own methods. I brought him around easy. Mama's way was too crude; she offended people. From the point of view of money, that was something we shouldn't do.

Maybe I was young and naive. Mama only cared about money, but she had to be that way; she was so much older. Probably in another couple of years I'd be the same. A person's heart ages with the years. Gradually, you get to be hard and stiff — like silver dollars.

这行了。我心中很明白——虽然有一点不满意她——除了干这个,还想不到第二个事情作。我们母女得吃得穿——这个决定了一切。什么母女不母女,什么体面不体面,钱是无情的。

三十八

妈妈想照应我,可是她得听着看着人家蹂躏我。我想好好对待她,可是我觉得她有时候讨厌。她什么都要管管,特别是对于钱。她的眼已失去年轻时的光泽,不过看见了钱还能发点光。对于客人,她就自居为仆人,可是当客人给少了钱的时候,她张嘴就骂。这有时候使我很为难。不错,既干这个还不是为钱吗?可是干这个的也似乎不必骂人。我有时候也会慢待人,可是我有我的办法,使客人急不得恼不得。妈妈的方法太笨了,很容易得罪人。看在钱的面上,我们不应当得罪人。我的方法或者出于我还年轻,还幼稚;妈妈便不顾一切的单单站在钱上了,她应当如此,她比我大着好些岁。恐怕再过几年我也就这样了,人老心也跟着老,渐渐

No, Mama didn't stand on ceremony. If a customer didn't pay in full, she'd keep his briefcase, or his hat, or anything worth a little money like a pair of gloves or a cane. I hated rows, but Mama was right. "We have to make every dollar we can," she said. "In this racket, you age ten years in one. Do you think anybody will want you when you look seventy or eighty?"

Sometimes, when a customer got drunk, she'd drag him out to a lonely spot and strip him of everything, right down to his shoes. The funny thing was the man never made a fuss about it afterwards. Maybe he didn't know how it happened, or maybe he caught pneumonia from the exposure. Or maybe, remembering how he got into that state, he was too embarrassed to complain. We didn't care, but some people had a sense of shame.

39

Mama said we age ten years in one, and she was right. After two or three years I could feel that I had changed a lot. My skin grew coarse, my lips were always chapped, my eyes bloodshot. I would get up very late, but I always felt tired.

I was aware of these things, and my customers were even less blind to them. Old customers gradually stopped coming around. As to new customers, though I worked still harder to please them, they got on my nerves. Sometimes I couldn't control my temper; I'd rant and rave so, I didn't recognize myself. Talking nonsense became a habit with me.

My more cultured customers lost interest because my "charming

的老得和钱一样的硬。是的,妈妈不客气。她有时候劈手就抢客人的皮夹,有时候留下人家的帽子或值钱一点的手套与手杖。我很怕闹出事来,可是妈妈说的好:"能多弄一个是一个,咱们是拿十年当作一年活着的,等七老八十还有人要咱们吗?"有时候,客人喝醉了,她便把他架出去,找个僻静地方叫他坐下,连他的鞋都拿回来。说也奇怪,这种人倒没有来找账算的,想是已人事不知,说不定也许病一大场。或者事过之后,想过滋味,也就不便再来闹了,我们不怕丢人,他们怕。

三十九

妈妈是说对了:我们是拿十年当一年活着。干了二三年,我觉出自己是变了,我的皮肤粗糙了,我的嘴唇老是焦的,我的眼睛里老灰不溜的带着血丝。我起来的很晚,还觉得精神不够。我觉出这个来,客人们更不是瞎子,熟客渐渐少起来。对于生客,我更努力的伺候,可是也更厌恶他们,有时候我管不住自己的脾气。我暴躁,我胡说,我已经不是我自己了。我的嘴不由的老胡说,似乎是惯了。这样,那些文明人已不多照顾我,因为我丢了那点"小鸟依人"——他们

英汉对照
English-Chinese
中国文学宝库
Gems of Chinese Literature
现代文学系列
Modern Literature

little love-bird" quality — their favourite poetic phrase — was gone. I had to learn to behave like a street-walker. Only by painting my face like a clown could I attract the uneducated customers. I spread my lipstick on thick, I bit them — then they were happy.

I could almost see myself dying. With every dollar I took in, I seemed to come closer to death. Money is supposed to preserve life, but the way I earned it, it had the opposite effect. I could see myself dying; I waited for death.

In this state of mind, I didn't want to think of anything. There was no need. I only wanted to live from day to day — that was enough.

Mama was the mirror of my coming self. After peddling her flesh for years, all that was left of her was a mass of white hair and a dark wrinkled skin. Such is life.

40

I forced myself to laugh, to act wild. Weeping a few tears would never have washed away my bitterness anyhow. My way of living had no attraction, but it was life after all, and I didn't want to part with it. Besides, what I was doing was not my fault. If death seemed frightening, it was only because I loved life so dearly. I wasn't afraid of the pain of dying — my life was more painful than any death. I loved life, but not the way I was living it.

I used to picture an ideal life, and it would be like a dream. But then, as cruel reality again closed in on me, the dream would quickly pass, and I would feel worse than ever. This world is no

唯一的诗句——的身段与气味。我得和野鸡学了。我打扮得简直不像个人,这才招得动那不文明的人。我的嘴擦得像个红血瓢,我用力咬他们,他们觉得痛快。有时候我似乎已看见我的死,接进一块钱,我仿佛死了一点。钱是延长生命的,我的挣法适得其反。我看着自己死,等着自己死。这么一想,便把别的思想全止住了。不必想了,一天一天的活下去就是了,我的妈妈是我的影子,我至好不过将来变成她那样,卖了一辈子肉,剩下的只是一些白头发与抽皱的黑皮。这就是生命。

四十

我勉强的笑,勉强的疯狂,我的痛苦不是落几个泪所能减除的。我这样的生命是没什么可惜的,可是它到底是个生命,我不愿撒手。况且我所作的并不是我自己的过错。死假如可怕,那只因为活着是可爱的。我决不是怕死的痛苦,我的痛苦久已胜过了死。我爱活着,而不应当这样活着。我想象着一种理想的生活,像作的梦似的;这个梦一会儿就过去了,实际的生活

dream — it's a living hell.

Mama could see that I was feeling low, and she would urge me to get married. A husband would give me food, and she could get a cash payment for her old age. I was her only hope. But who would marry me?

41

Because I had known so many men, I forgot completely the meaning of love. I loved myself — no, I didn't even love myself any longer. Why should I love anyone else? Still, if I were to marry, I would have to pretend, to say that I loved him, that I was willing to spend the rest of my life with him.

And that is what I did say — to several men. I swore it, but none of them wanted to marry me. The rule of money makes men sharp. They were quite willing to have an affair with me. That was much cheaper than going to a brothel.

If it didn't cost anything, I guarantee all the men would say they loved me.

42

Just about this time, I was arrested. Our city's new chief of police is a stickler on morals; he wants to clean out all the unregistered brothels. The licensed women can go on doing business, because they pay tax.

After my arrest, I was sent to a reformatory where I was taught to work — washing clothes, cooking, knitting. But I already knew

使我更觉得难过。这个世界不是个梦,是真的地狱。妈妈看出我的难过来,她劝我嫁人。嫁人,我有了饭吃,她可以弄一笔养老金。我是她的希望。我嫁谁呢?

四十一

因为接触的男子很多了,我根本已忘了什么是爱。我爱的是我自己,及至我已爱不了自己,我爱别人干什么呢?但是打算出嫁,我得假装说我爱,说我愿意跟他一辈子。我对好几个人都这样说了,还起了誓;没人接受。在钱的管领下,人都很精明。嫖不如偷,对,偷省钱。我要是不要钱,管保人人说爱我。

四十二

正在这个期间,巡警把我抓了去。我们城里的新官儿非常的讲道德,要扫清了暗门子。正式的妓女倒还照旧作生意,因为她们纳捐;纳捐的便是名正言顺的,道德的。抓了去,他们把我放在了感化院,有人教给我作工。洗,做,烹

how to do all that. If I could have earned a living by any of those methods, I would have quit my own bitter profession long ago.

I told that to the people at the reformatory, but they didn't believe me. They said I was a loafer, immoral. They said that if I not only learned to work, but also loved to work, I could become self-supporting, or find a husband.

They were very optimistic. I didn't share their confidence. They were very proud of the fact that they had "reformed" about a dozen women and found them husbands. For a two-dollar licence fee and a guarantee from a responsible shopkeeper, any man could come to the reformatory and pick a wife. It was a real bargain — for the man.

To me it was a joke. I flatly refused to be "reformed." When some big official came down to investigate us, I spat in his face. But they wouldn't let me go. I was a dangerous character. Since they couldn't reform me, they sent me to another place. I went to jail.

43

Jail is a fine place. It convinces you that there's no hope for mankind. Never in my dreams did I imagine any hole could be so disgusting.

But once I got here, I gave up any idea of ever leaving again. From my own experience, I know that the outside world isn't much of an improvement.

I wouldn't want to die here, if I had any better place to go. But

调,编织,我都会;要是这些本事能挣饭吃,我早就不干那个苦事了。我跟他们这样讲,他们不信,他们说我没出息,没道德。他们教给我工作,还告诉我必须爱我的工作。假如我爱工作,将来必定能自食其力,或是嫁个人。他们很乐观。我可没这个信心。他们最好的成绩,是已经有十几多个女的,经过他们感化而嫁了人。到这儿来领女人的,只须花两块钱的手续费和找一个妥实的铺保就够了。这是个便宜,从男人方面看;据我想,这是个笑话。我干脆就不受这个感化。当一个大官儿来检阅我们的时候,我唾了他一脸吐沫。他们还不肯放了我,我是带危险性的东西。可是他们也不肯再感化我。我换了地方,到了狱中。

四十三

狱里是个好地方,它使人坚信人类的没有起色;在我作梦的时候都见不到这样丑恶的玩艺。自从我一进来,我就不再想出去,在我的经验中,世界比这儿并强不了许多。我不愿死,假若从这儿出去而能有个较好的地方;事实上既

英汉对照
English-Chinese
中国文学宝库
Gems of Chinese Literature
现代文学系列
Modern Literature

Crescent Moon

I know what it's like outside. Wherever you die, it's all the same.

Here, in here, I saw my old friend again — the crescent moon. I hadn't seen it for a long time.

I wonder what Mama is doing.

That crescent moon brings everything back.

Translated by Sidney Shapiro

不这样,死在哪儿不一样呢。在这里,在这里,我又看见了我的好朋友,月牙儿!多久没见着它了!妈妈干什么呢?我想起来一切。